DEFIANT SYSTEMS

INFINITE VOID BOOK TWO

RICHARD RIMINGTON

Join our newsletter for exclusive access to 'The Survivors' - a prologue short story to the Infinite Void series.

Plus early reading access, discounts on new releases, and more exclusive bonus content:

Join here:
https://cutt.ly/rimington

The characters and events portrayed in this book are fictitious. Any similarity to real persons, living or dead, is coincidental and not intended by the author.

No part of this book may be reproduced, or stored in a retrieval system, or transmitted in any form or by any means, electronic, mechanical, photocopying, recording, or otherwise, without express written permission of the publisher.

Copyright © 2022 Richard Rimington

All rights reserved.

ISBN: 9798848500653

Dedicated to Indrani,

for being a comrade in hard times.

CONTENTS

Chapter 1	Pg 7
Chapter 2	Pg 22
Chapter 3	Pg 45
Chapter 4	Pg 72
Chapter 5	Pg 93
Chapter 6	Pg 120
Chapter 7	Pg 144
Chapter 8	Pg 168
Chapter 9	Pg 180
Chapter 10	Pg 226
Chapter 11	Pg 244
Epilogue	Pg 264
Infinite Void Series	Pg 270
Acknowledgements	Pg 277

Chapter 1

Cal was warm in his bed beneath a thick duvet. He felt soft toes wriggling next to his and the movement of someone's smooth legs against his own. Everything was quiet. Eevey was breathing slowly, still asleep. Cal opened his eyes a little and looked at her. Her long hair flowed around her face, framing her closed eyelids, her small nose, her lips. Her head rested against him, and he put his arm around her shoulders, feeling the gradual rise and fall of her chest as she slept. They were safe together on Vale Reach.

But that wasn't true. They weren't together on Vale Reach anymore. He wasn't on Vale Reach at all. His homeworld was far away, perhaps immeasurably out of reach. The path back was through the domain of malicious pirates. Vale Reach had likely been destroyed. All that would remain of his homeworld by the time he returned was drifting, burned pieces.

No, he realized that wasn't true either. Cal began to awaken more. He'd spoken to Eevey, not long ago, for the first time since his journey began, making contact through an FTL communications channel. Everyone onboard their starship had been able to contact home. She was alive. Vale Reach was still alive too. But something had been terribly wrong in that strange conversation.

He slowly opened his eyes and realized he wasn't in the small steel bed in his cabin aboard the starship *Fidelity*. He wasn't in any kind of bed at all but instead lay on a pile of flattened cardboard. The sounds of industrial work were rumbling all around him, but he was very much alone. Cal realized he was on top of a mound of discarded packaging material. He sat up gradually, trying to clear his head.

He was in the repair bay of a space station in a distant part of the galaxy where their ship *Fidelity* had docked for emergency repairs after suffering critical damage in an encounter with pirates and mercenaries. The crew from Vale Reach had little understanding of where they were. As one of *Fidelity*'s navigators, Cal knew that for a fact. But he wasn't sure why he was not on the ship. He thought back.

After his conversation with Eevey, he'd felt far more exhausted than he'd expected. Cal attributed it to the stress and turmoil of the past months. Seeing her had somehow released an emotional blockage in him. It was as though all his traumatic experiences had caught up with him. He'd gone for a walk in the wide-open space of the dock area to try and calm his thoughts. Then fatigue had overwhelmed him. It seemed he'd found this sheltered space, unobserved in an alcove of the repair bay, and passed out. He looked up. Hanging directly above him was the eight-hundred-meter length of *Fidelity*, roughly cylindrical like a cigar, its surface once smooth but now pockmarked with scars.

They were already so far from home. He was separated from Eevey by both time and space. With so many FTL jumps between them, time wasn't flowing the same for her as it was for him. He was slipping into the future. He couldn't even be sure how much time would pass for her before they would next be able to speak.

Keeping in contact with Vale Reach was not something the technology of their ship could support. The crew of *Fidelity* had only been able to successfully contact their homeworld once so far during the mission, using the equipment here on the repair station. From what he'd heard, the station was a strictly neutral and nonaligned facility. Cal had no idea if he was supposed to be experiencing morning or night in such unfamiliar surroundings. He began to feel drained again, his head dizzy. The deep ache he felt from weeks of stress still haunted his bones. He shut his eyes and lay back down, returning to slumber.

Memories of the call home returned. Eevey hadn't been alone—someone else had been there in his old apartment with her, seated at a chair in his old kitchen. She'd described herself as the Ambassador to the Tylder Empire. It had been an almost unbelievable thing to see, a strange woman from distant space. Cal wondered how she'd even been present on Vale Reach. Offworlders were prohibited on their homeworld due to a series of hostile treaties imposed by Vale Reach's neighbors, yet this Ambassador had seemed open about her presence there. Why had she come to his house in particular? What role did Eevey play in all this?

Cal began to slip deeper back into sleep. He'd spoken to neither his captain nor the other crew about the encounter. It unnerved him to think of Eevey within reach of that strange Ambassador. His mind replayed details of the bizarre conversation. Was the Ambassador even human? It didn't feel likely. She'd put her arm around Eevey. Was it a threat? Cal's mind obsessively searched each detail. He saw it all again: Eevey's smiling face, strained slightly by some concern that she wouldn't vocalize. The Ambassador in her purple dress, almost monstrous in size. The two of them sat side by side, appearing on a video screen, one face the most familiar to him in the world, the other alien and inscrutable.

"I know everything," the Ambassador had said. "I must warn you that if you continue to persist in this journey, I will be forced to direct my agents to terminate it for you. Don't go any further. Please. I'm asking you in the name of kindness. Are you so determined to throw your life away? I don't want to slaughter you all. I hope you truly appreciate how I've chosen to use my time to tell you that myself and in person."

Cal heard the words again, just as he'd heard them before. The Ambassador had threatened him all right. That was for sure. How could Eevey have sat by and watched as she said such things to him? In his memories, he felt the Ambassador watching him, her gaze suddenly piercing and intense. The fog of his dreams cleared, and Cal could see every detail of her unnatural skin. Her eyes glowed with burning brightness, whilst Eevey sat next to her, frozen in place.

"The first of these agents is already reaching you, Caladon," she said. "His name is Sarjan. He exists without a body. I have summoned his spirit from the depths of collective memory. My followers are present in every star system. There is nowhere for you to hide."

This is new, he thought in his dreaming state. He'd never heard that message before.

The Ambassador's eyes glowed ever brighter, pulsing like a strobe light, while her words became ghostly like an echoing whisper. "He is a man without fear and without limits. He has died already, endless times over. He exists as a mental template in my collection, his soul imprinted into many people, spreading as a latent virus, ready for my activation. At my command, the warrior Sarjan has been born again. He will see the world as I show it to him. Your starship and crew will pay a tragic price for your refusal to see sense and abandon your futile mission."

Black clouds appeared to fill the interior of his old apartment as she spoke to him. Cal was powerless to talk back, only an observer as the Ambassador spoke to him with a voice that felt real. He tried to ask her why she was so determined to stop them, whether she was truly speaking to him in that moment or just an apparition created by his frayed nerves, but it was no use. The sight of his old apartment disintegrated and fell away, but the Ambassador and Eevey remained, still seated in their chairs, floating in a void.

"Remember, Cal," the Ambassador said to him, her voice growing louder as her image flickered. "All of this can be stopped by you. You need only convince your starship to end its mission. Then there will be no quarrel between us."

Eevey's eyes opened, and the piercing white glare from the Ambassador emanated from Eevey too. "No quarrel between us," Eevey intoned ominously.

Cal awoke crying out in fear. The experience of the dream had felt more tangible than any other dream he could remember. He wondered if something otherworldly happening to him or if his grip on reality was just slipping. He'd had no chance to process the recent chaotic events of his life. It wasn't a simple thing to tell his commanding officers that his fiancée had become involved with a dangerous offworlder, but he knew he had to do it.

It would be even harder to tell them that he was worried about the content of his dreams. He would lose any credibility if he started talking about imaginary things. It was entirely possible that the dream meant nothing. The simplest explanation was that the vivid message was just a product of his exhaustion and his bizarre sleeping place. Perhaps he was getting paranoid.

He sighed slowly and sat up again. The Ambassador had demanded that their ship turn back. In all likelihood, it implied problems beyond his ability to understand. She had somehow gained access to their homeworld, to Cal's own apartment, to his partner. Their enemies were ready for them in ways they couldn't have imagined.

He willed himself to get to his feet. He was on leave from his official duties whilst *Fidelity* continued to receive its final repairs in the space station's central dry-dock area. Like much of the crew, he'd been assigned a few days of rest and recovery after the carnage they'd endured whilst crossing the Grand Highway of Thelmia.

Nearly a quarter of their ship's crew had been killed during an attack from two hostile boarding parties. Cal's body was patched up with adhesive bandages, covering the wounds left from where medics had removed metal shrapnel and bullet fragments from his flesh. It hurt, but he'd grown accustomed to the pain. He realized that he'd slept in his uniform.

At least the space station was kept warm. He looked around. They were guests in an unfamiliar environment, but they'd bartered for their time there. The repair bay was spartan but at the same time much more spacious than what he'd become used to aboard their cramped and experimental starship. He should take the chance to walk around freely while he could. He'd spent months confined to narrow corridors and likely would soon return to that state.

The space station held many thousands of people, all of whom seemed to be employed in some capacity, even the youngest children. None of them paid him much attention as he shuffled around the repair bay, his Vale Reach uniform clearly marking him as one of the ship's crew inside the immense central chamber where the starships were held for repairs.

Despite his dazed state, Cal was once again impressed by the size of the facility. He could see the entire length of their ship suspended above him, yet the chamber was pressurized and breathable for convenience. *Fidelity* was held in a tubular cavity at the center of the facility, surrounded by work platforms that could be raised or lowered. Like any rotational gravity environment, the weight of all objects pushed outward from the center of the station. Aligned with the spine of the repair bay, *Fidelity* shared the station's gravity. Workers sparsely covered the surface of the ship like a handful of ants.

From studying the other vessels at the space station, Cal had observed that *Fidelity* in fact maintained a relatively high internal gravity for an interstellar ship, but he couldn't imagine any lesser amount being comfortable in the long term.

The repair station's platforms were at a distance of around fifty meters from the surface of *Fidelity* so that the station's crew had quick access to it whilst also allowing room for large parts of starships to be moved into place. Cal could see how the platforms could be moved farther back to accommodate a vessel of wider radius. Steel cables ran from the repair platforms up to *Fidelity*'s open portals and vents, moving carriages and trolleys that would bring heavy equipment from the station to the ship. The cable cars were of a range of sizes, the largest able to move something like an entire thruster engine if needed, but they were mostly inactive at the moment. Cal had watched a few days previously as the workers had replaced an enormous exhaust pipe.

It seemed that the station held around ten other starships, all located in the central core of the station and separated by movable screens that were fixed at each end to give the ships some privacy like patients in a ward. At one point, the sights here would have amazed and awed him beyond words. Four months ago, he'd never seen a starship in his life. But being placed in mortal danger did a lot to quickly remove a sense of wonder and amazement. His life depended on starships and space stations. It had become the primary business that occupied his mind, filling him with near-crippling anxiety.

He watched the dock workers around him. The people who worked in this place seemed content. They were skilled at what they did, providing anonymous repairs far from any terrestrial land. He envied their sense of clear purpose and the security that their services seemed to bring them. The deal to repair the ship had been negotiated with them by *Fidelity*'s pilot, Marraz. Despite being born on Vale Reach like the rest of the crew, Marraz had somehow spent much of his life in space, or so he'd claimed.

Out on the repair platforms, Cal could walk in a wide circle without bumping into anything. Cal let his arms swing loosely by his sides and stretched his legs, subconsciously preparing for the challenge of traveling once more. Soon, they would set off on their journey again, and he would lose his ability to wander freely without colliding with some console desk or piece of machinery. Open space was the thing he missed most, other than Eevey, when living within the mazelike corridors of *Fidelity*.

The casualties so far among the crew were worse than he'd expected, yet the mission was still moving onward. Maybe that meant they were more successful than he realized. Cal had recently started to believe that reaching their end goal was actually achievable.

Fidelity's task was to secure protection for their homeworld and to prevent its occupation by a huge foreign military power called the Universal Legion, likely in the form of a treaty that would prohibit colonization of their planet. Their annexation by the Legion could begin at any moment. Securing an alliance of that kind for Vale Reach required their starship to reach a distant star system known as Ruarken, passing through lawless and dangerous territories. On multiple occasions so far, their modest vessel had almost been destroyed by pirates. But they had crossed the Grand Highway of Thelmia, and the worst of the pirates should be behind them. A mostly blank map now stretched in front. Vale Reach simply didn't know about what was so far out.

During that last encounter, they'd learned a long-forgotten secret about their homeworld, relayed by the leader of one of the pirate gangs that'd attacked their vessel. Their planet was the location of an ancient artifact known as the Seed of Steel, thousands of years old and hidden somewhere out of reach. The properties of the artifact were unknown, but it was clear that at least some offworlders out in space were already quite aware of its existence. The new developments were perhaps more dangerous to Vale Reach than beneficial, but the full ramifications remained to be seen. There was some chance the crew of *Fidelity* could use the information to aid their negotiations when they reached Ruarken High Senate, but it also made their world more of a target than ever.

Cal watched as a dockworker carried equipment into a large cable car. The man was working methodically, loading canisters of gas at a fast but steady pace. At least two dozen canisters were stacked in the carriage already, but the dockworker seemed to be accelerating. Others came to watch the man's actions, forming a small crowd.

The worker moved on to a group of crates, each containing cartons in bright-orange packaging. The others in the repair bay began to question him, but the man ignored them. One of them moved to block his path, and he impatiently pushed his way past. More people came to block him, their clear confusion growing. Cal watched the dispute. It wasn't normal—he could tell from their obvious concern.

The dockworker grabbed a large armful of orange cartons and forced his way through the small crowd to board the cable car. Several other workers stepped on board with him, but the man didn't hesitate to pull a lever that closed a door and detached the cable car from the repair platform. Cal got to his feet, his unease growing. The cable car began to ascend toward *Fidelity*. Cal anxiously walked a few steps, fidgeting with his hands. The cable car was soon far out of reach for everyone on the platform. He needed to tell someone aboard the ship what was happening. Cal searched his crumpled uniform for his communications device, his fingers fumbling as he tried to connect to *Fidelity*'s channels.

The people inside the cable car surrounded the dockworker. They were fighting, Cal realized, throwing punches. It was hard to make out much in the scuffle. Suddenly, the situation changed, as only the original dockworker was left standing. Somehow, he had fought off all his assailants, leaving them beaten on the floor.

Cal felt a heavy, horrified feeling grip his chest as the dockworker began to haul them over the railings and throw them out of the cable car, one by one. They fell down to the platform, hitting the deck loudly. A visceral groan came from everyone in the hangar bay. Cal's heart accelerated to a state of terror. There was no doubt it was murder.

His datapad finally connected to *Fidelity*, but the emergency channel registered as completely busy. The car continued to climb rapidly. In a handful of seconds, it would contact *Fidelity* near the main engine array. Gunfire broke out from around the platform, loud and sharp, as a handful of workers began to shoot at the homicidal man at the cable car's controls. Cal realized what was happening. The explosives on board would detonate when they collided with *Fidelity*'s hull. It was a suicide attack.

Cal looked around, trying to see if anyone could stop what was happening. The commotion and the shooting had attracted attention from all around the hangar bay. Many of the people seemed hesitant to fire guns, as there were still people lying unconscious on the floor of the carriage who'd be killed if the explosives were accidentally struck, though it would surely detonate anyway when it reached the side of the ship.

Cal saw a doorway hatch open in the side of *Fidelity*, and a man leaned out. It was someone he recognized, Major Rosco, one of his comrades on their journey. Rosco carried a Vale Reach military rifle. He took aim with it for a second. Cal had to get in contact with him, in case Rosco didn't understand what was happening. Cal had access to his private communication number. Rosco fired a shot. Cal thought he saw a spray of blood as the bullet struck the man at the carriage's controls, but he didn't seem to flinch. Rosco fired again, and the man took cover. Cal heard the sound of his datapad connecting to Rosco's earpiece.

"Rosco he's going to blow up the ship!" Cal shouted. "It's a suicide bomb."

"Roger that," Rosco said. He shot several more times, to no effect.

"It's still going," said Cal.

"I see that," said Rosco. "Maybe I can stop the machinery."

Rosco fired several more shots and hit the motor that pulled the carriage along the steel cable. The carriage came to an abrupt halt. Cal breathed an enormous sigh of relief, as though a physical pressure had been lifted from him.

He saw there was still movement inside the carriage. The dockworker was doing something. Cal reached into his uniform and pulled out a pair of binoculars. He could see the dockworker collecting the orange cartons of explosives and attaching them to some kind of harness around his body.

"He's up to something in there," Cal told Rosco.

The dockworker had swiftly attached as many explosives to himself as he could. Cal spotted a coil of steel cable bundled in his hand. Suddenly, the man leapt out of the carriage and hurled the steel cable at their vessel. It struck the side of *Fidelity* and somehow held in place. The dockworker gripped its length and swung underneath the ship, dangling from the hull. Cal's heart began to race again as the man climbed.

"Rosco, he's attached himself to *Fidelity* with some kind of line, and he's still climbing up! He's going to reach the ship soon."

Rosco leaned farther out from the hatch with his rifle. "I can't see him. Does he still have explosives?" Rosco asked.

"Definitely," said Cal.

The man ascended steadily. Cal moved to watch Rosco through the binoculars. Cal could see the frustration in his face. Rosco could get no clear line of sight to the dockworker, who was directly beneath the ship.

Cal felt himself panicking as he watched. Rosco was unsure what to do. The dockworker was still climbing, hand over hand. He had to have had immense arm strength. Rosco disappeared from the hatch for a moment then returned, carrying some more items that Cal couldn't identify. Cal saw him carefully attach a length of rope to the exterior of *Fidelity* by the edge of the hatch. With an uncomfortable surge of fear, Cal realized Rosco was planning to lower himself down and try to separate the attacker from the side of their vessel. If he came within range of the man's explosives, Rosco would be doomed.

"Rosco, if you go down there, you'll be in the blast range. It's too dangerous," Cal said.

"I don't see any other way to deal with this," he replied. "We have to protect our ship at any cost. I need to get this man away from *Fidelity*."

He took a deep breath and lowered himself down from the hatch on the rope he'd secured. His rifle was still tucked under his arm and attached by a shoulder strap. Rosco slid down the rope gradually, attempting to aim his weapon with one hand.

Cal watched him fire several shots. Blood splattered out from the climbing dockworker, but the man continued without slowing. It seemed impossible. Rosco fired several more bursts, hitting the dockworker again. There was no effect. Rosco hesitated for a moment, evidently sharing Cal's sense of disbelief. Then he fired at the metal cable that the man climbed up. It wobbled violently as bullets struck it, but its steel material was too resilient to break.

Rosco seemed to have another idea. He swung backward and forward, generating momentum, increasing the horizontal distance as he moved like a pendulum. Then he reached out and managed to grab hold of the dockworker's cable. Rosco wrapped his legs around the other cable to steady himself, then reached around to the other equipment he carried on his waist, the rifle hanging from its strap around his neck and his other arm still tightly gripping the rope that supported him. He took out a small welding torch with his other hand and began burning through the steel cable.

Underneath him, the dockworker began to increase his rate of ascent. He was getting so close to Rosco, but Cal resisted saying anything that would distract his comrade from using the welding torch. Any explosion would kill both of them.

The steel cable suddenly split and broke. In that moment, the dockworker threw himself upward and caught hold of Rosco's boot with both hands. The two men began to spin and dangle wildly, both hanging from the single rope that Rosco had secured. Rosco frantically kicked at the man, hitting the man's hand, but his attacker's grip was too tight to be shaken. Then Cal saw Rosco put the tip of his foot against the clasp of his boot and flick it open. The boot slipped off his foot.

The dockworker with his explosive harness fell, still gripping Rosco's boot, plummeting to the hangar floor below. He exploded on impact, and Cal dived for cover as the sound of shrapnel striking hard metallic surfaces rattled around the whole chamber. The deafening shock of the blast slowly faded as it reverberated in the environment. Cal looked around and saw as the smoke cleared that Rosco was climbing back up to the open hatch above him. There were shouts of anger and disbelief from the dockworkers, but Cal felt numb with the threat over. A wave of relief and fear came over him. Rosco was alive. The danger had passed, and yet the nature of the threats to their ship had changed. Cal sat on the hard metal platform as his adrenaline was replaced with a deep feeling of dread. He had to speak with *Fidelity*'s leaders immediately. Things were escalating.

Chapter 2

Rosco briskly marched down the corridors of *Fidelity*. Their time at the repair station was being cut short—the chance to rest was over. The crew had been ordered to return to the ship immediately. They were under attack once again, and it was too dangerous for them to be anywhere but aboard and ready for departure. They'd become scattered throughout the repair station but were now arriving via the cable car system at *Fidelity*'s open hatches. Rosco had ensured that thorough checks were being performed on each incoming carriage, given his bad experience just an hour before.

"Major Rosco!" he heard someone calling from behind. He turned to find Caladon Heit walking toward him.

"Operator Heit," he said in greeting.

"There's something I need to tell you."

Rosco felt a pang of concern. He'd learned not to underestimate Cal's issues.

"What is it?"

"Well..." Cal gestured for Rosco to step into an alcove with him.

Rosco reluctantly followed him then nodded for Cal to speak.

"So, you recall that when we first docked at the station here, we made contact with our homeworld through the FTL communications lines?"

"Of course," said Rosco.

"And then after the official calls were done, there was time for crew members to make personal calls back home?"

"Yes." Rosco began to have an idea of where Cal might be going with this.

"Well, I called my fiancée, Eevey," said Cal, "and I got through to her."

"That's good. I remember you telling us about her. How did it go?"

"Well, there was someone else there with her, in the flat. It didn't go great, to be honest."

Rosco looked down at the floor. "Oh, Cal, I'm so sorry." He patted Cal on the shoulder. "That's sad to hear. How are you holding up?"

Cal shuffled his feet and shook his head. He took a deep breath and hesitated, clearly struggling. "So, this person was... the Ambassador of the Tylder Empire."

Rosco stared at him. "Are you being serious right now?"

Cal nodded. "I mean, that's who she claimed to be."

Rosco reached for his communicator and brought it up to speak. He paused and looked at Cal again. "And she was an offworlder? Someone not from Vale Reach?"

"I mean…" Cal thought back to the woman. "She was around nine feet tall, with some kind of artificial skin, so… yeah, she's an offworlder."

Rosco activated his communicator. "Advocate Fargas? We have a situation. Come and meet me on the eastern outer deck. I think we need you immediately." Rosco disconnected. "The lawyer's on the way." He sent a note to Fargas, outlining what Cal had already said. "Are we in any immediate danger?"

"Maybe," said Cal.

"Goddamn it, Cal!"

Cal nodded. "Maybe it's not that bad? I mean, she didn't seem entirely hostile…"

Rosco sighed. "I need to bring Captain Haran in on this as well."

"The captain?" Cal sounded nervous.

Captain Haran had been badly injured when the pirate-boarding parties attacked their ship, suffering a skull fracture. She'd been recovering and recently transferred to the onboard infirmary as part of the crew's return to the ship. Rosco had been operating as temporary captain for several days since her injury, but she was awake and recovering and would expect to be kept up to speed.

Advocate Fargas appeared, walking down the corridor. "He did what!?" Fargas shouted. His wrinkled faced peered out from within his voluminous blue robes. He looked angrily at the busy corridor around them. "Get someplace private!" he barked at Rosco and Cal.

Rosco ushered them into a nearby room and locked the door.

"You spoke to the Tylder Ambassador?" Fargas asked. He seemed to be hyperventilating, almost struggling to speak.

"Yes," said Cal. "She was—"

"Mother of God, the actual Tylder Amb—do you understand there is protocol to be followed if you've made contact with a technocratic diplomat?" Fargas restrained himself from shouting further, then gestured for Cal to continue speaking.

Rosco placed his datapad on a nearby table, and Captain Haran's face appeared on its surface. Her head was still thickly wrapped in bandages. She didn't say anything but watched.

"Well," Cal began, wide-eyed in trepidation, backed into a literal and figurative corner. "I called Eevey, and she answered. But she wasn't alone. The Ambassador was there, waiting for me. Apparently, she'd calculated that I was certain to call Eevey at that moment."

"So, she knows who you are?" Fargas asked.

Cal nodded. "She claims to know who all of our crew are. She's determined our identities."

Rosco maintained professional composure, but it was unnerving to hear.

Fargas growled slightly in barely suppressed frustration. "I suppose that extends to me too…"

Rosco had never seen those emotions from the lawyer. Nothing had particularly fazed him before now.

Fargas turned to Cal. "So, she was waiting for you on that call? Why?"

"To deliver a message. She told us to turn back. To abandon the mission," Cal said. He relayed the Ambassador's ultimatum and the entire conversation as best as he remembered it.

Rosco folded his arms. "Vale Reach needs our operation. That's not an option."

"What is the Ambassador even doing on Vale Reach?" Captain Haran asked, her voice a dry croak.

"I don't know. Apparently, something that involves Eevey and some others," said Cal. "Eevey mentioned working for the Ambassador now."

"Working with her? How?" Rosco demanded.

"Professional employment, I assume. Eevey worked as an anthropologist in the region around the capital city. I don't know exactly what projects she was working on. She kept those private… She was doing historical research, last time I was there. Nothing that I imagine could be related to what we do."

"And how long have you known Eevey?" said Fargas.

Cal was a little stunned by the question. "Four years."

"So the Ambassador is assembling people for some project on Vale Reach," Captain Haran said. "What more do we know about that?"

Cal sighed and shook his head. "I guess we didn't get into the specifics of it. There was a lot going on in the conversation. But whoever this Ambassador is, she's active now on Vale Reach and doesn't seem to be hiding herself."

"Surely, it's illegal for an offworlder to be on Vale Reach," Rosco said. "The Binding Treaty prevents any foreign influence on our planet."

"She could easily get a diplomatic exception," Fargas said with a wave of his hand. "Hell, I managed to get one. It's not that hard."

They were quiet for a moment, each calculating the ramifications of what they'd heard.

"Could that be related to what happened in the repair hangar bay?" Captain Haran asked, rubbing her bandaged head.

"That's under investigation," said Rosco. "We should have some findings soon." He turned to Fargas. "Who are these agents that the Ambassador mentioned?"

"Anyone. Could be anyone," Fargas murmured.

"Did I do the right thing by declining her demands?" Cal asked quietly. "I might have gotten ahead of myself when I said it... I guess I had an emotional moment. I was thinking about all the people who died in the attack on the highway."

"The Ambassador already said that she wouldn't prevent the Legion from occupying our land," said Rosco.

"Which means we continue without change to our mission," said Captain Haran.

Cal exhaled in relief. "Maybe the call went well, then? At least it's all over now."

"The call is over, at least, that much is true," said Fargas. "The damage is done, so to speak. But yes." He nodded. "You did the right thing."

There was a knock on the door, and they all paused. Rosco hit the unlock button and opened the door a few inches.

The ship's new chief engineer, Leda Palchek, was outside. "Major Rosco," she said, "we've gotten word that something's abnormal about the dead body in the repair bay."

"What?" Rosco said. "The man who attacked us?" He lowered his voice. "Is there much of him left?"

"What I know is that there's a crowd forming down on the platform below the ship. They look disturbed. There's definitely something happening down there," she replied.

Rosco frowned. "If it wasn't for the other station workers that were killed, we'd need to assume the station had turned against us, but that can't be true." He sighed. "Something has gone terribly wrong for them, hasn't it? I got close to that man. He was deranged. It didn't seem natural."

"I think we need to go down and investigate," said Leda.

Rosco could tell that she was already prepared to leave the ship, with bags of gear on her back and attached to her utility belt.

"We can do that soon. Don't leave the ship without me." He shut the door then quickly opened it again. "I mean it."

Leda was already walking away.

*

Cal and Yendos surveyed the main screen on *Fidelity*'s cylindrical bridge. They shared the task of determining exactly which FTL jump routes the ship should attempt as it continued the mammoth task of reaching the Ruarken High Senate.

The bridge was a hive of activity, as the starship was prepped for launch as soon as possible. Crew performed checks and tests as *Fidelity*'s reactor awoke from hibernation and powered up to high capacity. The repairs would have to suffice as they were, Cal thought. They needed to leave without drawing any attention to their departure.

He and Yendos had a frosty professional relationship and had experienced several disagreements already. Supposedly, they were united by a common purpose of finding the best path through the stars for *Fidelity* to reach the Ruarken Senate, but the imbalance of their knowledge made cooperation difficult. Cal was still suspicious of Yendos's real motivations, as the man was an offworlder with no ties to Vale Reach and whom they'd found stranded on a barren planet.

It seemed too convenient. For that reason, Cal's role on the bridge included ensuring that someone from Vale Reach agreed with Yendos's assessments when directing the ship.

Yendos claimed to be an explorer who'd crashed on an isolated world along with his assistant, Ontu. He was a giant within *Fidelity*'s confines, standing nearly twice as tall as Cal did and wearing a black leather space suit that he never removed. He'd offered his services as a navigator in exchange for being taken on board, despite the strict secrecy of *Fidelity*'s operation. Though Yendos had undoubtedly contributed to the success of their journey so far, Cal had good cause to question his techniques when calculating jump routes. *Fidelity* had not always arrived exactly where they intended.

Cal was academically trained. For years, he'd studied the limited mathematical data that Vale Reach had recorded from the transit points in their local star system. It was something that had occupied much of his youth and his short professional career, but the material available to his homeworld was just so sparse. He had been refining his model thoroughly over the past weeks. When he observed a new transit point, he could calculate the major destinations to which it could lead.

His sense of success had been short-lived, however, as Yendos had revealed to the crew the existence of many other hidden exits to the transit points, either secret or forgotten, difficult to detect, and perhaps even harder to successfully reach. Cal was greatly bothered by how little they knew of what was ahead. Vale Reach's handful of star maps had ceased to be relevant after they'd crossed the Highway of Thelmia. The ship had no real understanding of the path forward. And yet, Yendos claimed he could predict what was ahead.

"I was here very many decades ago. I can follow my feet," Yendos said, his voice emitting from a small metal speaker built into the front of his hood.

"Obviously, that's not possible," said Cal.

"I thought the idiom from your language would correctly convey the situation," Yendos replied.

Cal was quiet for a moment. "So you're telling me the only way for us to know which way to go is to just blindly follow whatever you say? At each junction, you'll just have an idea for us?"

"I've been here before," said Yendos. "I'm certain of this. But the memories are proving harder than I'd hoped for me to access. An understanding of astral directions is built into me. Once I'm able to orient myself with a star system, the ordering of my memories becomes clear to me."

"I guess that's just a 'yes,' then," Cal muttered, rubbing his chin as he looked at the star map. The path behind them was covered in intricate labels of data that they'd recorded. The star systems ahead were virtually blank, except for a single glowing point that floated ahead of them like the light at the end of the tunnel: Ruarken. "You are completely certain that your path leads us here?" Cal pointed at it.

"All paths can lead there, from the right perspective," said Yendos. "But yes, we will be able to enter their territory from this direction. That much, I know."

Cal considered that for a second. "I'm not sure that we've really considered much about the shape of the Ruarken's territory. How spread out is it, as a place?"

"The High Senate is the most significant place in their empire. It's very dense. As I recall, they define themselves as a federation rather than an imperial territory, but that's often a technicality in practice. Ruarken is small, in spatial terms. They maintain a well-guarded perimeter, with the High Senate at its core. They have several highways they rigorously maintain, allowing them far-reaching access. We won't be approaching from any of those highways, though."

"Why not?"

Yendos turned to look down at him. "News has reached me about your meeting with the Ambassador. Her agents are not to be underestimated." Yendos nodded to the screen. "She'll have fail-safe precautions established along the highway routes. But within the Senate, her influence will be much more diminished. The Ruarken can identify their own people. There, she has to play by the same rules as everyone else."

Cal thought back to that inhuman woman in his call with Eevey. Yendos spoke of the Ambassador with reverence, even fear. "Is it true that the Ambassador controls many entire planets by herself?" he asked. He hated being dependent on Yendos for information.

"She doesn't need to," Yendos replied. "When she tells a planet what to do, they follow the instructions."

"Except for Vale Reach, thanks to us aboard this ship. We're defying her," Cal said.

Yendos was silent for a moment. "We are, indeed." His emotion was hard to read. He seemed nervous in a way Cal hadn't seen before.

"If we reach Ruarken Senate, our mission is complete. We can try and put this all behind us, maybe go back to our regular lives," said Cal.

"Agreed," Yendos said. "So, we need to finalize our next jump coordinates for your captain. I take it you'll be following my suggestion?"

"Have you seen this?" Cal waved his datapad at Yendos.

Yendos paused. "What is that?"

Cal was overjoyed to have secret information of his own. It was a briefing document sent to *Fidelity* by government operatives on Vale Reach via the FTL communication lines of the repair station, just before the ship's departure. "Reports from the homeworld, sent to the senior officers of the bridge, such as me." Cal wasn't entirely sure why he'd received it. "The situation on Vale Reach has changed," he said.

"How so?" Yendos asked.

Yendos was trying to read the datapad as Cal continued waving it. Cal realized he was smiling too much and adopted a serious face. "It says the Universal Legion has started orbital construction projects. So far, just empty frames and modules."

"Time for your planet grows short," said Yendos.

"Yeah." He suddenly felt very sad. "Yeah, I guess it does."

"It shows the Legion are not waiting for any further authorizations," said Yendos. "They're preparing their infrastructure for their occupation."

"So far, it's all just orbital stuff, mostly premade objects being moved into place. It doesn't impact us yet."

"It sets precedent," Yendos said. "It can be used to justify any further action."

"Damn." Yendos was right again.

"This is the beginning of the next stage for you. The calm before the storm is over. And whilst time is against you more than ever, it appears you have no desirable jump routes ahead." Yendos gestured at the screen. "I take it you'll be following my recommendation?"

Cal redirected his gaze to the star map. He thought for a while. "We can avoid time debt if we pass through here." He pointed to a particular jump point on the large diagram.

"I was intrigued to see if you would pick that. It's an active battlefield reclamation zone."

"Battlefield reclamation? As in, the battle is over, yes?"

"Indeed so," said Yendos. "One century previously. A large Makron invasion fleet was destroyed here by a combined-alliance force. Fortunately, that's now just history for this region."

"The Makron?" Cal was getting edgy from the number of unpleasant shocks in their journey. "The Makron are present here, in this area?"

"No longer the case," said Yendos. "The entire power of the Greater Makron Empire is less than that of the rest of the galaxy combined against them, but not by a very large margin. As a consequence, only a severe threat of Makron invasion is enough to unify a significant coalition against them. Otherwise, the opposition to them is highly disorganized."

"That opposition would include us?"

"True." Yendos offered a small shrug. "As a consequence, the Makron can afford to intrude into hostile territories without incurring any dangerous losses, from their perspective. The rate and intensity of the attacks depend on the personality of the particular overlord in command of the fleet. Some are more cautious than others. The largest waves of Makron incursion reach far indeed, but their holdings rarely last. They extend, and then they crumble. It is amazing that they can afford to be so wasteful. Regardless of their excesses, the next system should be safe for *Fidelity* with a competent pilot to navigate us around the designated danger zones. That at least you do have, in the form of Marraz."

"According to the data that we downloaded at the repair station, the dockworkers tagged the system as having"—Cal paused for a moment in disbelief—"unexploded ammunitions, heat-seeking minefields…" He hesitated as he kept reading. "Space acid, dormant vessel hulks… Yendos, you can't possibly be serious about this. How will we be safe in there?"

"The majority of explosive material has been collected and dismantled, as have the other threats. The system is registered as dangerous, as the cleanup process is not complete, but navigation of it is quite possible."

Cal looked at him. "Can you guarantee that?"

"I'm risking my own life here as much as anyone else's, aren't I?" he replied curtly.

"There has to be a better route. A route that doesn't put us in mortal danger."

"Alternative routes exist." Yendos waved a hand then raised a finger. Cal noticed that it had a built-in laser pointer of some kind. Yendos indicated a few paths with his laser. "But they will require several additional jumps, probably through territories that will demand payment in exchange for allowing your passage. Let me be honest with you, Cal." He paused. "Why are we debating this? What alternative does *Fidelity* have to following my guidance? You may have updated your data banks with publicly available material, but I've seen more planets than the average space farer does in five lifetimes. If I say a route is best for you, you should probably choose to do what I say."

Cal's jaw muscles clenched in frustration as he considered the other routes. They were all too far off course or beyond the power of their FTL drive to achieve without time debt. "We don't really have any choice, do we?"

"Not if you want to get to Ruarken within six months."

Cal let out a long exhale. "How long do you think it would take for the Universal Legion to finish building one of those orbital structures above Vale Reach?"

"Maybe a week," said Yendos. "Maybe less."

"Damn," Cal said again.

*

Rosco and Leda stepped out of the cable car and onto the repair platforms. Rosco had noticed on the journey down that Leda had a small trail of stitches in the side of her neck. They seemed new, and not related to the other minor injuries they'd all sustained in the journey. He decided not to ask about it yet.

A crowd of dozens of people in dockworkers outfits had assembled, facing away from Rosco and Leda. None of them had noticed their arrival, focusing instead on something at the center of their huddle. Rosco could tell from their body language that something was very wrong.

"Should we introduce ourselves to them?" Leda asked Rosco.

"I suppose we should."

As they approached, the crowd turned to face them with hard, suspicious gazes. The emotion was raw, even venomous. The *Fidelity* crew had become intensely unpopular.

Rosco raised a hand in greeting as he spoke. "I'm Major Rosco from the starship *Fidelity*. This is Chief Engineer Palchek. We were attacked by one of your dockworkers earlier in the day."

An old man with a short white beard emerged from the crowd and pointed a finger at them. "Who are you, really?"

"I assure you that we're just travelers on a routine diplomatic journey. My name is Major Rosco, and I am the acting captain of my ship."

"You're something more than that," the old man said. There was a moment of hostile silence. His expression softened slightly. "You don't know much, do you?" He gestured for them to come forward, and the crowd separated a little more to let them through.

"Know about what?" Rosco said quickly, but he walked to where the old man indicated.

Leda followed slightly behind him. Rosco saw something moving on the floor behind the crowd, and became aware of hissing and bubbling sounds. "Oh gods," Leda gasped in disgust.

There was a dead body on the floor, presumably the remains of the man who had attacked Rosco, but it writhed and twitched chaotically. It was indeed bubbling, with thick white foam emerging from the dead man's insides. The corpse was far more intact than he'd expected. He'd heard the explosion triggered by the falling man's impact. The limbs were missing, yet the body was barely burned at all. It was regenerating, he realized with shock, its flesh knitting back together. "What the hell is happening to this thing?" he asked Leda quietly. "Is he coming back to life?"

She'd turned pale, a look of deep revulsion on her face, but she resisted the urge to look away. "I don't think so," Leda murmured. "There's not enough material left for that. His insides have somehow turned to goo... Parts of his organs are liquefying. Surely, he can't create any new matter..."

"We've never seen anything like this," said the old dockworker.

"Never?" Rosco asked.

"Never," the man repeated.

Rosco whistled. "What do you think this is, Leda?"

"I think he's digesting himself for more energy," she said. She squatted to take a closer look but kept herself at least two meters away. "His body looks like its breaking down parts of itself to repair the other parts. He's gaining muscles and losing organs. But as I say, it looks like he's just too damaged from the explosion to reform."

"That could explain how he lived after I shot him so many times," Rosco said.

"We knew this man," the old dockworker murmured, "or we thought that we did. He was a father and a husband before he became this thing here. He attacked people who were like his family. Do you have any explanation at all for what has happened to him?"

Leda looked at Rosco. "I don't know what to suggest."

"It means this dock is no longer safe for our ship," said Rosco. "It's been compromised, even if the people here don't know how."

"Look." Leda pointed urgently. "Look at the face."

Much of the crowd groaned and turned away. At least one person vomited. The man's skin dissolved violently into foam that shot up in droplets. The foam slipped away to reveal the face of a remarkably different individual with new skin and different features.

Leda narrowed her eyes. "There's no scientific explanation for that unless… Is he regrowing into someone else? What could cause that? A virus? Genetics?" She turned to look up at Rosco. "Whatever it is, they should burn it to dispose of it."

*

On *Fidelity*'s bridge, the atmosphere suddenly became quiet. Cal looked up from his console, where he was inputting detailed commands for the upcoming FTL jump. At the far end of the bridge, the main entrance portal opened, and a figure moved through, slowly and slightly hunched over.

"Captain on deck!" an officer shouted, and they all saluted the new arrival.

Captain Haran walked through the silent, awestruck group, bandages still covering the top of her head. She ascended the stairs to the captain's chair, took her seat, and looked directly at the main screen.

"Thank you, officers," she said quietly, with a slight smile. "All crew, return to your duties. Communications, give me a channel to the whole ship."

Cal heard the muffled click of the all-ship speaker engage.

"*Fidelity*, this is Captain Haran speaking. Our purpose remains unchanged. We have learned more of the mysteries of our homeworld. We now understand that the people of Vale Reach possess an ancient relic, possibly dating back to mankind's earliest exploration of the stars. Its powers are unknown. It likely remains buried deep under the earth of our world. This information had been passed to us by hostile pirate forces, but we have good reason to believe its veracity."

Cal remembered the words of the Lizard King's minion, Tarufa, and her cackling laugh as she'd taunted the wounded bridge crew. He still struggled to understand what had motivated her.

"We must stay resolute," Haran continued. "This new knowledge only heightens the danger our homeworld faces. It increases our value as a target. At the far side of our journey lies our destination… and safety. Our mission remains for us to secure the protection of the Ruarken High Senate for our home. If we fail, the world we return to may be an industrial wasteland or worse, if we are able to return at all.

"The signs for us are good. Our mission so far has succeeded. We know our lands remain intact. The Vale Reach government urges us on. When our mission began, each of us heard the original broadcast from the Universal Legion that threatened our world. They are willing to kill as many people on Vale Reach as they need to achieve their demands. They feel no remorse or doubt. Remember that. Our journey matters above everything. It is the only path to a future with dignity and life for the people of our world."

Despite his cynicism, Cal felt a surge of pride. They truly were fighting to save the existence of billions.

Captain Haran signaled to disconnect the communication line. "Now, open a private channel to the pilot's compartment," she said.

The communications officer nodded.

She frowned as she regarded him through the video feed. "Operator Marraz, don't expect that I've forgotten your dishonesty. You withheld information from us. You were aware of the Seed of Steel's existence and said nothing to us. Perhaps you're too accustomed to being surrounded by pirates and deceitful lowlifes, but here amongst the Vale Reach Navy, you would be stripped of your position if it were at all possible. Do not forget that your loyalty is to your birth world of Vale Reach and no one else. Consider this your last warning."

"Yes, Captain," came the reply from the pilot's compartment. "I've always had Vale Reach's best interests at heart, I swear to you."

Captain Haran disconnected the communication channel.

Before long, the ship was prepared for its final approach to the next transit jump. A new message appeared on the main viewing screen. "Captain, we're receiving an unknown transmission," said an officer. "It's a live signal."

Captain Haran's face darkened with concern. "Put it through to the main screen."

An image of a face filled the screen, female and artificial but not the Ambassador. It was Tarufa, the leader of the pirate warband that had attacked them. It'd been less than a week since Tarufa had stood on *Fidelity*'s bridge, having killed the mission's original leader, Councilor Theeran. Her blue complexion and metallic silver eyes loomed over them.

"*Fidelity*, why do you appear to be about to destroy yourself?" she asked, a perplexed expression on her face.

"You have no right to demand any information from this ship," Captain Haran retorted.

"Captain Haran, how refreshing to see you up and active," said Tarufa with a sinister smile. "I feel you owe me a debt of gratitude after what I did to those Legionaries who attacked you."

"You're owed nothing," said Haran. "Your crew killed many of us."

Cal wondered where Tarufa could physically be. The transmission showed only a close view of her face, but she seemed alone and not on the bridge of any ship.

Tarufa cleared her throat. "I went to a significant effort to rescue your ship from the grip of the Enforcers unit that had arrested you. Wiping out an entire vessel of the Universal Legion is no trivial task, you know? Members of my own crew were killed. And now, you seem to be sailing directly into a minefield, about to throw away my good work."

"Disconnect her," Haran said to an officer.

"How is she speaking to us, sir?" Cal asked.

Haran gave him a stern look.

"It's impossible unless she's somehow passed through the highway with us," he added.

Tarufa shrugged. "I may have installed some simple listening devices in your bridge. Nothing too invasive, just enough for me to keep an eye on you and send the occasional FTL message from far away."

There was a pause.

"Did you contact us simply to offer your sincere advice?" Haran asked bitterly.

"My advice is for you to reach Ruarken intact and unexploded," she replied in a flat tone. "Don't throw your lives away."

"We are passing through a reclaimed battlefield system to approach Ruarken by the fastest possible route," Haran said with a snarl. "We'd be traveling faster if you hadn't wrecked much of the interior of our ship."

"So risky." Tarufa shook her head. "No room for error there."

"We have a skilled pilot, don't we?" the captain replied.

Tarufa gave a sharp burst of laughter, her eyes revealing genuine amusement. "That you do. That you do. Can Marraz hear me?"

"No," Haran said.

"I don't believe you. Marraz, you scoundrel. Everything depends on you." Tarufa shook her head in clear disbelief. "May the gods have mercy."

☐

Chapter 3

Fidelity jumped to a new star system. Leda heard a ripple of discomfort from among those on the bridge. Cartographer Yendos had briefed the ship about what they should expect to find, but Leda still felt that he'd underestimated how hazardous this region would be. The scanning signals that *Fidelity* transmitted as light rays returned back to them over a period of several minutes, and so the map of the star system was continuously populating with deadly warnings. The more details that filled in on the map, the more tenuous their position seemed.

Leda saw that the devastation was quite unlike anything they'd seen before. It implied titanic vessels and the destructive power of societies millennia more advanced than their own. She noticed laser scars and huge blast craters in moons and the shattered fragments of comets that spun at chaotic angles. The fighting had been protracted and intense. Each side had taken desperate measures. She felt a pang of fear that one day Vale Reach could look like these moons did, an uncomfortable thought that the entire bridge crew surely shared. They could have been looking at their future.

The hazardous regions formed the shape of a jagged claw, she thought, one that seemed to reach out to seize the planets in the system. The symbols on the star map were spiked and sharp, some were pooled like liquid where the tides and currents of orbital gravity had pulled them, whilst other remnants of the battle were more randomly scattered. Entering many regions would mean certain death, whilst others were flagged with unknown levels of danger.

No-one would intentionally have done this to their own star system. The pattern of hazards was permanently destructive, somehow bordering on careless. Leda concluded that the weapons had been deposited by starships that were minelayers. She envisaged vessels leaving a steady cloud of dormant objects in their wake.

They registered the dead hulks of many destroyed warships. The space was far from unpopulated—junkyards floated near dense clusters of derelict ships, where the recovered and recycled remnants of the vessels were held in storage. It was a massive operation. Smaller ships were all around, still harvesting material from the more inaccessible regions.

As an engineer, Leda felt most stimulated in such moments. By her personal assessment, the abandoned predatory weapons were the worst aspect—they could hunt anything that came within range. Fortunately, many small-scale scavenger ships were flowing through the system and had left messenger buoys stationed in space, marking the distances at which passing vessels would be safe. *Fidelity* would depend on those anonymous messages for its survival. The buoys seemed distributed haphazardly, but Leda's instincts suggested that they would be reliable. They needed them to be, or their mission and lives would be over quickly. The scavengers themselves paid no attention to *Fidelity*—their ship was of little value to any who observed it.

"Senior officers, give me your appraisal," Captain Haran said.

"There's no shortage of potential problems, obviously," said Major Rosco. "It's not as bad as the pirates' nest we entered, but… it leaves us with limited options. It looks as though the battle here occurred just a few years ago. Are we sure it's been a century?"

"The cleanup operation has been gradual," Advocate Fargas responded. "To tell the truth, it's likely been neglected due to corruption. It's all just been labeled as generic hazardous waste so they can leave it for private scavenger crews to deal with. By dragging the process out, they give more time for unregistered reclamations to profit from what they acquire and funnel it to black market clients."

"I'd like to highlight that what we see here is still within the parameters that I described to you," Yendos said. "My guidance is accurate. This is a risk that we all agreed to take, and it is quite manageable."

Leda's attention became drawn to the furious rate at which Cal seemed to be calculating, jabbing his finger at his console's keypad and frantically scribbling notes.

It seemed that Leda was not alone in observing him. "Operator Heit, do you concur with that assessment?" said Captain Haran.

Cal continued to work in a frenzied fashion for several more seconds. He dropped his pencil and made eye contact with the captain. "It's all within the parameters that Yendos predicted, yes. This star system matches his description," he said with a sigh. "We need to finalize our path through."

"We're getting a call from the pilot's compartment," an officer called from the bridge.

"Put him on-screen," said Captain Haran, still barely keeping the distaste from her voice. "Operator Marraz," she said as the image of him in the pilot seat appeared. His actual position was beyond the front of the bridge, in a private compartment. "I trust you are aware of the life-and-death nature of the task we now require from you?"

"Yes, sir." Marraz sounded focused and busy, still in the middle of his own calculations. "Do they use the phrase 'threading the needle' in the Vale Reach Navy?"

"They do," replied Haran coldly.

Leda could see it would be a highly complex task to traverse the system. The calculations would need to be precise. Fortunately, precise calculation was the very nature of space travel.

The speeds required to cross a solar system in a useful time were too immense for the nuclear engines of a typical starship thruster to be able to achieve much meaningful change.

When a starship moved between planets, it had little control of its velocity. Instead, the gravitational wells of large stellar objects were used to change direction or speed. Their winding path through the star system would require them to make a great many such maneuvers in succession.

The engines on the ship could reorient *Fidelity*, nudging the vessel off course. It was a gradual process, but it allowed *Fidelity* to aim itself at a particular planet and select the specific angle of its approach and exit trajectory. But there was no way *Fidelity* could bring itself to a halt. They were always moving forward.

When docking with other ships or space stations, *Fidelity* could match its speed to the orbital velocity of the station and create a state of no relative motion in geosynchronous orbit. Nothing in space was ever stationary, but if objects shared a common position and common vectors, then a stable environment between the two could be established.

"I can do it in thirty-two gravity boost maneuvers," said Marraz, still visible onscreen.

"Thirty-two?" Haran clearly didn't believe him.

The route he described appeared on Leda's console display. She immediately began to dissect it for weaknesses. It zigzagged from planet to planet and around the entire star system, curling around itself like a knot as it wrapped around gas giants and rocky dwarf worlds.

"It goes back and forth. Thirty-two gravity maneuvers are what it will take to reach our desired transit point out of here. That's roughly five days. It avoids any lethal regions. I can stay awake for the entire process, but if you've got any extra stimulants you've been holding back from me in the med bay, now's the time to let me have them. Flying with a buzz is the right way to do this."

Leda heard Captain Haran's angry response to him, but she'd stopped listening. She was becoming lost in the details of the map, fascinated by the specifics she found in Marraz's plan.

*

Deep into the night, Leda stared at the ceiling. She lay in bed, her eyes open in the darkness. Her mind raced, calculating in many directions at once. Their own vessel was so fragile. The engineers had considered ways to upgrade *Fidelity* in the repair station, but the ship's very simple hull couldn't be integrated with the available hardware that they'd seen. The eight hundred meters of *Fidelity*'s length had seemed gargantuan when Leda had first laid eyes on the vessel, but now, it already seemed pitifully too little.

Hardware was free to be taken in this system, she considered. It drifted unclaimed between planets. Over ninety years had passed since the battle, but the urgent warnings and the scavengers all around showed how many remnants of war were still present despite such a length of time. Valuable material awaited harvesting deeper into the dangerous zones. Obviously, it was all a risk. But *Fidelity* was too vulnerable if it had no means to protect itself. Surely, there had to be something available that they could successfully take, some action that would enhance their position in a significant way, but even to see it was a challenge.

Leda reached up to touch her head and felt the stitches in her skin then moved to the others in her neck and back. The clinic on the repair station had told her that they would naturally dissolve after a few more days. So far, she had only hesitantly tested her implants, which were designed to speed up her nervous system in short, controlled bursts. She hoped they'd help her escape any dangerous situations.

Leda wasn't sure how her implants would operate within the legal system of Vale Reach. Foreign technology was strictly forbidden on her homeworld. Her personal upgrades would create some difficult questions for her to answer at the end of the mission.

None of the other ship crews *Fidelity* had so far encountered were without some kind of cybernetic modification. It was plainly obvious to Leda that a conventional human body was too fragile for the demands of living in space. Out between planets, those who weren't augmented would face life as an inferior class.

The general outline of an idea came to her, bringing specific structures and requirements. The flow of data and power rapidly became intricate as the blueprints took shape. The core of her idea was fully formed, but she needed to tease out the specifics. Leda took out her datapad and sent an urgent message to Cal.

"What?" he replied in confusion. "What is this? What is happening?" He seemed weary and disoriented.

"Cal, we need to talk about starships." She'd already studied the photographs of the Enforcer ship that had attacked them as they reached the Grand Highway of Thelmia, and of the pirate vessels in the Lizard King's lair.

"Now?" he asked. "Really? Does it have to be now?"

"Yes. I need to go through some layouts about specific starships abandoned in this system. You can help me do that."

Cal groaned, mumbling incoherently, but Leda sensed he agreed with the task. She knew it was an area that interested him.

"This one." She sent a specific data file to him. "Cross-reference it with these other spaceships here. And these too." She sent more. "What do they all have in common?"

There was a long silence on the line. She waited patiently for him to respond. "They're modular," he said with a gurgle.

"Exactly." Leda laughed in satisfaction. "I need you to find more examples."

*

The next morning, Leda arrived on the bridge with a bundle of papers under her arm. She'd risen from bed early then sat in the canteen for an hour, psychologically preparing herself for what she planned to do next. She got herself to a highly caffeinated state. What she was about to do would risk her credibility and her standing among the senior officers.

The bridge was still quiet when she entered. Out of the twenty crew present, most were wordlessly focused on monitoring the consoles in front of them. A handful of them conferred in small groups, but none paid any particular attention to her.

Marraz was twenty-four hours into the series of maneuvers that would successfully navigate *Fidelity* through the death trap of a system that surrounded them. Leda's plans would affect him, too, but for the time being, he didn't need to be distracted. Captain Haran was the most important member of her audience.

Leda walked to a central point in the bridge, faced Haran's captain's chair, and stood at attention.

After a moment, Captain Haran regarded her. "Chief Engineer Palchek?"

Leda began to speak. "Captain, I've conducted a recent evaluation of our ship's performance during the mission so far. These results are troubling." For fifteen minutes, she laid out a detailed analysis of the problems that *Fidelity* had faced. With virtually no weapons or defensive systems, their only strategy was to either hide or flee whenever they encountered unfriendly ships.

It had been a good approach in the early days, but it was also severely limiting them. In many situations, *Fidelity*'s protocol was simply to retreat when the route ahead was unsafe. That was not going to be an option going forward. The situation on Vale Reach was growing ever more urgent—the latest transmissions revealed that the Universal Legion had already begun construction work. No spare time remained. Even a single failed transit jump could severely impact their chances of reaching the Ruarken Senate within a suitable time.

Captain Haran said nothing as she listened to Leda's report. So far, Leda had stuck to the facts, very intentionally. Making contact with the homeworld had increased the pressure everyone felt. Seen from far away, their society seemed fragile and close to falling apart. Leda knew she was appealing to very real concerns that all of the crew, and Haran perhaps most of all, must have felt. She laid out each point in detail, describing the constraints each aspect of their ship faced. People paused their work to observe what was happening. All eyes on the bridge focused on her.

"The root cause of these problems is essentially our state of 'blindness,' not just in terms of our scanners and our star maps, but our computer systems. We don't have the right technology to properly access and investigate any of the database systems around us. There must be records in existence for all these star systems, as they're clearly populated. But the primitive state of our ship's internal network prevents us from seeing any of this information."

Next, Leda highlighted pieces of the hardware abandoned around them in space. She connected her datapad to the main screen and indicated several parts of their route back and forth across the star system, as well as the derelict ships within close reach of their path. Leda was quick to outline her proper understanding of the dangers present. She hoped the crew would understand where she was going with this, but they still couldn't have predicted the full scale of it.

"So, the next step for *Fidelity* is to extract a complete server module," she finished. "That means the communication arrays, the processors, the internal power supply... everything. These systems are far too complex for us to reverse engineer and build our own. We have to take one and restore it back to functionality aboard our own vessel."

"This is all certainly promising to consider, Chief Palchek," Captain Haran said.

Leda continued as though Haran hadn't spoken. "So far, we've observed multiple cultures using similar computer protocols, quite unlike anything on our own homemade Vale Reach machines. We are 'blind' because we cannot properly connect with any other databases we encounter. The server modules we can obtain will allow us to search for star systems that are friendly to our cause. It will change our mission from a gamble to a carefully calculated operation." Leda pressed a button on her datapad, and an image of a derelict starship filled the bridge's main screen. "Code named Gamma Alpha Epsilon Four-Oh-Two, but we'll need to devise a new name for it. It's around three times *Fidelity*'s mass, but crucially, it appears mostly intact, with no visible laser damage. It also has useful secondary assets, such as several complete weapons sockets located in external positions, easy for us to detach."

Captain Haran opened her mouth as if to speak.

"But how would we get within reach of it?" Leda continued quickly. She had to outline all the crucial elements quickly. "There's a solution for that too. We've actually learned a great deal about intercepting objects since we set off from Vale Reach. We've seen several techniques in action for vessel capture. Elastic cables are the key. Even for friendly exchanges, it seems likely that one vessel will often need to reel in the other to bring them together. Fortunately for us, our target is derelict and so has an extremely predictable position. It's not going to be evading us in any way. If we can make contact with just a single cable, we can tow the ship behind us and then bring it in closer to harvest its parts. We have explosive charges in our supplies for that, along with our projectile launcher. I can brew some kind of sticky glue that'll help our tow cable attach to the ship. Our own vessel won't have to deviate from its current route in any way."

Captain Haran had fallen silent, observing what was occurring in front of her.

"I propose this," said Leda, selecting a file on her datapad once again. An image of a new spacecraft, *Fidelity* but in a form that didn't exist yet, filled the screen. A ring of metal alloy support frames was welded together to encircle the hull. At either side were two rotating turrets onto which weapons had been mounted. The ship featured additional antennas, secondary reactors, and even a mockup of a shield generator. The image varied in its transparency, revealing interior details. Accompanying it was a list of required materials and the work times for each stage of the process. "This image is just for aspirational purposes."

"Chief Palchek, your face has gone purple. Please, sit down now," Haran said urgently.

"What?" She felt dizzy, became faint, then collapsed onto the floor of the bridge.

*

Leda opened her eyes slowly. She saw Cal.

"Damn, Leda, you were hyperactive back there. Are you feeling okay now?" Cal asked.

She was in the infirmary, she realized, as her vision cleared, and she became aware of her surroundings. She could hear the nursing staff somewhere in the room, but given that only Cal was by her bed, the situation couldn't have been that serious. She tried to respond, but it was still difficult for her to speak.

"You turned purple, man," said Cal. "Really dark purple." He looked at her suspiciously for a moment. "It didn't seem natural."

Leda tried to shrug in a nonchalant way, but that wasn't easy when she was still dizzy.

"You just kept talking and talking, and it became faster and faster. Unbelievably fast. Then you passed out and hit the floor, but it doesn't look like you bumped your head too badly. Stress and exhaustion, the doctors are saying. Don't worry—no one blames you for anything. I mean, we've all been through a hard time, especially you…"

Leda shut her eyes and tuned out the sound of Cal talking.

"So, tell me," Cal said, his voice quiet and conspiratorial, "how did you produce all that? I mean, I remember that when you called me last night, you were just figuring things out. You had no idea what you were going to do. I found some of those drifting hulks that your data's based on. And then you turn up today with fully developed blueprints? You had every margin of error calculated when you showed it all to Haran. You're essentially finished with those designs. There just weren't enough hours available for you. How did you find the time, Leda?" He waited for her to answer, gesturing for her to say something.

She didn't reply, pretending to be sleepy. Leda heard a knock on the door and the sound of Rosco's voice. She opened her eyes and peered around the room again. Rosco appeared at the doorway that led to the small area her bed was in. "You doing okay, Leda?" he asked.

"Yeah." She suddenly felt foolish and tried to sit up, though she was concerned to note that her muscles felt weaker than expected.

Rosco was smiling. There was something strange about the expression on his face. She realized there was something he had to tell her.

"What is it?" she asked.

Cal was smiling, too, she noticed, and looking at the floor.

"You made a strong impression with your presentation on the bridge," Rosco said.

Leda was starting to experience regret as her mind cleared. Perhaps she hadn't fully considered the reception her speech would get.

Rosco crossed his arms. "We're doing it." He looked expectant, waiting for her to comprehend.

"As in?"

"We ran the numbers," said Cal. "It all looks solid. Even the risk is minimal, since *Fidelity* doesn't have to deviate from its position."

"The senior officers all discussed it whilst you were out. Marraz in particular loved the secondary upgrades that you outlined. I think he's desperate for better hardware," said Rosco.

"Plus, it'll get us to Ruarken in much fewer jumps," said Cal.

"So…" Leda murmured. She fully opened her eyes and grinned. "It's happening."

*

DEFIANT SYSTEMS

Rosco left Leda's infirmary room. She was fine, despite the disturbing color that she had turned on the bridge. It had been as if she'd had some kind of seizure. Recycled air and rotational gravity were probably putting all kind of strange pressures on their bodies. His communicator began to beep—Captain Haran was calling him to an unscheduled briefing. He headed to meet with her in the ship's conference room.

She didn't say anything as he came in. Haran stood rather than sitting in any of the chairs, so Rosco remained standing, too, in the presence of his commanding officer. "We have a problem, Major Rosco," she said. "It's my personal problem, but I'm going to make it your problem too. We have a period of time unaccounted for on the bridge of this ship."

"When you were knocked unconscious from your injuries by the Enforcers?"

"The problem runs deeper than that." She quickly shook her head. "There was a period where no commanding officer was present on the bridge. The ship was, in effect, under the command of pirate forces."

"Yes." He hadn't considered it in quite that way. "The pirates were in full control."

"We have no idea what they did during that time. Tarufa just admitted that she's planted listening devices. They could have compromised our systems in all manner of ways. They could have attached tracking equipment, devices that are beyond our ability to detect. We are facing a security breach that opens up potentially unlimited questions."

Rosco frowned and nodded. He'd been driven out from the bridge by the intense fighting.

"And after the pirates left, once she'd eliminated the Enforcers, Tarufa just decided to let us keep our ship and sent us on our way to Ruarken." Something in the captain's demeanor expressed her doubt. "That's what she wants us to believe." Haran paused.

"Why?"

She pointed at him. "That's exactly what I'm wondering. She achieved some kind of goal here, and I believe someone on our bridge assisted her. Some kind of agreement was made, likely one contrary to Vale Reach's best interests, in exchange for Tarufa returning control of our ship to us. There are three candidates I've narrowed it down to. Yendos, the navigator; our pilot, Marraz; and of course, Advocate Fargas."

Rosco gave a sharp intake of breath in displeasure. "They're all vital to our operation in some form. They may be potential security risks, but can we relieve any of them of their duties? Marraz is irreplaceable at the current moment. Yendos knows more about the route forward than any of us, though Operator Heit can cover the basics of navigation. And Fargas, well… we'll need him when we get to Ruarken, if any of this is going to work. With Theeran gone, he understands our legal case better than anyone."

Councilor Theeran had been the mission's original leader, one of many killed by the pirates during the attack.

"Do not trust any of them, Rosco," she said. "And do not under any circumstances let them seize control of the bridge. This is a Vale Reach military ship, and it represents the people of Vale Reach. There is an unbroken chain of trust that extends from the homeworld to me and through to you. That's what ensures we protect the people back home. As long as we remain officers of Vale Reach, the mission isn't over."

Rosco nodded but hesitated for a second. "Captain, I have to ask something… Are we still certain that continuing onwards is in the best interests of our homeworld? In case we fail, has there been any progress in the negotiations between Vale Reach and the Universal Legion? Could we negotiate with the offworlder Ambassador who's in Arkstone City?"

Haran didn't seem displeased but appeared to be studying him carefully. "Councilor Theeran asked himself such questions every day. It was a calculus that consumed him. Perhaps it even made him too blinkered in his focus. He never wanted the Seed of Steel to come to light—he felt it would only endanger our planet and our people. Once we give away our rights to the Seed, even to the Ruarken High Senate, we have no leverage remaining."

"I know you have covert channels to report how the mission is going," he said.

"Before we left, Theeran set up a group of people on Vale Reach who he could count on to take action to protect our world, of which I am a member. Even the Vale Reach government itself cannot be fully trusted to be free of infiltration." She paused for a moment. "Theeran's dead now, likely betrayed by someone on this ship. He left a thick bundle of documents for this ship to follow in such an event."

"And that's our guide?"

She nodded. "Even if we receive contradictory orders from the capital. It's time you were brought into the group, Rosco. Should the situation on Vale Reach change in a way that negates our mission, then Theeran's comrades will send a specific code word to me. Until we hear that word, nothing stops the journey."

*

At the designated time, *Fidelity* launched its projectile on a precisely calculated path. The payload consisted of an adhesive fluid connected to a long unspooling wire. No automated weapons were in the area. They'd detected traces of unexploded ordinance but nothing that would actively hunt them.

Their operations on the captured vessel would need to be complete before *Fidelity* reached the next planet in the system to conduct a gravity-well maneuver in almost fourteen hours. At any time, they could disconnect and jettison the remnants of the hulk, prepare to enter the gravity well, and accelerate to their new speed.

On the bridge, the crew fell silent as they awaited confirmation of a successful hit on the target. The other vessel had a mass several times larger than their own, so *Fidelity*'s thrusters would have to work hard to ensure that their ship didn't change course once the connection was made.

Cal watched their ship's display screen show the relative position of Gamma Alpha Epsilon Four-Oh-Two. The whole of *Fidelity* was suddenly pulled in a particular direction. The crew held on tight to their surroundings, and the derelict ship's point on the map began to move. They congratulated each other as the position number ticked away like a countdown. The cable connecting the two ships had stabilized, and they could begin reeling it in like an immense fish on a line.

"It needs another name," Captain Haran said. She selected *Tenebrous* as its designation.

Over the next few hours, whilst the cable retracted, Cal studied the derelict vessel as it came into position at the rear of *Fidelity*. The bridge gathered very accurate visual images—like most starships, it was approximately conical, with circular decks arranged around a central core. It was around a kilometer in length and three hundred meters in width. Unlike *Fidelity*, the ship had the luxury of a painted exterior, a white color that had been stained with dust, with red areas containing some kind of symbolic lettering. No light whatsoever emerged from the ship, making every viewing port and vent seem like black holes. There were a few weapons, large laser cannons that were dozens of meters in length, similar to some others that *Fidelity* had seen. They would demand far too much power for *Fidelity* to be able to use. Cal noted signs of superficial damage on the ship, dark soot and crumpled areas where it had struck debris. A single huge hull breach had been punched into the front of the ship, presumably the mortal wound that had disabled it.

Fidelity's scanning had identified at least one hundred similar ships of this type in the star system, leaving little doubt that the vessel was once one component of a large and efficient military system.

Eventually, *Tenebrous* was only thirty meters behind *Fidelity*. *Fidelity* was moving at a constant speed and rotated so that the front of the ship faced *Tenebrous*. Rather than inserting the crew via shuttles, *Fidelity* would use its boarding tubes, flexible pipes that could reach one ship from the other.

Cal continued to vigilantly study the derelict vessel, his anxiety growing as the prospect of entering it neared. He scanned it for energy signals, using every tool at his disposal, but found no infrared signs and no movement. It was completely dead, surely. He remained concerned about the possibility of defective ammunition being buried inside, though nothing had dislodged or discharged during their abrupt capture of the vessel. He still watched warily, glad he wouldn't take the first steps aboard the dark ship.

*

Rosco stood by the metal exit hatch with five other members of the Vale Reach security team. It was a circular portal, scarcely wider than his own height, but it had seen a lot of action so far. Several hostile boarding parties had passed through its frame during their battles in the previous sector of the galaxy. Since then, it'd been entirely replaced with a heavier model, its thick structure a shiny steel in contrast to the rest of *Fidelity*'s interior and welded in place in a simple but neat fashion. On the far side, out in space, was the machinery for extending the boarding tube. The tube itself could rotate separately from the hull of *Fidelity*, reducing the extent *Fidelity* would need to alter its artificial gravity to engage with the other ship. *Tenebrous* was spinning at an off-center angle, probably due to a collision with some other object. Internal gravity would vary significantly throughout the ship.

Rosco heard a loud metallic clang accompanied by a tremor through the walls as the boarding tube made contact. There was a simple display monitor attached to the wall by the hatch, displaying the tube swaying slightly in the vacuum of space. The flexible metal segments creaked. The boarding tube was pressurized with breathable atmosphere, but it still needed to be tested for pathogens. The offworld crew members that *Fidelity* had gained were better suited than the Vale Reachers to the task. Rosco awaited the arrival of Cartographer Yendos, who would test what was on the other side.

Rosco heard heavy footsteps but was surprised to see a different figure arriving, as tall as Yendos and wearing the same black leather bodysuit and hood that was never removed. "Ontu," said Rosco. It seemed Yendos had chosen not to join their mission but had sent his assistant instead.

Ontu bowed in acknowledgment—he rarely spoke directly to the crew. Rosco didn't feel it was respectful to ask if his skills were equal to those of Yendos, but he considered the possibility.

"Major Rosco, may I volunteer my olfactory senses for your expedition?" Ontu asked as though sensing his unease. The loose black hood covered his face but on the surface was a series of small dials and vents. "I will vouch for the quality of the air conditions."

"Glad to have you," Rosco muttered. He turned and nodded at the rest of the squad.

They each carried a pistol and a rifle from the Vale Reach armory. Three of the officers carried weapons they'd collected from dead Enforcers. It was vaguely reassuring to be heavily armed, he couldn't deny, but when faced with a grimy airlock, the limitations of their guns became clear. All the weapons fired some kind of small pellets or hollow bullets that would minimize damage to the starships themselves.

Rosco noticed that someone else had joined the security officers. She was getting good at sneaking into things. "Leda, you shouldn't be here," he said with frustration. "Are you just chasing danger at this point? You still have bandages on, for gods' sakes."

She shook her head. "You need someone to assess the structural damage inside."

It was true, he had to admit. He didn't say anything.

"I can verify that each region of the ship is safe for entry," she said. "And if no one from engineering goes with the security team, you won't be able to identify any of the machinery you discover. No offense to your technical abilities."

"You are not coming aboard that ship until it's secured," he said. "Wait here until I or someone from the security team confirm that it's totally safe for entry."

"You're welcome to board the ship first," she said, waving him onward. "But you'll need me there before long."

Rosco didn't have a good counter argument. The security team attached the helmets to their space suits, and Rosco turned and opened the hatchway to reveal the rattling interior of the boarding tube, lit by weak electric light. The far side was thirty meters away, but somehow, as he looked at it, the distance seemed farther than that. All the signals indicated that the clamps had safely engaged with *Tenebrous*. Rosco led the squad into the boarding tube, and they closed the hatch behind them. *Tenebrous* was still spinning slower than *Fidelity*, so the effects of rotational gravity decreased as they neared the other end of the tube. They reached the far side, and Rosco faced another portal, identical to the one he'd just passed through. It was smeared black with grease over freshly machined metal.

"Ready?" he asked. The squad affirmed. He pulled a lever, and the portal opened to reveal darkness. A thin hail of dust drifted in toward them. The yellow lights of the boarding tube illuminated nothing beyond a few feet of floor decking on the other side. Rosco and the squad activated their lamps, casting bright white beams into the far side. It was an empty corridor.

Rosco's heart was beating quickly, and he tried to calm himself. They were looking into a bulkhead space of some foreign design, eerie but perhaps unremarkable. Rosco checked the atmosphere monitors in his suit. This region was sealed somehow, and so their environment had not depressurized, but bulkheads on a damaged vessel couldn't be trusted. They needed to establish the structural integrity of the environment.

"Let's go out and determine the extent of the pressurized zone. Watch out for any loose airlocks or stress fractures in the hull. If a rip blows you outside, it won't be easy to retrieve you." He stepped onto *Tenebrous*. "We already know that this ship has taken significant impact damage on its front, so there are decks that are breached to the starboard side of our current location."

The squad spread out, staying in close radio contact. Around every corner and shadow, they half expected something to leap out at them, but the ship remained as silent as a corpse. Before long, they encountered sealed doors with no pressure on the far side, marking the edge of the habitable area. Beyond there, the decks were exposed to the void. Other pressurized corridors led farther away. Rosco didn't want to split up the group in such an unknown place, so he ordered the squad to remain together.

"Major, I've found something," an officer reported.

Rosco hurried to join the man. His heart skipped a beat when he saw the thick black residue that was smeared across the walls under the illumination of the white beams from their torches. It was old blood splatter, unmistakably so, likely caused by a fatal wound given its size. It resembled an impact mark, Rosco thought, as though a whole body had been thrown hard against the wall. So far, it was the only trace they'd found of the ship's original inhabitants. The officers surveyed it, but no one spoke. The only sound aboard *Tenebrous* was a pervasive metallic creaking from all around.

"A lot of things could potentially cause that," he said eventually. "It's too ambiguous for us to draw much conclusion. We already know this ship was damaged. We can't turn back because of some blood splatter, so let's keep moving, and keep alert. Any sign of any human remains yet?"

"None yet," another officer reported.

"No bodies at all," said Rosco, "which indicates that they were able to successfully abandon the ship." The sense of stillness aboard *Tenebrous* was becoming oppressive. He wanted it jettisoned and far away from *Fidelity*. They had six hours remaining to complete the operation. The sooner that they began recovering material, the better their chances. "Have we confirmed absolutely no sources of danger near our entry point?"

The squad agreed.

"All right. Let's bring Engineer Palchek on board. She can start marking out the correct demolition points."

By detonating charges at key points, *Tenebrous*'s structure would break apart, shearing into pieces that could be retrieved and then lashed to the outside of *Fidelity*'s hull in a somewhat crude fashion, ready to be properly attached when time constraints were not so urgent. If *Fidelity* missed its turning maneuver, they could sail into a fully armed minefield and be destroyed.

Leda came aboard in her own sealed space suit, accompanied by several other engineers from the ship. They examined seemingly mundane features of the new vessel with great interest, checking door hinges and air vent filters and taking photographic evidence. Ontu was also shuffling about, continuing to sniff at things.

"Everything is well preserved here," Leda said to Rosco. "It looks undamaged. We should see what else we can find—there could be plenty of material to extract."

Rosco looked up a dark corridor that led to a junction at the farthest end of their visibility. No one had been beyond that point yet. "How's marking the points for the demolitions going?"

"Good." She indicated a group of engineers who worked with handheld devices. "We can measure through the walls here. We're building a rapid image of how this ship is put together and which of the key support beams will need to be cut through." She nodded to the unexplored junction again. "Shall we see what's back there?"

Rosco agreed. It was time to move out from their initial beachhead position. He waved for two of the security officers to join him. "Let's expand the perimeter. The engineers will need to get beyond this point." The three security crew moved ahead through the darkness, their rifles ready.

More hours passed by as the engineers worked and Rosco's security team confirmed which sections of *Tenebrous* were safe and secure. Each group worked methodically, taking no chances. Before long, a significant portion of the ship was clearly marked on their networked map as they collectively created an image of *Tenebrous*'s interior.

The engineers began planting their explosive charges, small packs of volatile chemicals that would dissolve critical pieces of the ship's internal support structures. Before the ship could be broken apart, however, they still needed to identify an appropriate computer system that could be extracted in its entirety—preferably something powerful. Rather than figure out the complex process of how to remove it, they would simply detach the whole piece of *Tenebrous* that contained it.

Rosco opened a door to a small room, shone a light inside. Leda was nearby, and he signaled for her to join him. "Come see what you make of these."

She studied a dusty collection of rectangular machines. As Rosco kept watch outside, he could hear her muttering to herself. After a few minutes, she reappeared at the doorway. "I have some good news and some less-good news. They're both kind of the same thing. Which do you need first?"

"The bad news," he said quickly.

"We need to bring Cal over here."

"Seriously?" Rosco was dismayed. "He's really not going to like that."

"I've found some computers here that have files still accessible. I can see what looks like files for star systems that this vessel recently visited, but I'm not entirely sure that's what they are. If Cal can confirm it, then we've identified our primary asset."

"Can't we just download everything and send it to him?"

Leda shook her head. "No, these machines aren't compatible with our own computer systems in that way. That's the entire problem. I have some equipment that can physically measure what's on the screen, but it's a slow process. We have to be selective, given our time constraints. Cal has the knowledge to determine if these machines are exactly what we need."

Rosco stared ahead. "Yeah, he's definitely not going to like that."

☐

Chapter 4

Cal stood at the edge of the boarding tube, regarding the interior of *Tenebrous* with disdain. "I didn't need to come here, you know."

Rosco shrugged. "That's not what Leda advised."

Cal narrowed his eyes but didn't step aboard. His dome helmet covered his entire head, despite the atmosphere of *Tenebrous* having been confirmed as breathable. "She claims to have found star charts on this wreck?"

Rosco nodded. "She thinks so. She's not entirely sure. That's what we need you to evaluate."

"That could give us an opportunity to verify what Yendos has been telling us." He hesitantly stepped onto the other ship. "This could give us an objective way to test if he's been telling us the truth." Cal looked around. Other members of the engineering and security teams could still be seen going about their tasks in the area. "You've stationed the whole security team in a perimeter here?"

"Yes," said Rosco.

Cal nodded. "So, we'll get an alert if any movement is detected? Okay. All right. Okay, then. Show me where you need me."

Rosco led him a short way down the dark and narrow corridors, grateful that Cal didn't seem to have noticed the blood splatter in the background.

Cal kept his eyes on his immediate environment, regarding *Tenebrous* with a sense of disgust. They arrived at the room in which Leda was working, her white flashlight visible, waving ahead of them. Cal stuck his head around the door then disappeared inside to join her.

Rosco kept watch outside and prepared to organize more security patrols. After ten minutes, he checked back into the room. Leda was exactly where he'd left her, and she and Cal huddled next to each other—it was as if she'd multiplied from one to two.

Rosco cleared his throat. "How's it looking? Anything good?"

Cal looked over his shoulder. "Yeah. I can recognize a bunch of this. It's pretty interesting, actually. We won't be dependent on any guesswork for future systems. We need to get this server setup back onto the ship."

Rosco nodded. "Excellent. The engineers report they've nearly finished marking out points for demolition." As he turned back to the hatchway leading to *Fidelity*, his communicator beeped. Someone was contacting him.

"We're registering movement from the depressurized areas. Lots of movement," an officer reported urgently. There was noise on the line, and it became harder to hear what he was saying.

"What's happening?" asked Rosco.

There was more noise and disruption on the line. "Identified what hit *Tenebrous*..."

Rosco heard a sound like fists beating against flat metal. It came from a door several meters back from their location in the corridor.

"Oh hell, everyone, helmets on! Brace to depressurize!"

Everyone hurried to reattach their helmets, ready for the door to burst open. Then a light on the door panel came to life, and the door opened smoothly. There was no rush of air out. A figure stepped through, moving falteringly into the lightless corridor. More stepped out from behind, a jumble of arms and legs tangled tightly together. Their bodies were hard to see in the dark.

They appeared not to wear space suits, their limbs slender as though they wore nothing at all and yet somehow rubbery and synthetic. Metal sockets gleamed on their chests, and each had a thick bundle of pipes wrapped chaotically around a shiny dome helmet on their heads. The dome helmets were featureless but rotated unpredictably, suggesting that the wearers were examining the world around them.

Rosco rapidly took several steps back, speechless.

The creatures continued to emerge through the door slowly, as though dazed. They appeared human, with muscular anatomy visible across their skinny bodies, but the way they moved was unnatural and unnerving.

Dozens came through, filling the corridor. Rosco, Cal, and Leda were separated from the other members of the expedition.

"What is this?" Rosco asked into the communicator. "What are we dealing with here?"

"This ship was struck by a boarding torpedo, sir," one of the engineers reported.

Rosco put the words together after a moment of confusion. "But that must have happened nearly a hundred years ago."

"It's reactivated. We don't know why."

Rosco looked over his shoulder. Cal and Leda were still in the small room with the computers, wearing their helmets and looking at him, awaiting answers. They had no idea what was happening. He immediately saw that the room they were in was a dead end with only one exit.

"Get out of there now!" He waved urgently.

"We're not finished reviewing the data," said Cal.

"You are now. Something's coming. Get out, hurry," Rosco replied.

They scrambled to the door and looked out.

The humanoid creatures had begun to advance down the corridor toward them. Even more had emerged through the opened doorway, yet they still moved gradually, almost painfully and stiffly. He heard crackling and popping sounds, like ice being added to a warm beverage.

Rosco tried to contain his trepidation. "They're thawing. They've been frozen."

Leda came out of the room and took several sudden steps back from the corridor, clearly horrified as she saw them. "These are Makron."

Cal jumped out of the room. "There's no way back to the ship! Oh gods, we're trapped!" He waved his hands around in blind panic for a moment.

Rosco kept his rifle aimed low. They could back away from the Makron at a speed equal to their shuffling advance, but that would push them deeper into unexplored areas of the ship. "Security squad, do you have a clear line of sight on the intruders?"

"Affirmative," came the reply.

"Don't open fire unless we have no choice. We've not seen any aggression from them yet."

The nearest creature seemed to study him as it ambled forward. It raised both arms, as though reaching out.

"I really don't like these things," Leda said.

A larger Makron suddenly appeared through the doorway, standing head and shoulders taller than the rest and far heavier in build. It knocked down the other Makron as it pushed its way through the multitude, moving at a decisive march.

"Okay, we're getting the hell out of here," said Rosco. He turned and pushed Cal and Leda down the dark junction. They turned and ran through unknown corridors.

"This way," Leda directed.

"You don't know this place," said Rosco.

"I memorized most of the interior scans," she said. She hit a button to open a door and led them into another corridor.

"Are you doing okay, Cal?" Rosco asked.

Cal had stopped saying anything. Rosco looked back at him and saw that Cal had turned white, as if in shock. "Just keep moving, okay?" He patted Cal on the back as they ran, moving as fast as they could through the unfamiliar confines of the lightless ship.

"How can they still be active after ninety years?" Leda murmured.

Rosco connected his comms line to the bridge. "Captain Haran, we have an emergency situation! An unknown boarding party is active here, suspected to be Makron units. Secure the boarding tubes to *Fidelity* immediately."

"Confirmed," Captain Haran said quickly. "Most of the engineers and security team have reembarked to *Fidelity*."

"Officers Heit and Palchek are with me. We've become separated from our ship's entry point. We're going deeper into *Tenebrous* to stay out of contact with the Makron."

"I see. Stay in communication. I trust you to handle the situation, Major," Haran said. She sounded sorrowful, he thought. "We'll try and devise a solution for you at our end."

They passed through another doorway into a narrow junction, the white torchlight beams of their space suits whipping through the black halls as they searched the area ahead of them.

"Have we tried just talking to them?" said Leda.

"It's worth a try. I'll tell them to stop." Rosco came to a halt, and the others stayed behind him.

"Be diplomatic, if possible," said Leda.

They heard the sound of something heavy approaching, and they began to back away from the junction.

Rosco raised his rifle. "Let's see if they can be reasoned with. If they suddenly rush toward us, I'm ready for them." He nodded to the weapon and aimed carefully ahead.

Leda and Cal exchanged uncertain glances and backed farther away.

From around the junction, dozens of the smaller creatures emerged, some walking, others crawling along the walls and the ceiling like insects. Their arms and legs all seemed to move in unison as they collectively scuttled toward him.

Rosco turned back. "Oh hell, keep running."

They sprinted deeper into the pitch-black starship.

Rosco opened the comms line to *Fidelity*. "Captain Haran, do you have anything that can help us?"

She reappeared on the line. "Major, the Makron have reached the boarding tube. *Fidelity* is going to disconnect from *Tenebrous*."

The news felt almost painful. He decided not to tell Cal and Leda. "What else?" he asked the captain.

"The engineers were able to get some close scans of the Makron boarding torpedo as it was powering up," she replied. "It was dormant the whole time."

"They're coming out of a boarding torpedo," Rosco told Leda. He saw her thinking on this, even as they ran along. "Leda, connect to Captain Haran with me," he said. "Cal, you too."

"A boarding torpedo?" Leda asked Captain Haran. The group weaved their way deeper into the ship, vaguely following Leda, though Rosco had no idea if she understood where she was going.

"It's large, maybe a third of the whole length of *Tenebrous*," said Captain Haran. "There could be a huge number of Makron onboard. It must be designed to invade and overwhelm enemy ships"

"They could be all around us, then." Leda slowed slightly. "They could be pouring into the ship corridors from all directions. Fuck! They could be right ahead of us!"

"They've awakened because we came here," said Cal.

"Think about it!" Leda said as they progressed into another the dark corridor. "Why are the Makron only just coming out of their torpedo now?"

"It's like they never awakened when it first struck here," Cal said.

"Exactly," she replied.

Rosco aimed his rifle back the way they'd come from but saw nothing. The sounds of a horde of feet on metal were still near. They kept hurrying along.

"They went into stasis when *Tenebrous* was abandoned by its crew. We must have awakened them when we arrived," she said.

"The torpedo kept them frozen for ninety years?" said Cal. "It has the energy to do that?"

"I've got a theory," Leda replied. "Captain Haran, send me the latest scans of the boarding torpedo."

"Done," the captain replied. "There's not much."

Leda glanced at her datapad without slowing her pace.

"I was right!" She scanned through diagrams as she ran. "It's a parasite. This boarding torpedo doesn't have its own reactor. It's somehow drawing from the power grid of *Tenebrous* to wake itself."

Cal was audibly wheezing. It sounded like he was hyperventilating, struggling to breathe. He stumbled for a moment. "I need... I need to..." He couldn't speak.

Rosco brought them to a stop. "Breathe slowly. Inhale through your nose, and exhale through your mouth." He couldn't afford for Cal to pass out and collapse. Rosco turned and kept watch over the corridor for a moment. They heard heavy footsteps stomping on the metal deck. The larger Makron abruptly appeared round the junction. For an instant, he was clearly visible in the light of their torches without the horde of smaller Makron crawling around him.

The arms and legs were muscular to an almost grotesque degree. Thick armor plating covered its neck, chest, and thighs, and an angular steel helmet covered its head. It had the same rubberized coating as the rest of the Makron and was armed with a gun, but Rosco didn't have time to examine the weapon closely. He saw multiple barrels on it and that the weapon seemed equally as bulky as its user.

He couldn't risk any firefight. "Keep moving. We're getting out of here." He chose a doorway and suddenly pushed the other two through it.

Leda was still urgently scrutinizing her datapad as she hurried along. She glanced up nervously. "We need to cut the link between the torpedo and the reactor on *Tenebrous*. Let's go this way." She led them down a new passageway, as dark and unfamiliar as ever.

Rosco made sure that Cal stayed in front of him and didn't fall. They were depending on no Makron emerging from ahead of them. If that happened, they might have no options left.

Rosco and Cal turned a corner together, Rosco almost dragging him onward. They saw Leda at an open doorway ahead of them, far wider than anything else that they'd found in the ship so far. Inside was a large chamber. She rushed into the dark area, almost sprinting, the other two hurrying after her.

They were in a huge, circular space with what looked like some kind of reactor at the center. It was a tiny fraction of the size of the one onboard *Fidelity*, Rosco saw, even though he knew nothing about reactors. There was a glint of light in the deep darkness. "Watch out!" he shouted as he spotted something moving around.

Leda skidded to a halt, struggling to stop herself in the low gravity of *Tenebrous*. Three of the small Makron creatures were skulking around the base of the reactor. Leda hesitated. The creatures hissed and scurried about in agitation but didn't come toward her, instead defending the reactor as if it was their prize. Rosco held his rifle ready.

They could hear the scraping, clanging noises coming from all directions as the Makron horde approached them. Rosco saw that the chamber they were in had many doors leading in from all around.

"Is this what you need?" he asked.

Leda nodded, still wary of the Makron creatures in front of her.

"Cal, seal these doors!" Rosco yelled.

"What about the damn Makron already in here?" he replied.

"Well, a lot more are coming, so seal this place up now."

Cal rushed from door to door, hitting the buttons to close them. The room was a large space, and so it would take him maybe half a minute to reach every door. The sounds from outside continued to get louder.

"If I can't shut that reactor down, the Makron torpedo will keep on awakening them," said Leda. "I need to get to work on it immediately." The skulking Makron creatures hissed angrily as she gestured to the reactor. They were still mostly hidden in the shadows, and Rosco kept his battle rifle aimed on them.

He wondered what would happen to the Makron already awake, but shutting down the torpedo had to be a useful step.

"Leda, you don't have any idea how this reactor works," said Cal, still running from door to door. "You can't just start taking it apart—you'll flood the room with radiation."

"Well…" She hesitated. "There's a development I need to tell you about. Back on the repair station, I had some work done. Medical-type work. Enhancement."

"What did you do?" Rosco felt a new sense of alarm.

"I have an implant in my brain. It essentially slows everything down for me. I can use it now, when I try to handle this reactor. I'll have much more time to figure things out."

"What!?" shouted Cal from the other side of the room.

"Leda, we'll have a serious discussion about this later," said Rosco. "Are you sure this implant is going to work?"

She nodded. "I still need to get close to the reactor though." One of the small Makron began advancing toward her. Leda backed away.

"Maybe I can subdue this thing," said Rosco. He gave his rifle to Leda and flexed his fingers. The creatures were smaller and thinner than him., but he knew they could have some kind of hidden strength. They had no weapons that he saw—they seemed to be almost cowering yet enraged. Rosco didn't want to cause unnecessary deaths. The event could eventually become a diplomatic incident for Vale Reach, and he preferred to avoid that. "Have you got all of the doors closed, Cal?"

"One more to go." He sounded exhausted.

The Makron in front of them were getting close. Rosco stepped forward and punched the nearest on the front of its helmet as hard as he could. His thick gloves absorbed the energy. The Makron flew backward and collapsed. Rosco prayed it would not get up. "That's one down."

He heard a popping sound and saw gleaming steel blades emerge from the hands of the remaining two Makron.

"Oh shit," he muttered, drawing his pistol as quickly as he could.

One leapt at him immediately. Rosco stepped away as it sliced toward him, and he jumped back as it stabbed at him again. He held his pistol low in one hand and fired four shots that seemed to all strike the Makron's body. It fell face-first to the ground.

The other Makron was already attacking him, slashing with its blade. Rosco saw how jagged the edge was, shaped like some kind of industrial tool. It was too close for Rosco to dodge. He raised an arm in defense, and the sharp blade gouged his shoulder and scraped his back. "Fuck!" Rosco shot the Makron in the face, cracking its helmet, and it tumbled back like the others. The first fallen Makron still wasn't moving.

Leda didn't wait for any invitation. She jumped over the bodies of the Makron and reached the reactor. It was over three times her height and extended deep into the floor. The exterior was encased in a curved metal shell with no obvious parts for interaction. The machine was surrounded by a series of computer consoles, but they were as black and lifeless as the rest of the ship.

"Leda, are you completely sure you should open that thing up?" Cal gasped as he hit the final door button. "It's unknown technology, and you don't really know what you're doing…"

"Not yet, I don't," Leda muttered, sounding almost pleased. "The process with the implants takes a moment to engage." She sat cross-legged on the floor.

"This isn't how I envisaged things going," said Rosco. His shoulder burned, but he'd dealt with plenty worse. At least the room around him was still pressurized. He held his rifle tightly in both hands. "Are you…"

Leda's head began to twitch wildly, thrashing back and forth.

"Gods alive! Are you all right? Is she all right?" he asked Cal.

Cal shrugged, his eyes wide open in horror.

Leda's arms rose up rigidly, as if she was in a trance, and her hands trembled violently.

One of the touch panels on the door to the room changed from red to yellow. "What does that mean?" Rosco asked.

Cal hurried to the door to examine it, still short of breath.

Rosco aimed his rifle at the door. "Be careful."

Cal quickly examined the panel. "It's unlocking. Someone's opening it from the other side." Cal pushed frantically at the panel a few times. The light went red again. "I've canceled it."

One by one, all the other door lights around the room turned from red to yellow. "Oh no, oh no!" said Cal. He looked around, filled with panic for a moment, then dashed toward another door. "Rosco, can you cancel these other door-open commands like I am?"

Rosco felt a jolt of trepidation. Technical work was outside of his skill set. "I can try… I mean yes, I'm sure I can do it."

Rosco ran to the nearest door. The symbols on the display panel were all totally foreign and unreadable to him. He pushed a few colored shapes. How had Cal done it? He looked over his shoulder.

Leda was still in some kind of seizure. Suddenly, it stopped, and her eyes opened. "I'm ready!" She sprang to her feet and almost threw herself at the reactor. She pulled and tugged at the exterior, detaching pieces and examining what was inside. Leda worked in a blur, rapidly checking the interior of the machine, rushing around to study different angles.

Rosco turned his attention back the control panel. It was still yellow. Some kind of spinning wheel seemed to be counting down. He jabbed his finger at some of the symbols until it finally turned red again. He ran to the next door and tried to do the same again.

"I'm not physically conditioned for this kind of activity," he heard Cal say between audible wheezes. They couldn't keep shutting down the door commands indefinitely.

"Leda, are you making progress?"

She grabbed a panel on the reactor and wrenched it aside. "Soon, soon. I've nearly got this thing figured out," she said rapidly. "This is the interesting part. I need to open the fission chamber and manually engage the control rods. All I have to do is pull out a particular bundle of wires, and it'll go into shutdown. The Makron torpedo will stop awakening once that happens."

"Open the fission chamber?" said Cal. His voice was almost too hoarse to speak. "Is that going to melt our insides?"

"I gained augmentations in more than just my head. Some are in my spine and my hands. I can do this in… twelve percent of a second. For that duration, our space suits will protect us."

Cal stumbled as he ran to the next door and fell to the floor. He groaned as he pushed himself back up to his feet.

Rosco silently prayed for Leda to be correct. It was literally all in her hands. For a second, she moved as a blur. More metal panels clattered to the ground, followed by a hail of smaller components and finally a bundle of wires. She suddenly stopped and swayed on her feet, almost limp, then collapsed backward.

Cal and Rosco both yelled her name.

She raised one of her hands into the air. She was waving at them, Rosco realized, signaling that she was fine. The room suddenly became quieter. An electric hum that Rosco hadn't even noticed before had ceased. They could still hear the sounds of hands beating on all the doors.

"Leda, they're still coming!" Rosco said. "What should we do now?"

She didn't have a response. The red panels on the door faded to darkness, leaving the white spotlights of their suits as the only light penetrating the blackness. Rosco backed away from the door and quickly raised his rifle. "Are these going to stay locked?" he asked Cal.

Cal shrugged, on his knees, regaining his breath.

A metallic screeching began from another door, the sound of some kind of power tool cutting into it.

"They're still trying to get in. Cal, get away from those doors. Fall back to the center of the room."

Cal and Rosco quickly moved to stand by Leda, facing outward from the reactor. Leda was sitting, but she seemed dazed and unable to speak.

"The ones that've already woken up aren't going back to sleep," Cal said.

"There's probably far too many of them for us to fight," said Rosco.

Cal turned to look at him. "I don't feel like surrendering to these guys."

"Don't give up yet," Rosco told him.

"Major Rosco, report your status," Captain Haran said through his communicator. He hadn't been sure whether the signal would penetrate so deep into *Tenebrous*.

"Captain, Leda thinks that we've disabled the power supply for the boarding torpedo," Rosco said.

"That's confirmed, Major. Activity from the boarding torpedo has stopped."

Rosco felt a minor sense of relief at the positive news, but it wasn't enough. "The Makron already awakened are still active. We're trapped in here. They have us surrounded."

The captain paused. "What are you chances of survival, Major? Do you have Heit and Palchek with you?"

"Chances of survival if captured by the Makron, sir, I think we have to assume are low. Their level of aggression has been steadily increasing. And yes, I do have Cal and Leda with me."

"You have to try and hold out in there, Major," said Captain Haran. "We'll develop a solution for you. Two hours still remain until we must disengage from *Tenebrous* for our maneuvers."

Rosco had almost forgotten about the original purpose of their operation on this ship. "How successful were the engineers?"

"They managed to plant most of the explosives. It's likely that we'll be able to salvage our targeted assets on *Tenebrous*."

The sounds of power tools seemed to multiply around them, once again coming from every direction.

"We could break apart the ship," said Cal. He looked alert, but he didn't seem enthusiastic for what he was saying.

"What do you mean?" said Rosco.

"Detonate the chemical explosives," said Cal. "Crack the whole hull open right now. Split the ship."

"With us on board?" said Rosco.

"I don't think any of the explosives are near to us here. The blasts won't harm us," Cal replied, "but it'll rip apart the ship, maybe even tear through this central chamber here. The ship will fully depressurize, and we'll lose gravity."

"We'll be thrown out into space," said Rosco, "but so will the Makron."

Cal looked around at the doors as the sounds of things crashing against the far side grew ever louder. "We have our space suits." He patted his chest, though he sounded doubtful.

"Are you hearing this, Captain?" Rosco asked.

"We could be recovered from space," said Cal. "Right, Leda?"

Leda seemed to be having trouble staying awake. She still sat on the floor, her head against her knees.

"There's no guarantee that we'll be able to retrieve you from the debris field of *Tenebrous* in the time remaining," said Captain Haran.

With a piercing metal shriek, one of the doors into the room was wrenched upward, creating a gap almost one foot high.

Rosco made a tough decision in that moment. He knew exactly what he had to do. "Captain, detonate the explosives."

"No, wait!" Cal cried. "Rosco, your space suit is ripped. You'll die."

"I know, Cal," he said. "But you and Leda might be fine."

"Goddammit, there has to be something more we can do!" Cal shouted. He rushed over and investigated the wound in Rosco's shoulder, prodding at it with his finger.

In the darkness, Rosco could see things creeping through the gap under the raised door.

"The elastic inner suit is mostly intact," Cal said. "It'll maintain the pressure around your chest and neck but not your arm. You need oxygen!"

"There's no time, Cal." Other things were in the room with them.

"I won't accept that." To Rosco's amazement, Cal grabbed one of the Makron bodies from the floor. He studied the tubes of its body, where they came out of the Makron's suit and into its neck. Cal ripped one out and pressed a button to open his own dome helmet. Cal gave the pipe a sniff. Rosco was dumbstruck. "Not this," Cal muttered, dropping the pipe with a queasy grimace. He ripped another pipe from the Makron and sniffed that. He put the pipe into his mouth for a second. Despite everything, Rosco was disgusted.

Cal nodded and closed his own dome helmet again. He dragged the pipe and the Makron toward Rosco. "I know you've got a vent back here," said Cal. Without asking permission, he pressed the Makron's pipe against a socket on the neck of Rosco's space suit. Rosco felt a faint spray of oxygen against his face. "You'll have to hold the connection tight with your hands, but you'll be able to breathe. We need to form a seal. I'll help you with it. We can take it in turns." Cal hesitated as he realized what was about to happen. "Oh fuck, time to do it. Here we go," he muttered. "Leda, are you ready to depressurize?"

She gave a thumbs-up and grabbed hold of his leg. They would stick together.

"Detonate it."

Tenebrous ripped apart.

☐

Chapter 5

Fidelity's three shuttles were basic, derived from the design of a rotary-blade atmospheric craft with the turbines replaced by a series of rocket engines mounted on rotational gimbals. It was effective, assuming its occupants didn't need to travel particularly fast.

There wasn't much time available. There was no way Marraz could be spared from his work to fly the shuttles. If he became somehow incapacitated and couldn't return to the pilot's seat before the two-hour deadline had run out, *Fidelity* would likely be destroyed. Nothing was worth that risk.

Several other trained pilots from the *Fidelity* crew could serve as backup shuttle pilots, but instead, a more unlikely figure had volunteered to operate the rescue craft. After some debate, the captain had agreed to it. Ontu barely fit into the seat, his knees against his elbows. He held the flight stick between finger and thumb. Yendos had assured Captain Haran that Ontu was one of the galaxy's finest pilots—and that he had played no role in the crashing of Yendos's previous ship. Despite his status as Yendos's junior, Ontu had more years of flight experience than the Vale Reach officers, and he was familiar at flying in highly hazardous vacuum environments. Ontu appreciated the vote of confidence from his master.

Out in space, the area around *Fidelity* was chaotic. The plan to harvest parts from the derelict ship had been a success, and *Tenebrous* had split into a vast cloud of debris. Ontu had experienced some private doubts as to whether the Vale Reach engineering crews would be able to achieve their ambitious plan, but they'd proven him wrong. Any rotating ship would naturally disintegrate if the structural beams creating its internal tension were broken.

Behind him, Vale Reach's other shuttles were being launched to retrieve the precious pieces of starship hardware that were floating freely amongst the remnants of the destroyed vessel. Even a small shuttle could pull a huge load in microgravity. Ontu wasn't collecting material—his task was solely to find the missing crew.

In the process of breaking apart, many of the internal compartments on *Tenebrous* had disintegrated. This had all happened within fifty meters of the exterior of *Fidelity*, but the blast was designed to push any debris away from their ship. Around the shuttle was a thick jumble of ripped steel decking, furniture, and wiring. It clattered persistently against the shuttle's exterior, alarming Ontu as he gradually and gently used the shuttle's engines to dig deeper through the cloud of wreckage.

Suddenly, he heard the sound of something beating on the side of the shuttle. It was shockingly loud and so forceful that he felt it reverberate through the whole interior around him. Something heavy had latched onto the side of the shuttlecraft. None of the Vale Reachers had such mass or strength. Ontu pushed some buttons and pulled a lever, rapidly spinning the shuttle around. Whatever had been there was wrenched free and hurled out into space.

Ontu paused, slightly dizzy, and took stock of the situation. A countdown on his screen listed the time remaining till the shuttles would have to return to *Fidelity* for the final time. If he ventured too deeply into the shifting pieces of the *Tenebrous* wreck, the shuttle could become crushed. A voidcraft designed for the task at hand should be equipped with a set of mechanical arms on its exterior, but *Fidelity*'s shuttles did not have any such luxury. Instead, he nudged things with the wing tip of the shuttle and pushed his way through.

The ruins of the ship were like a tangled wall floating in front of him. He'd reached a dead end, but Ontu felt sure there was an area beyond. He had to try to reach it. He hit the forward accelerator. There was a crash, and he broke through the layer of shredded metal ahead of him. On the other side, amidst the chaos, he saw a familiar set of bodies floating in space.

*

"Honestly, I think that went well, overall," said Leda.

Rosco and Cal stared at her in disbelief from their own beds in the infirmary.

Cal's whole body felt in so much pain that he couldn't determine which part was the worst. The doctors had told them that they'd suffered no permanent injuries. Rosco had suffered badly from oxygen deprivation out in space, but he seemed to be returning to good health.

Cal was grateful that he didn't remember much of their time in the vacuum. He harbored a lingering fear that the memories would suddenly and unexpectedly return to him. What he did remember was the silence and the loud sound of his own breath rattling inside his helmet. Time had seemed to stretch to infinity, with no stimulation or any input other than the feeling of Rosco and Leda in contact against him.

Together, the three of them had held the oxygen pipe that was still attached to the Makron drone against Rosco's helmet, creating an airtight seal and alternating as they each became tired. The tendons in Cal's hands had burned with pain. He hadn't dared to look around, but in his peripheral vision, he'd seen the immense pieces of *Tenebrous* silently spinning as they drifted in the void. Their survival had been a long shot, but with no alternative, he'd managed to wait, willing with all his energy for his body to hold off death.

"Leda, we're lucky to be alive," Rosco croaked, adjusting the tubes running into his nostrils.

"But the mission was a success, Major," Leda said. "All the pieces of the vessel that we targeted have been recovered. We've secured them to the outer surface of *Fidelity*, ready to use once we're somewhere more convenient. If anything, the mission went perfectly. We got ourselves into danger only because we became separated from the main group."

"That was also your idea," said Cal.

She nodded. "That's true. That was my fault. I can see that, and I should have slowed down a little."

"We're lucky our own ship even found us," said Cal. "Time was getting very short. *Fidelity*'s shuttles aren't designed for search and recovery. Given the low odds of getting us back, I'm surprised Captain Haran was willing to risk sending the shuttle out for as long as she did."

"Given that our group included the chief engineer and her head of security, there was no way she wouldn't have attempted a recovery," said Leda.

Rosco began to mutter angrily to himself. "We are going to reassess how you take risks, Leda. Especially in light of what I now know about your implant."

"Yeah, Leda, what the hell? That sounds absurdly dangerous to just plug things into your brain," Cal added.

"Given that we survived our encounter with the Makron, I think my implants have demonstrated their value. The Makron intimidate even the Legion according to what we've heard. My implants are exactly what saved us."

"Leda, are those implants enhancing your positive attitude?" Cal asked. "Serious question. Because I can't see any other way for you to put an upbeat spin on this whole experience."

"Things didn't go that badly," she insisted, "other than us getting blown out of *Tenebrous* into open vacuum. That is one area that went poorly. But we recovered the computer systems, exactly as we needed to do."

"Leda, did you say you had implants in your head, your spine, and your hands?" Rosco asked. "That seems like far too much to add to yourself all at once."

"That's the right way to do it, Major," she replied. "All of the pieces are linked. They form a set. If you want to really speed up your nervous system, that's really the minimum. The brain for decision-making, the spine to communicate, and the hands for acting."

"Sounds expensive too," Cal said. "You don't have that kind of money. Did you get this done in some dodgy back-alley place on the repair station?"

Leda sighed. "That's a very subjective term."

"Gods alive, Leda." Cal sat up in bed as he became animated. "You'll be lucky if your brain doesn't turn to mush. Was it even clean? Or was it grimy? You could get an infection. Was it even a doctor you met? What if it fails? Who will you complain to? Have you thought about any of these risks?"

"Yes, Cal, I've considered all of those risks." She shook her head.

Cal thought for a second. "Do they actually work properly?"

"Yeah, they do pretty much exactly what I hoped they would."

Cal nodded slowly and lay back down in bed. "That's interesting."

"My brain is in incredible condition," Leda added. "It's never felt stronger."

"I'm sure the medics will have logged and identified what you've done," Rosco said wearily.

They sat in silence. Cal thought Rosco would have stormed off if he could, but they were all stuck together, bedridden.

"What about him?" Cal pointed to the fourth bed in the room. On top of it lay the Makron drone, unconscious and immobile. It was the one that Rosco had knocked out, and it had no bullet injuries. The medics had been stunned to discover a remarkably human body beneath its vulcanized skin, and they had injected enough sedatives to keep it unconscious indefinitely. Somehow, it had survived without its oxygen supply for the two hours that they'd drifted in space.

It looked very different in the light of *Fidelity*. All kinds of features were visible. Cal studied it. The easiest way to describe what he saw was that its skin had been replaced with a synthetic substitute, dark brown in color, that gave it a lean and almost skeletal look. Its hands had been replaced, too, ending in metal sockets that were currently empty. No serious attempt had yet been made to remove the steel helmet covering its head.

"Why exactly did we bring it on board?" Cal asked.

"To learn from it," said Rosco. "This could be what we're up against. We need to know how they work. This one will be easy enough to contain, from what we've seen. Vale Reach has to be ready to face something like the Makron one day."

"I can't believe it survived," Cal said.

"I heard the doctors say it consumes oxygen at a very slow rate," Leda said.

"I can believe that." Rosco had an edge of bitterness to his voice. "I experienced it myself."

"We don't need it waking up. What if it can talk to the others somehow?" Cal asked.

"The other Makron?" Leda raised her eyebrows. "For a while, other Makron were floating around in space near us, but that's not the case anymore. They drifted away after *Tenebrous* split. Apparently, *Fidelity* got a good look at the Makron boarding torpedo too."

Cal attempted to sit up again but then gave up. "What do you think happened to them?"

"After Marraz navigated us round the planet for the next gravity boost, I think most of them would have fallen down into its gravity well. Meaning they struck the hot atmosphere," Leda said.

Rosco began to cough violently and reached out, hands fumbling for a container of water as he went pink in the face.

"Damn." Cal looked horrified. "I almost feel bad for the Makron."

"Maybe they didn't burn up!" Leda sounded like she was trying to console him. "Maybe some are still out there now."

"I don't want to think about that either," he replied.

Leda tilted her head at the fourth bed. "At least now, we can experiment on this Makron sample."

"Leda!" Rosco shouted in the middle of his unpleasant coughing. "You've done enough experimenting with things you don't understand. Do not interfere with this thing until we've established whether we can communicate with it. Maybe we can reason with it."

Cal lay flat again, feeling himself grow tired. Their voices faded away. His eyelids became heavy, and he let them close.

*

He fell deeply into sleep, shedding layers of perception as he drifted away. He was too exhausted to maintain any sense of his surroundings. *Fidelity* faded from his mind, and he was pleasantly alone in the spaceless dimension of his own thoughts. Anonymous shapes flickered and whirled around him.

He saw Vale Reach, his homeworld, pale green and shimmering. It looked perfect. It was an idealized image, more radiant than the single time that he'd actually seen it through *Fidelity*'s monitors when night was clouding its surface.

He was rushing toward the world as though falling, but he welcomed the feeling. It was like a warm embrace. The hills and grasslands swept as far as he could see, like a rippling green canvas.

He saw familiar pieces of coastline flying past, familiar towns and valleys where he'd spent his youth. His hometown. His apartment, even—he floated down in front of it. He could see Eevey through the window, sitting in the sunlight at their kitchen table, looking out toward him. She clearly couldn't see him, though. She stared straight ahead, strangely rigid.

Cal floated in and joined her. Still she didn't move, staring like a statue. The light within his apartment seemed much grayer than the shimmering daylight outside. He felt a voice, booming like thunder. He couldn't hear the words, but the force and meaning of them were clear. There was flickering like a bright electric discharge.

"You are only following the path I have set for you."

It was the Ambassador's voice, he realized. The flickering light was just as he'd seen it the last time that he'd recalled his encounter with her.

"There is nowhere you can go where I will not follow." There was a crash of thunder and lightning again, the thunder rumbling as deeply as the voice, and the lightning flickering on the edge of his perceptions as though searching for him directly.

He felt the Ambassador watching him.

"Turn back, and you will find me merciful." He saw Eevey's mouth moving. She, too, was saying the words. "My agents will find you," the voice said. "There are always more to come."

The Ambassador had been inside his flat, he remembered in the dream. She'd been a monstrous, alien thing to him despite her pleasant appearance. He'd seen her only from the waist up and through a camera, but he felt her watching him every time he closed his eyes. Electric white light crackled again. What did that mean? Was he being manipulated? Of course he was. It was a trap. The Ambassador had laid countless traps for them. Even his dream was a trap.

He looked at Eevey. Already, she seemed farther away from him, as though slipping into the distance. He wanted to try and speak to her. He might never be with her again.

It might all be over. The dreams and memories could be his only chance. He rushed to the table, his face next to hers.

Light crept out from under her eyelids. Her eyes seemed both closed and open at the same time. The light swirled around her like thick, viscous liquid. Then Eevey opened her eyes fully, and blinding white radiance dazzled Cal. He was stunned. Though he could still see Eevey's outline, everything else from Vale Reach was gone. Cal blinked, and Eevey became the Ambassador. The two of them merged, the same person with four arms and both heads, growing and changing. The hybrid swayed back and forth. Then the Eevey parts shriveled, and the Ambassador towered over him, taller than he'd feared possible. The purple robes she wore became a tsunami rushing toward him.

Cal felt terrible doubt. Eevey was working with the Ambassador. She'd directly told him. He knew it to be true. He just didn't know what he could possibly do in response to it. He couldn't let go of his old life and sever his connections with her. He would be left with nothing. He didn't want to go back to his life before he'd met Eevey.

The colossal wave of the Ambassador's robes crashed over him, smothering him. He tumbled into the lightless depths, kicking and thrashing as he fell into nothing. Raging winds and angry whispers whipped around him like a violent storm.

He saw himself in the blackness—his own face, his own eyes. They morphed into the features of another, regrowing with bubbles and froth. He became Sarjan, the man who'd attacked them at the repair docks, another of the Ambassador's thralls.

When he awoke, it was dark in the hospital ward. The other two were asleep in their beds.

He questioned whether he should go to Captain Haran to tell her he'd had another nightmare about the Ambassador. He'd likely be considered an idiot or a lunatic for complaining to his superiors about a dream. Whether he was correct or not, they would lose all trust in him as someone to be relied on.

He wondered if he could trust his own thoughts, his dreams, or even his own body. He couldn't begin to answer the question. He was helpless to know if he was truly going mad. The Ambassador had done something to him—he could feel it. It involved that damn flashing white light, whatever that had been. It was sending messages into his brain. Could he have been hypnotized? Or perhaps he needed no hypnotizing at all. He couldn't walk away from anything that involved Eevey. The Ambassador had ordered him to come back to Vale Reach. Had Eevey become her agent, as it seemed so many had?

The warning in his dream had been unambiguous. But it hadn't contained any new information. It could all have been a manifestation of his anxieties, a product of his fear. The dream could just have been a dream. He felt his doubts fade as he returned to a state of waking, but some trace of them remained. Things were happening in Eevey's life on Vale Reach that he didn't understand. The time debt he was building up in small amounts with each FTL jump was causing her to experience more time than him— several years more by the time of his return, and that was if nothing more went wrong. Was she happy being alone, waiting for him to come back? Could their relationship last against something as fundamental as time itself?

For a moment, he was lost in his thoughts. If their mission to Ruarken wasn't successful, only a ruined Vale Reach would remain to go back to. Eevey would suffer. She and all of Vale Reach needed him to be on the path he was on, the path that would lead to *Fidelity*'s arrival at Ruarken and safety for their world. There was still a way back to her. There was a path through which a return to his old life was possible. There was still time for everything to be fine in the end.

*

Marraz slumped in his chair. His marathon task was over. He'd been at the controls of *Fidelity*'s cockpit for five straight days. Although he desperately wanted to rest, he no longer desired to exit the cockpit immediately. Setting foot outside would almost be too much of a shock to his system after so long. He'd do it later. To simply relax his mind was his top priority.

Fidelity had reached its constant traveling velocity after the final gravity-boost maneuver. They'd looped around the mass of a heavy giant, correcting course using two moons, followed by a series of crucial reflections off six outer dwarf planets to avoid the copious minefields and colossal acid sprays that had drifted around over the decades. The transit point was straight ahead of them. This place wasn't the most challenging star system that he'd ever navigated, but perhaps it was the hardest that he'd done alone. The Vale Reachers depended on him, but they couldn't help him much.

The final approach for making contact with the transit point still needed to be calibrated, but the bridge crew could handle that themselves. *Fidelity* had to enter the transit point with its FTL drive already running to generate a harmonic resonance that would rematerialize them in the next system. That was navigation's work, not the pilot's. Small rockets on *Fidelity*'s exterior would make tiny adjustments to ensure that their angle of approach would translate into what they wanted in the next system. They would avoid time debt beyond the loss of a few days.

Marraz took his hands off the control stick and rubbed his thumbs. His right thumb had been blown away in a gunfight a few years back and replaced with a carbon synthetic. Sometimes, it itched. Sometimes, he preferred it to his original, such as in moments like now when his hands felt on fire. He breathed slowly and shut his eyes. His cockpit in the nose cone of *Fidelity* was at the very front of the bridge, where he could feel the turning forces with the most precision. His display screen was black, showing a true image of space outside, including the white spots of the star field. The pattern varied across every system, yet each would give a person their place in the universe if they knew exactly what to look for. Despite everything, it was good to be in space.

*

Fidelity arrived in the next star system and detected no imminent danger, in stark contrast to their previous jump. From her hospital bed, Leda studied the construction work outside *Fidelity* on her datapad. Multiple pieces of *Tenebrous* were still crudely lashed to the side of their ship. As quickly as possible, the engineering crew began salvaging what they had gathered.

Fidelity had one hundred and twenty voidsuits in its inventory, more than enough for all the available engineers and some additional labor. One great advantage of the vacuum was that without gravity, even the largest object could be moved by human power.

The engineers positioned themselves across the exterior of *Fidelity* like a carpet of ants. Slowly, in teams pulling cables, they moved the massive pieces of *Tenebrous* into usable positions. Some groups went in search of intact computer hardware and communications arrays. Around the ship, other parts of useful hardware were quickly attached using small spot welds that would be heavily reinforced later on. The engineers sat back and admired their work. The ship looked very different already.

An armored nose cone that would protect against collisions with junk or laser strikes had been added. The engineers had also welded a cage of additional support beams around the entire hull. Smaller objects, such as strips of exterior lighting, antennae, and lenses for sensory attachments had all been collected and were in the process of being wired to the ship's power grid. Some would perhaps ultimately not work, but if even only a fraction were functional, the difference would still be noticeable. Enough electric cabling had been recovered from *Tenebrous*'s interior to replace parts from *Fidelity*'s original construction. The work wasn't beautiful, but it would suffice. Almost without the workers fully realizing, a new vessel was taking shape before their eyes.

*

Cal was back at his desk on the ship's bridge. For once, he appreciated it. He planned not to leave his seat for several weeks. He told himself that it could be a good experience. It would certainly be easier on his body.

Rosco and Leda had returned to their own positions on the bridge as well. Cal could tell from her behavior that Leda was frustrated that she hadn't participated in the construction work, but they were in no condition to return to outside space. Despite the controversies around her decisions, she remained the chief engineer. The bridge crew had all agreed to her plan, after all, collectively signing off on the undertaking.

Now, they would activate the newly enhanced bridge systems that had been harvested from *Tenebrous*. That would be the real test of Leda's ideas. Cal had seen some of the plans, but nothing was guaranteed until it was fully operational. She was already becoming vindicated as each hour went by. The physical scale of the ship's modifications made an impression on them all.

A moment of quiet settled on the bridge as they waited for the new programs running on the ship's screen to initialize. Trying to build a computer from scratch was futile, it was clear to see, but *Fidelity* had already got some of the recovered parts working. The power connections would be the critical issue. Whatever they used needed electricity to run. They'd calculated which cables were for energy input and carefully plugged the *Tenebrous* processors into *Fidelity*'s power supply. A handful of terminals from *Tenebrous* had even been transplanted onto the *Fidelity* bridge, with strange, unrecognizable keypads that were covered with new paper labels.

The *Tenebrous* equipment was old, but from Cal's own assessments, it would meet the requirements to access the publicly available information networks of all the worlds that they'd so far encountered.

"Let's turn it on," said Captain Haran.

The text on the main screen shifted to reveal a new set of features. *Fidelity* immediately began collecting data from every satellite network it could register in the star system. A vast directory of information was in the process of forming, an encyclopedia of cultural knowledge. Much of it was junk, but it was comprehensive.

Cal was enthralled by the list of planets. *Fidelity* could access clear information about the political situation of each star system before they arrived. Yendos would still have the upper hand in interpreting how to use the transit points, but the path ahead was no longer his alone to predict. They had regained some ability to question Yendos's decisions. Cal relished it.

"It's a success, Leda!" he exclaimed.

"I knew it would be," she replied.

"We've detected a group of messenger beacons broadcasting an urgent alert," another officer said.

Captain Haran pressed a few buttons on her chair, and an analysis of the beacons appeared onscreen. Each message was fully translated and labeled with the time and coordinates of where it had first appeared.

Cal read them with a sense of wonder. It seemed that the collection of messenger beacons was the one thing that separated this modestly populated star system from the others they had seen. They floated at key locations. He counted ten. *Fidelity* had seen objects like these before but never ten of them arranged intentionally. They were positioned to provide total coverage of the star system, all acting as relays for each other.

"Multiple transmissions are recorded on the beacons in layers at different times," said Yendos. "It appears several different parties have manipulated these devices."

At least five messages were identifiable in the analysis of the beacon, Cal saw.

"Three of these are minor legal warrants and technical readouts," said Fargas. "Probably of little interest. The other two matter more."

"Put the first on-screen," Haran commanded.

Important Information from the Universal Legion, Cal read, immediately growing tense.

"There's no doubt that the Legion are active in this area," Haran said. "That's far from ideal. Although they have no reason to suspect us of being in this side of the galaxy, they're still fundamentally opposed to what we're doing."

Cal kept reading: *You are entering a Successionist Zone. Rogue nations are operating without constraint.*

The integrity of interplanetary law cannot be guaranteed beyond this point. Established treaties may not be enforced. Financial compensation and insurance liabilities may be voided upon entering.

Pacification campaigns are still underway. Beware of active rebel elements targeting any shipping related to Universal Legion activities.

Report all lawless elements to the nearest Legion garrison.

It all sounded faintly familiar. What were the crew of *Fidelity* if not successionists, at least in the Legion's eyes? Succession was all a matter of perspective and of legal standing. Perhaps Vale Reach wasn't as alone as they'd thought they were. The situation of their homeworld had to be just one example amongst many—that'd always been one of the hypotheses that justified *Fidelity*'s expedition.

"The next layer," said Fargas, "looks to be a clear attempt to overwrite the previous one. The original message is still visible, but perhaps that's unavoidable."

"Or perhaps it's intentional," said Haran.

Declaration of Self-Rule, Cal read. *Welcome to the Liberated Zone.* He raised his eyebrows. They hadn't yet been welcomed anywhere before.

You are entering the territory of the Free Nations. We do not recognize the authority of outsiders to dictate our laws.

The Crusaders of Freedom defend this region.

Cooperation with the Universal Legion will not be forgiven.

Fight for justice.

Cal sat back and let out a breath in admiration. They were significant words, an open declaration of war against the entire Universal Legion and its belief in its unlimited jurisdiction. Or maybe, Cal considered, whilst at war with the Legion was the easiest time to make such a challenge. It wasn't hard to demand justice in the middle of a fight.

"Do we trust these beacons?" Captain Haran asked.

"The message from the Legion is authentically signed by them," said Fargas. "It's very likely to be real. As for the rebels, that's harder to verify, of course."

"But why would anyone falsely claim to be in a rebellion against the Legion? A declaration like that, any sign of open resistance, it's not something the Legion will tolerate," said Haran.

"All the information coming in from other star systems shows that the Crusaders of Freedom are a real and active group," said Leda.

"If we go in there, we could be entering into a war zone," Rosco added.

"We just managed to get out of one," an officer on the bridge said.

"That was an abandoned battlefield," said Rosco. "There's a difference."

"How big is this Liberated Zone?" Captain Haran asked. "What are our options for going around it?"

"Some coordinates within the beacon indicate the zone's perimeter," said Cal. "They're pretty far away from here. It's a very big region that's in front of us." He highlighted a collection of coordinates on-screen.

"Yendos, can you add to this?" Captain Haran asked.

Yendos nodded. "Oh, yes." He added several more labels to the map.

"By the gods," Captain Haran said.

A sense of awe passed over the bridge.

"Ruarken System," Cal murmured to himself. "It's on the other side."

"We'd have to pass directly through the zone," said Haran. She turned to Yendos. "That's correct, yes? If we pass through the middle of the zone and reach the far side, we can reach the Ruarken Senate?"

Yendos was silent. As ever, his strange black hood covered his face, but his posture was indicative of his thoughts. He put his hands together and reflected on the question. Even Yendos hadn't fully absorbed the ramifications of their new data, Cal realized.

Yendos raised one finger and traced strange patterns in the air. "From that system at the edge"—he aimed the laser from his hand at a specific spot on the large screen—"a jump into the Ruarken System can be achieved."

There was a quiet gasp on the bridge. For the first time since they began their mission, nearly eight long months before, Cal felt some of the unbearable weight and pressure subside. He felt real hope, and it surprised him.

"Would our vessel be legally permitted to enter the Ruarken system from that location?" Haran asked Advocate Fargas.

"If we transmit a handful of the relevant codes, which I have already prepared, we'll be granted entry under a temporary visa. We can take it from there," Fargas said. "So, Captain, are we going into the Liberated Zone?"

"There are obvious and significant risks to entering a territory where the Legion are confirmed to be operating," Haran said.

"The Legion operate everywhere," Fargas replied with a shrug. "But perhaps they operate slightly less in here, if these messages are to be believed."

"Yendos, brief us on possible routes that go around this zone." Captain Haran turned to Cal. "You, too, Operator Heit. What are our alternatives?"

"There are routes around anything," said Yendos, "but they are often not appealing. I can see several different routes that would circumvent the entire Successionist Zone, but for your vessel, time debt would become a significant issue."

"That's true," Marraz said from the pilot's cockpit. "We need an almost direct route for our best chance to end up with minimal time debt."

Cal felt his hopes grow. If they could avoid the effects of time debt, they could one day return to their old lives on Vale Reach—something that he almost dared not imagine. "That checks out," he said. "From what I can see of the transit jumps ahead of us, we could progress though the Liberated Zone without any major risk of straining the FTL drive, assuming our thrusters are running as normal."

Captain Haran's face didn't give away any emotions. "Major Rosco, provide us a security analysis."

Rosco brooded. He didn't look happy—his eyes were tense, and his jaw clenched. "It's dangerous—that's confirmed. But is it any more dangerous than the star systems that we'd encounter on the other routes? More to the point, does time debt allow us any option? The pressing danger to Vale Reach may be the deciding factor. With the Legion beginning construction above our homeworld... I think we have to take every shortcut we can get."

"We must balance the danger to the ship with the danger to our world," Haran said.

"We can't afford any conflict with even a single vessel from the Universal Legion," said Rosco. "We all remember what happened before. But it'll be easier to avoid their suspicions this time. If we're cornered again, their systems will register us as from a distant part of the galaxy. Our design will be unfamiliar. Any indications that our ship is from Vale Reach should be unrecognizable to the untrained eye. Frankly, the Legion forces here probably haven't even heard of Vale Reach. Our cover story is that we're lost and confused, and we stick to that no matter what."

"We could learn from these people," said Leda.

Captain Haran raised a skeptical eyebrow at this statement.

"It seems these Crusaders have been in conflict with the Legion for many years. We can see how they do it, how it's possible," she continued. "We might find something that we can use ourselves in the future."

"Will the rebels be hostile to us?" said Haran.

"It's possible," said Rosco. "But the presence of the rebels might also help us avoid the Legion. It depends. Will the Legion be distracted and spread thin? Or will they have increased the intensity of their patrols compared to 'regular' space? Consider this, Captain." All eyes on the bridge focused on him. "Did the Legion delete the self-rule declaration from their messenger buoys?"

"They did not," Haran replied.

"Were they unable to delete the message?" Rosco asked. "That seems unlikely from a technical perspective. So that means the Universal Legion does not fully control this place."

Captain Haran smiled very slightly for a moment.

"This isn't their land, no matter what they might say. The words of the beacon prove it, simply by their existence," said Rosco.

"We proceed onwards, then," she replied. "As a simple traveler who has no business with anyone."

The *Fidelity* bridge crew reviewed everything they could about the next system, deeper into the so-called Liberated Zone, or the Successionist Zone as the Legion called it. They accessed the commonly available files in their current region, showing numerous transit-point exits and many planets with high-density human settlements ahead of them. Cal noted that the two features usually went hand in hand. There was a light amount of traffic between the transit points, most of which registered as commercial. There would be no way to tell if Legion ships were present until they actually arrived.

Cal scanned through the data himself, accessing it through his own console. One planet stood out from the rest and, on its surface, one city in particular. Photographs had been collected from that world's public transmissions, general images that indicated the state of things. The damage to the city was severe. Cal wasn't a security expert, but signs of a war were obvious.

The city hadn't been obliterated, though, which the Legion was easily capable of doing. Clearly, the attackers had desired to preserve it in some way, though they hadn't been careful with it either. The bombardment looked untargeted, deep holes blasted into the city at almost regular intervals. Repair work had been done, but from the looks of things, it amounted to little more than a cleanup operation. It was difficult to gauge how old the bomb craters and collapsed buildings were. Any transmission that was sent through a transit point, as these were, would be out of date to some degree.

Cal saw that other officers on the bridge were looking at the same thing.

"Do we suspect the Legion at work here?" asked Haran.

"They are post revolution," Fargas replied with a clinical air.

Cal searched more deeply into the material their new computer system had generated.

"Despite their relatively developed infrastructure, the governments over there are in a transitional state," Yendos said.

"Meaning they've experienced a recent regime change," said Captain Haran.

"Multiple regime changes in succession," Fargas added.

"Is there a chance that could be the cause of the damage?" Major Rosco asked.

"The damage is caused by the Legion," Yendos replied. "I've seen the pattern before."

"The city was accused of harboring criminals." Fargas was reading documents at a speed far beyond anything that others could manage. Cal was partially reminded of Leda and her handling of *Tenebrous*'s reactor. "So, the Legion installed a new governor who would provide it with what it wanted, which in this case seemed to be transferring some group of prisoners. Of course, the new governor didn't survive for long once the Legion left, and now, they're close to having no governor at all."

"It seems the population was not appreciative of their new governor's actions," said Yendos.

"When the Legion left, taking the rebel prisoners with them, they also took most of their offworld military units. Those remaining are just patrolling the key installations… but they're nowhere near able to control the whole planet," said Fargas.

Captain Haran nodded. "Perhaps we'll be the least of their concerns. Make the jump then study the situation directly as soon as we arrive. We'll begin crossing the Liberated Zone."

*

They arrived on the other side of the jump. The information they received from these worlds now expanded far beyond the limited signals that had been beamed across the transit point, though the transmissions were still highly disorganized and chaotic.

It seemed that a state of anarchy was spreading across the continents of every populated world. Some messages contradicted others. Clearly, there was a range of angry opinions across each planet. Some of the broadcasts sounded entirely detached from reality. After discarding the messages that seemed unhinged, they found that an approximate consensus existed on the state of things.

Anti-Legion rebel agents were spread throughout all of the worlds. Efforts to remove them hadn't been effective. No one claimed to be in contact with the rebels directly— that would have been far too dangerous. But another common thread was discovered: a moon orbiting a gas giant just one star system away. The rebels had originated there.

It seemed likely that the rebels were as numerous as they claimed, Cal thought. This place was simply the first system that they'd encountered beyond the beacons. It was inevitable that *Fidelity* would encounter some kind of rebel force before it finished crossing through the Liberated Zone. An unexpected encounter or even an ambush could be disastrous. And yet the rebels would likely share ideological similarities with *Fidelity*.

Captain Haran gave the order to cautiously approach the moon.

Chapter 6

They didn't detect any armed military vessels as they approached, which Leda took as a good sign. The moon was a mix of isolated settlements and the occasional heavily developed city, with some mineral-harvesting stations. Some of the settlements showed signs of damage similar to what they'd observed in the previous world, but the destruction seemed older.

Rosco would travel down to the moon to attempt to establish contact with the crusaders who'd left their message with the buoys at the edge of the Liberated Zone. Leda wouldn't travel to the moon to explore it, just as she hadn't been able to participate in the construction work outside *Fidelity*. She'd been ordered to stay at her post on the bridge despite her objections.

She suspected she was on probation after the discovery of her unauthorized augmentations. It was frustrating, and she struggled not to feel angry, but the directive from Captain Haran had been clear, so she begrudgingly acknowledged the necessity of following it. There was nothing much on the moon that particularly interested her, anyway.

Rosco's destination was a ball of green rock. Leda studied it, seeing its color as shockingly bright in the white light of its nearby sun. It wasn't green from foliage but from the natural mineral powder of the dusty ground. The effect was unlike anything she'd previously seen. Scans showed that water existed deep underground and was pumped upward by a series of huge artificial facilities dotted around its surface. There were no oceans at all but vast mountain ranges that towered up almost into space.

Fargas had come up with the communication strategy their expedition would use. Leda wasn't surprised. The man was gifted at manipulation.

Fidelity positioned itself to travel directly toward the green moon and make a close pass through its atmosphere. They would be visible to anyone on the surface. The security staff had studied the scans of the moon and confirmed that there were no hidden weapon systems that they could detect. In theory, there was no danger to the ship, but as was often the case during their journey, the unknown threats concerned them the most.

The green moon grew nearer. As usual, *Fidelity* had entered into the star system from the transit point at the system's edge with a velocity that would take them to their target in under a day. A shuttle dispatched to the planet would need several gravity maneuvers to decelerate before safely attempting to contact the ground. With *Fidelity* clear of the minefield regions, Marraz was available for the challenging task.

A message appeared on the bridge. "We're being sent a transmission," the communications officer reported. "It's directly beamed, sent specifically to us. They're using one of the common languages that we can translate using what we have on file."

A video appeared on-screen, showing three people with their faces covered and a flag behind them. They wore green uniforms, carried guns, and stood at ease as they spoke into the camera. Their words sounded calm, although there was no way to understand them without translation. After a few seconds, readable text appeared to the side of them.

The organization declined to identify itself, but they told *Fidelity* that it had been detected by local organizations on the moon below. *Fidelity* was accepted at its word as a collection of travelers from distant regions with little understanding of where they found themselves. All of those points were entirely true, Leda thought.

An invitation was sent, received, and verified by the ship's newly enhanced computer system, asking them to come to a small town on the moon and introduce themselves to the local authorities. They claimed to be members of the provisional government of the moon, but they also seemed to be in hiding.

Given the clearly patchwork nature of *Fidelity*'s exterior, it was abundantly obvious that *Fidelity* had little in terms of material value to offer. *Fidelity*'s landing party was being directed to a rendezvous in the middle of nowhere. That didn't seem to be a good sign in terms of legitimacy, but it stood to reason that any legitimate government would be under duress given the pressure from the Universal Legion. For establishing a contact with the rebels, it could be a promising lead.

Leda was summoned to the ship's conference room. Down in the launch bay, the shuttle was being readied for the journey to the planet below. Inside the conference room, she saw several other members of the engineering department around the table along with Advocate Fargas, who hunched alone in the corner. He seemed impatient, drumming his fingers faintly against the table. There was a pensive air to him, not normally visible when he was addressing others.

He was several centuries old, she considered, at least ten times older than she was. The people of Vale Reach could guess only vaguely what a mind like his must be like on the inside. Perhaps he thought so little of the engineers that he didn't feel the need to maintain his normally impenetrable professional demeanor.

Captain Haran came in and swiftly took a seat. The engineers stood to attention at her arrival then seated themselves again. Leda looked back at Fargas. His face had completely changed to a stony visage that would not have been out of place on a marble statue.

Captain Haran took a deep breath. "Soon, we are likely to make contact and establish diplomatic relations with a foreign military organization more powerful than our own. History tells us that this moment must be approached with great caution. I am referring to the rebels on the planet below, but the argument equally could apply to the Ruarken Senate. Everything discussed in this meeting is highly confidential. You have all been chosen from within the Vale Reach crew as reliable at maintaining secrecy."

Captain Haran paused for a moment, surveying them all. The room was soundproof and blocked even the engine's noise. "We can't be sure what they already know about us and Vale Reach. Previously, we have encountered offworlders who were somehow aware of the Seed of Steel. A fully defined policy must be in place before we can address the matter with any outsiders." She flattened her hands on the table. "What do we know? Technically, I wasn't conscious when our crew first learned of its existence."

Leda had seen Haran be attacked by the Enforcers. The bridge had been destroyed, and Leda had fled along with Cal and Rosco. "It's an ancient artifact," she said. "That's what everyone understands. Operator Marraz described it as a weapon. He seemed to know plenty about the Seed. If I may ask, Captain, why is he not here for this discussion?"

"Our pilot, Marraz, has already been interrogated and debriefed and his responses recorded," Captain Haran replied. "He was very much aware of the Seed for the duration of our mission, and his deceit has been proven. He will not be part of our discussions here."

Leda nodded. Marraz was in many ways a hardened criminal. She trusted that Captain Haran had extracted all information of value from him.

"What else do we know?" the captain demanded.

"It was apparently originally the property of the Tylder Ambassador," another engineer offered.

Captain Haran nodded in thoughtful acknowledgement. "That's the same individual who contacted Caladon Heit over the FTL communication lines."

"Does that mean that this Ambassador physically dates back to the prehistory of our planet?" Leda asked.

"It does," Fargas replied. "She's at least five thousand years old. I can assure you that's considered formidable anywhere."

"It's not lost on me that we're dealing with a potential enemy that's as old as human civilization on our homeworld," said Captain Haran.

"She has an array of multiple bodies." Fargas said. "She's changed form so many times, it's actually debatable whether there's anything original left in there at all."

"Why is she so determined to stop us, as Operator Heit reports?"

"To put it simply, she's afraid that she'll lose control of the Seed of Steel if we form an alliance with Ruarken High Senate," Fargas replied. He waved his hands slightly as he spoke to the captain. "If she is permanently unable to retrieve her artifact, that's the worst-case scenario for her."

"Why's she unable to retrieve it?" Haran asked. "We've confirmed reports that she's down on Vale Reach's surface right now."

"That's a good question," he said. "Perhaps one more suited to the engineers."

Leda spoke up. "We've heard reports that it's buried deep under Vale Reach. The mountain ranges of our world have unexplored tunnel networks that predate any of our records. It stands to reason that her artifact, whatever it is, must be lost within the tunnel systems. If she's searching for it, she hasn't found it yet."

"If she finds the artifact, perhaps she'd lose interest in our entire mission," the captain replied.

"If you lose the Seed of Steel, you have no leverage at all, nothing to offer the Ruarken High Senate," said Fargas. "You would once again be without a hope to stop the Universal Legion."

"Perhaps, so we move to the next vital point. What exactly does this artifact do?" Haran asked.

"Unknown," said Fargas.

"They call it an artifact, but perhaps we can presume it's a device of some kind," an engineer said. "I doubt it's going to be something ceremonial."

"It'll be advanced technology," said Haran, "yet we have no idea of its capabilities."

"Whatever it is, it's enough for a five-thousand-year-old being to be fixated with getting it back," said Leda.

Fargas smiled slightly. "I suppose she is becoming fixated with it."

"We're not handing over that kind of power till we know more about what it's capable of," said Captain Haran. "It would be profoundly unwise of us to transfer control of the Seed to anyone if we don't understand what it could do to our planet. We follow the plan originally devised by Councilor Theeran. We deny any knowledge of the Seed until we are forced otherwise. The less outsiders understand about what our world contains, the better."

"There is an alternative," said Fargas. "Something more reliable, in fact. You could offer rights to the Seed of Steel to the Ruarken Senate as soon as possible. Your improved communication systems now allow you to make long range contact with Ruarken far ahead of what was previously scheduled. You could trade giving them access to the Seed in exchange for their assistance in arranging your safe passage to the Senate, as well as maybe an agreement to form some kind of alliance with your world. It's the perfect bargaining chip. It ensures everything you want."

"And what would Ruarken do with the Seed of Steel?" Captain Haran asked. "Are we to simply trust that they'll be benevolent custodians of us all?"

Fargas looked surprised. "Someone has to control it, and the Ruarken are as good as any. It's foolish to believe you'll find anyone more suitable."

No one said anything. Haran and Fargas stared at each other disapprovingly. Leda became uncomfortable, and she was normally fine in such situations. Without Fargas to enable their crew to navigate the corridors of power once they reached Ruarken High Senate, the entire mission might not be successful. It simply wasn't possible to remove Fargas from their operation, and he probably knew that.

"You are dismissed from the bridge, Advocate Fargas," said Captain Haran.

Fargas grimaced then got up from his seat and left.

*

Rosco sat in the shuttle as they cruised down through the moon's atmosphere, studying an enormous collection of maps and documents. Three others were with him: Advocate Fargas, Cartographer Yendos, and Marraz flying the craft. The rest of *Fidelity* would remain in orbit, awaiting contact from Rosco to update them on the mission's progress. It had been decided that a small party was the safest way to meet the rebels.

Marraz would stay near the shuttle once they'd landed. He had the skills to get them back up into orbit against the planet's surface gravity using the small engines of the shuttlecraft and could leave in a hurry if anything went wrong. Yendos claimed he had great experience in crossing wilderness on foot and that he'd visited more planets than even he could possibly count, whilst Fargas was perhaps their best chance of successfully negotiating with whomever they encountered.

Rosco was the only person from Vale Reach aboard. Marraz was half Vale Reach in origin, but he seemed so different from them, his outlook changed from spending years as a pilot in deep space. If Marraz was taken at his word, then his loyalty was as much to Vale Reach as anyone else on *Fidelity*, but it was hard to trust a career criminal.

The other two had no inherent loyalty to his world, Rosco thought. Both Yendos and Fargas would have grown up in conditions far beyond what Rosco could imagine, probably as citizens of wealthy and powerful nations, where they'd been able to establish their careers. They both had knowledge that far exceeded his, yet he was in charge of the mission to the green moon. Captain Haran had been emphatic about that.

He remembered her warnings not to trust any of the other three men he shared the shuttle with. Each had potentially conspired with pirate leader Tarufa when she'd seized control of *Fidelity*. Haran had warned him to be on his guard. The mission was his responsibility. The offworlder advisors were his to direct, no matter if they began to believe otherwise.

"Is the shuttle fully prepared for landing?" he asked Marraz.

"Yes, sir," Marraz replied. He seemed happy to be outside of *Fidelity*.

Rosco's objectives were clear. He was to contact whatever rebels were present. If safe, he was then to establish how *Fidelity* could efficiently cross through the Liberated Zone and reach Ruarken. If they were ambushed somehow on the surface, Marraz had been instructed to return them to the ship immediately. Rosco wouldn't hesitate to give the order, if the situation required it. Given the nature of the message *Fidelity* had received, there was no evidence to suspect they'd face harm from the rebels. He was even authorized to inform them that they and *Fidelity* shared similar goals of undermining the Legion. Ultimately, curiosity toward *Fidelity*'s unique status would likely be their best protection.

*

The shuttle touched down next to a small settlement. From their position on the mountainside, Rosco could see just how basic the place was, no more than a collection of cabins and a few larger central buildings. Numerous paths led through the hills, and Rosco could see the signs of other settlements in the distance. The buildings were made of stone and what appeared to be gray wood, though he could see no trees. A dozen people emerged from the dwellings, waving at the shuttle before they had even exited. They were expected, despite doing nothing to broadcast their arrival.

Yendos and Fargas were quietly comparing notes with each other. Rosco couldn't understand the language they were speaking. It annoyed him, but it was unreasonable to order them to stop talking.

As the shuttle door opened, he caught a whiff of air that was almost indescribable. He realized it was only his second time on another planet. The air pressure felt unnatural, as though the whole world was eerily silent. He was tasting the chemicals of the air and the minerals in the rocks. He felt lightheaded, and his vision blurred for a moment. The others seemed unconcerned and barely even looked outside. The powdery green ground was even brighter up close, but Rosco saw dark-gray rocks like slate buried around on the surface too. The ambient temperature was reasonable, at least.

After waiting a moment to clear his head, Rosco removed his safety harness and stood. He had to take the lead, as both their security officer and mission leader. He put his head out the door and saw the small group of people watching them. They wore loose brown jumpsuits. Their mouths were covered by scarves, but the rest of their faces were visible. They seemed to view the newcomers with a detached and nonchalant air. Clothing hung on drying lines between the rooftops, and barrels of water stood in the shadow of the buildings.

Rosco had a pistol kept on his belt but made sure to carry no other weapons. He waved back to the locals as he stepped out of the shuttle, the other three emerging behind him. They each looked so different, he realized—Rosco in his Vale Reach uniform, Yendos in his black leather, and Fargas wearing bright-blue robes, plus Marraz's own dirty and personalized outfit that he insisted on.

The locals shouted a few words, presumably of greeting. Yendos replied to them in a similar-sounding language.

"Any idea what they're saying?" Rosco asked Fargas, who stood adjacent to him. The sky above was dark with long blue streaks, as though in twilight, with thousands of stars visible.

"No," said Fargas. "This one's a little beyond me but not the cartographer, it seems."

"We're being directed to sit indoors whilst we wait for our hosts to arrive," Yendos said to them.

"Fine with me," Rosco said.

They were ushered toward the doorway of a nearby stone cabin. Up close, the cabin was solidly built, with the gray bricks cut to be regular and even some decorative carvings in the wooden beams that made up the ceilings. Inside was dark. The windows were small, but enough traces of natural light came in for Rosco to see the basic furniture at the sides of the room. It seemed like the cabin was used for meetings, but no people were inside. "So, the villagers here aren't who we're supposed to meet?" said Rosco.

"Apparently not. They aren't very talkative," said Yendos.

Rosco could tell this settlement had been inhabited for a long time, given the general age and level of dust in the buildings. The cabin was clearly not a residence but maybe a communal space. There were mattresses arranged in one corner of the room but no signs that anyone permanently lived there. A few villagers came into the room with them and indicated for the four of them to sit on the wooden benches and chairs along the sides of the room.

"These people are here to spy on us, aren't they?" Rosco asked.

"Almost certainly," Fargas replied. "They'll take a good look at us and report back to someone."

"At least there's no chance they can understand what we're saying," Rosco said. The Vale Reach language would be impenetrable to them.

They settled into the rustic chairs in the dimly lit room. The villagers watched them but made no further attempt to speak to them. After a while, most left to attend to other business.

After an hour or so, their surroundings began to grow noticeably darker.

"Have we reached nightfall?" Rosco asked.

"Impossible," said Yendos. "Did you not observe the moon's rotation as we came down in the shuttle? We have fifty hours still till nightfall."

Rosco stood and looked out a small window. The doorway to the cabin was still open. Thick whisps of white cloud looked to be drifting in from the distant mountains. The air was still eerily silent, but faint howling could be heard from far away. "A storm, perhaps," said Rosco. He turned to Marraz. "Can our shuttle handle a serious storm? It's pretty exposed on the mountainside here."

Marraz shrugged. "Gods, I don't know what the weather is like in this place."

Rosco was unimpressed by his answer.

"Okay. It'll do a lot better if we anchor it properly so there's no way the wind can drag it around," said Marraz. "There's a tarpaulin stored inside—it wraps around the whole thing to protect all the vents, et cetera, though I've never actually done it."

A pair of locals entered the cabin and spoke to Yendos.

"It's a storm, all right," said Yendos. "They seem a little concerned. Apparently, we must expect to be here a while longer now."

Rosco turned to Marraz, and the man nodded. "All right, let's go wrap it up."

*

Rosco and Marraz both stood on the roof of the shuttle, trying to drag the huge piece of canvas across its surface as the wind steadily increased around them. Gravity on the moon was noticeably less than he'd initially realized, producing an uncomfortably low level of friction on top of the shuttle. It wouldn't matter much if he fell off, but he still felt alarming to be unstable whilst so high in the air.

The elastic waterproof cover was a tight fit over the shuttle, and it was a difficult task for two men. Rosco regretted not ordering Yendos to help them with the manual labor. The dark and empty sky they'd seen on arrival had filled with white mist that seemed to hover just above them, gradually descending. Marraz looked stable on his feet, making it appear easy to balance. As Rosco understood, the other man had lived under low-gravity conditions for years on end.

Marraz had seemed unconcerned by the sky at first, but Rosco had noticed that his pace of work had increased as the storm clouds crept nearer. They needed to shout at each other over the rising sound of the wind as they aligned the tarp and cleared it from any points where it became snagged. Rosco noticed how Marraz's Vale Reach accent grew thicker as they worked, till he and Rosco spoke in nearly the same way. It felt incongruous with the bright clothes and hairstyle that viscerally reminded Rosco of the void pirates they'd encountered.

They climbed back to ground level. Rosco kept one hand gripping the corner of the tarp and held the ladder with the other. To Rosco's surprise, Marraz jumped from the top and dropped gracefully to the ground. Rosco joined him at the bottom of the ladder. They attached the bottom of the tarpaulin to the edge of the shuttle's metal feet. Then they sheltered under the tarp for a second. A zipper would close it behind them to complete their work.

"I should put the electronics into safe mode!" Marraz shouted over the rushing wind. He pressed a button, and a door in the shuttle opened. He went inside, and Rosco followed to take cover from the elements. Only a handful of dim lights lit the interior. Marraz moved to the pilot's cockpit and began flipping switches. The few remaining lights began to fade. Rosco waited behind him.

Marraz paused for a moment. "You know, Major, I really am determined to be a useful part of *Fidelity*'s mission," he said.

"You are," said Rosco, "an integral part." His voice betrayed a hint of disapproval.

"I signed up for it before you did, you know?"

"Is that so?" Rosco remembered their first meeting in the lunar construction bay on Vale Reach's moon.

"I didn't have to return to Vale Reach." Marraz looked as though he didn't mean what he said. "Well, I suppose I did. Not having a choice is exactly what my position was." He shook his head. "I have family on Vale Reach, friends… all the people from before I left. I knew they were still back there, living their lives. It was inspiring to know everyone was happy without me, and I was far away, dealing with my own problems. They could live in their world, and I was away in mine, in a place that suited me. It was ideal. But… I need that to stay true." He looked miserable. "I need for there to be a Vale Reach and for that to be where my family is. Without that, I don't think I'd be able to carry on."

"Vale Reach is the only planet I've ever lived on," said Rosco, stating the obvious. "But I can imagine what you mean. Why did you leave Vale Reach in the first place?"

"My father was a void-kin," Marraz said, "but by the time I was getting ready to leave, he hadn't visited me in years. But I remembered his tales of adventure. I remembered them better than I remembered him. I felt I had seen those places myself. I used to look around at the town in Vale Reach, and I just knew I couldn't spend the rest of my life looking at such a small place. It's like I wouldn't forgive myself if I did. Of course, I have a feeling that made me act like a complete asshole toward my family and everyone else. I wasn't a great guy in those days. I guess I wasn't really a great guy in the years that followed either, but…" He shrugged slightly. "I'm trying to make amends. I've seen bad things that happen in space. Terrible things. I can't let anything like that happen to Vale Reach. And…" He hesitated. "I don't think I could hurt someone innocent anymore, actually. I think I'm done with crime and violence." He paused for a second, obviously deep in thought. "I mean, technically, this whole mission is criminal, but other than that."

"There's nothing criminal about it, according to our own laws." Rosco realized the logic was slightly tenuous as he said it. "What was your relationship with Tarufa? When she broadcasted to our bridge on the Highway, she made it clear she knew you pretty well."

Marraz sat back for a moment and closed his eyes. "She was a mentor, I guess you could say. Maybe that's a little flattering. Maybe she was just my superior officer. She ruled the ship through fear, of course. I knew nothing about her when I was assigned to be on her ship. I had nothing, really, and I'd joined a criminal gang to make some money. The gang traded material back and forth with the pirate ships in the region… and eventually, I ended up aboard Tarufa's ship. It was only semi-voluntary in the beginning, but it's never smart to complain too much about that."

"Weren't you two comrades?" Rosco's gut instincts told him it was true.

"Eventually, I guess I became some kind of curiosity to her, and I even became part of her bridge advisors. She has an active mind, compared to the other pirates. She's never settled. She has schemes going on that the rest of her crew never knew about. You're giving her what she wants, you know. She wants to see the Seed of Steel end up with the Ruarken Senate. I think she killed Theeran because he would never have allowed that to happen."

"Tarufa killed Theeran? Our official reports say the Enforcers did it."

Marraz shrugged. "I don't know for sure."

"And Tarufa just let you leave one day?"

Marraz laughed. "Obviously not. But I did successfully leave one day. When I saw signs that the Legion's world-breaker ships were being directed to Vale Reach, I knew I had to go back. I could arrive faster than any of the Legion ships could. When I reached Vale Reach's orbit, Councilor Theeran's organization detected me and made contact. I shared what I knew. Without me, none of this mission would be happening at all. Think about it, Rosco. Why would I undermine any mission that I myself helped to begin?"

"You didn't organize this mission." As the commanding officer, Rosco was trying to remain neutral as he listened to the man's story, but something about Marraz's sudden need to be earnest was compelling to him.

"I instigated the mission, then," said Marraz. "My arrival prompted this whole operation to start."

"That's partially accurate."

"You can trust me, Rosco," Marraz said. "I want to save Vale Reach just as much as anyone. Just as much as you. I'd rather die than see our world ruined. Only…" He paused.

"Go on," Rosco said.

"We can't stop Vale Reach from changing. We can stop the Legion from taking over the land… but we can't stop technology from arriving. Not anymore. And that's going to change everything for us, permanently. There's no way Vale Reach can continue to live as it has before. I think we need to be prepared for that. We need to be prepared to upgrade our planet in a very short span of time, once the opportunity comes. Either way, I think there might not be much of the old Vale Reach left when this is all done. We can't win, you know?"

Rosco patted him on the shoulder. "The past is always traveling away from us. And the future may not be something we can understand. It'll be our descendants who can have the chance to create a better place than we can imagine. Everyone's descendants, I mean." He was childless. He had no idea if Marraz was too.

"Vale Reach will never even remember us," Marraz said. "Especially not if we die lost in some obscure back end of the universe. You can just step out of people's lives and out of reality once you come out to space. But fuck it. I wasn't planning on being remembered. And I have memories that I'm glad will disappear with me."

The last of the lights faded to black, leaving them completely in the dark inside the shuttle. They both knew their way around the interior.

"Let's see what havoc Fargas has managed to cause back in the cabin," Marraz joked.

"Do you trust him?" Rosco asked quietly.

"He wants us to get to Ruarken," Marraz replied after a moment's consideration. "I'm damn sure of that."

"No ulterior motives?" Rosco asked.

"Of course he has those," said Marraz. "He's a three-hundred-year-old lawyer with a history of disciplinary issues. I'm sure he has a mountain of stuff he's covering up. But on this journey, at least, our interests are aligned, his and our world's. Theeran believed that, and I do too."

"He was just unconscious when Tarufa took over the ship?" Rosco asked.

"We all were, for the most part," said Marraz. "She didn't say much, just went about her business doing something on the bridge. Who knows what."

"Who knows," Rosco repeated.

Marraz and Rosco returned to the stone cabin. The wind had grown intense, whipping the rocky dust around in a way that was sharp against their skin. They rushed toward the door, pushed it open, and hurried in. As their eyes adjusted to the dim interior, they saw dozens of people sitting on the floor, arranged around Yendos's unmistakably large form. The group gazed up at him almost in adoration.

He was mid-sentence, talking in an unknown language, waving his hands. Storytelling, Rosco realized. The crowd watched in a state of raptured amazement. Rosco came to a halt, too confused to react. Yendos continued, unconcerned, his large hooded head turning left and right as he emoted about some series of events.

Rosco turned to Marraz in disbelief. "Why does Yendos never tell us any stories?"

"*Fidelity* has no children on board to hear them," said Advocate Fargas, somehow appearing at Rosco's side. "Yendos loves to perform for children."

"Wh-What? That man gets stranger and stranger…"

As the story reached some sort of conclusion, Yendos's voice and posture grew despondent. The locals got to their feet and moved to hug him in an embrace, all holding him in their arms. He accepted their condolences.

"Anything I should know about?" Rosco asked.

"Family history," Fargas said. "He'll tell you when he's ready."

*

A powerful storm rolled in. More villagers, far more than Rosco had been expecting, piled into the cabin till the room was packed. The noise was terrifying, with thunder like artillery explosions. The strange, silent atmosphere of the planet only seemed to heighten the blasting sounds of electrical discharge.

They heard wind-blown debris scraping against the sides of the hut. They all huddled and waited, the violent forces too frightening to allow sleep. Rosco stared at the wooden beams of the dark ceiling. He'd seen no signs of industrial technology on this world yet. Hours went by. He checked his watch—eleven hours had passed. He was experienced at living in the mountains during his time on exercises with the Vale Reach army, but the alien nature of this place left him unsettled. The villagers seemed more wearied than threatened by the storm. It wasn't uncommon to them, Rosco could tell.

Eventually, the storm cleared, as storms always did. The villagers who'd huddled together in the cabin filed back outside, and the *Fidelity* crew followed, ready to stretch their legs and see open sky. When Rosco stepped onto the rocky ground once more, he saw that the locals were already preparing for a trek, gathering their equipment and filling backpacks. Somehow, they were immediately ready to go.

Rosco turned to Marraz as the man exited the cabin. "We're going onwards."

DEFIANT SYSTEMS

*

Without any discussion, eight villagers joined the *Fidelity* crew, and as a group, they set off into the mountains. Rosco could tell how life aboard the cramp confines of *Fidelity* had reduced his own physical fitness. Fargas seemed to be struggling with the hike the most. The man was in poor physical condition, audibly struggling for breath during difficult stretches of the journey. Even Marraz, who was lean and muscular but perhaps not used to the endurance needed to travel far on foot, experienced some difficulty. He would be better in a fight than on a trek. Yendos, contrary to the slightly bulky nature of his outfit, handled the hills with impressive ease. He alone could keep up with the local villagers, who walked up steep rock faces as though out on a stroll.

They traveled up narrow paths, winding their way along ridges and around razor-thin peaks. In the far distance, Rosco occasionally saw flat, wide plans. They looked to his eyes to be almost like an ocean, but he knew from studying the nature of the moon that they could only be sand, an endless expanse of more fine powder. He had no idea where they were heading or even any ability to ask the people around him, but the villagers directed them with purpose and confidence. It seemed that everything was going according to plan.

The skies looked to be perpetually black, save for the alarming whiteout of the storm. Whatever atmosphere they were breathing was entirely transparent. The rocky green ridges extended as far to the horizon as he could see.

Fargas waved to Rosco as they walked, signaling for Rosco to join him as he wearily shuffled along at the back of the group. Rosco fell back to join him. "We need to prepare what you're going to say when you meet the rebels at the far end of this journey," Fargas said.

"How sure are you that it's the rebels who'll be awaiting us?"

"They must be. There's no other point to all this precaution. We're being taken to meet someone with some degree of authority. That means we'll likely be interrogated. If they seem too eager for information, then you should be coy with them. Seem on the fence, as though they need to earn your interest."

"Okay," Rosco replied. "I understand."

"You have to use guile, Major. Cunning."

"I can do that."

Fargas looked unconvinced for a moment. "If they don't seem very enthusiastic, then you react with surprise," he continued, "as if it just doesn't make any sense for the two of you not to be in an amicable alliance, as if it makes so little sense that you hadn't even considered it as a possibility! In a subtle way, make them feel foolish for questioning you."

"Okay. Yes."

"If they seem to know everything about us already, then they're fishing for more information. Give them a few little crumbs to keep them interested."

"Understood."

"And if they claim to know nothing whatsoever about who we are, that's a sign that this is all turning into a trap. There's no way they wouldn't know anything about us if they're bringing us this far."

Rosco nodded. "If it's a trap, we can't do much about it."

"Remember to trust your gut instincts above everything else. It's all very simple. Now, let's clarify some other scenarios…"

☐

Chapter 7

The group came to a halt. Rosco looked around but found nothing that distinguished their location from any other point on their journey, somewhere amidst the endless pale, pastel-colored hills. Three of the villagers used small sticks to clear dust and dirt from a patch of ground next to the trail, revealing what looked to be an old rug buried under the earth. They pulled the rug aside, uncovering a metal hatch that had been painted blue, small enough that only a single person could enter at a time.

"Tunnels," Marraz noted.

"It's a sensible choice," said Rosco. Rock and earth made an effective barrier against surveillance if the manual labor of excavation was manageable.

The villagers knocked on the hatch with a distinct rhythmic pattern then waited for a response. They received the sound of a different rhythm in return. The villagers listened carefully, their faces wrinkled in concentration, then knocked another rhythmic pattern in response. There was a back and forth for several rounds until at last, the villagers appeared relieved and satisfied. There was a metal grinding noise, and they heaved open the hatch. One of them went down first, and the others gestured for the crew of *Fidelity* to descend the ladder that led inside. Rosco naturally took the lead.

Traces of electric light shone from a distant lower level. Rosco could see nothing else of what was below him. Descending was an act of faith. After what felt like several minutes, the narrow shaft suddenly expanded into a larger room, and after a few more seconds, Rosco was standing on a flat rock floor, looking around him at a natural cavern that had been enlarged by human activity. There were a few metal crates scattered around and a heavy round door like that of a bank vault at one end. Otherwise, the space seemed empty.

Rosco waited for the remainder of their party to reach the bottom. He was a little surprised that Yendos made it through the hole, but the man seemed accustomed to fitting into narrow spaces. Rosco noticed that the round vault door at the far end was open by about two feet. He could go through, though he couldn't see the other side. Once again, the villagers gestured for Rosco to move forward, but they waited at a respectful distance, clearly intending to go no farther themselves.

Marraz, Yendos, and Fargas paused, choosing that moment to allow Rosco to discover first what was on the other side. He was ready to show confidence. He walked up to the opening and went straight through.

On the far side, he immediately saw two men. One stood close in front of him, taller than Rosco by several inches and imposing. He wore a uniform unlike anything Rosco had seen before. The outfit was the same green color as the surrounding rocks, covered in pockets, and with several ornate silk scarves wrapped around his body, each a vivid mix of materials. On the man's chest were insignia badges that seemed to contain precious jewels, which also featured on a cap that the man wore on his head. The uniform's flared ruffles had to be for aesthetic rather than practical reasons.

The other man in the room wore an identical uniform but with no cap. His skin was dark, and he had large eyes and a relaxed, almost cynical air. He sat behind a desk, his chair hidden in the dark, at a simple table that included small chairs for visitors. The furniture appeared to be made of the same gray wood as the cabins in the village. Both of the men looked to be offworlders. There was a lamp on the desk that cast a warm yellow glow over the space, but no other objects sat on the desk's flat surface. The man at the desk smiled for a second as he made eye contact with Rosco, but it was polite and perfunctory, an act of basic diplomacy.

The man standing closest to Rosco indicated for him to stop then said something in a language that Rosco did not understand. He'd immediately encountered an obvious problem.

"I don't understand," Rosco said. "I may need a translator." He sounded slightly apologetic. His lack of language skills was making their operation appear amateurish.

Fargas stuck his head through the vault door, peering around inquisitively. He made eye contact with the two offworlders inside and said a few words to them in a foreign language. Then he came into the room to join Rosco, almost scurrying. At some unspoken command, the vault door sealed shut with a clang, leaving Rosco and Fargas in the room with the two men.

"He's going to search us for weapons," Fargas said to Rosco. Rosco noticed suddenly that the man behind the desk was surrounded with some sort of transparent barrier, like a glass wall.

Rosco raised his arms as the man closest to them checked him and Fargas for weapons, first with a small handheld device then feeling with his hands. Rosco nodded to where his small pistol was kept, and the man removed it. Then they were waved ahead, and the man who searched them stood back against the wall. Finally, Rosco and Fargas were seated on the wooden chairs in front of the desk.

The man behind the glass barrier spoke.

Fargas translated. "His name is Lieutenant Norik."

"Major Rosco," Rosco introduced himself, speaking clearly. He pointed to his companion "Advocate Fargas." Then he turned to Fargas. "Tell him we're the representatives from the ship in orbit."

Fargas spoke to the man but didn't get much response. It appeared that the information was obvious.

"Tell him we're here to establish friendly contact between our ship and the people who control the Liberated Zone," said Rosco.

Fargas spoke to the man again.

The man sat up very gradually then said something brief.

"Why friendly?" Fargas asked Rosco.

"We have common goals of working against the Legion."

"I try speaking with you directly," the man said slowly. His accent was very strong, and it took Rosco a few moments before he realized the words were something he could understand.

"You can speak my language?" Rosco asked.

The man shook his head. "No. But over the years, I have trained in the basic form of linguistic assembly." The words came much slower than normal, but Rosco could piece together what it all meant. "It's been many years since I had a new subject to test myself on. Please. So that I know I have not become weakened in this area. I will adjust soon. You are an unusual party. A member of the revered cartographers' guild and a void-kin are outside, and here we have"—he gestured to Rosco and Fargas and hesitated—"a rich man and a soldier. Did I say that correctly? I don't want to offend."

Fargas smiled for a moment. It was rare to see him so pleased. "I'm a lawyer."

"And I am Lieutenant Norik, a member of the Crusaders of Freedom. I have no doubt you've heard of us. We are the only people fighting to defend the indigenous lives on these planets. We noticed your ship in orbit. Perhaps you would like to tell us who you are?"

"We are travelers from distant worlds. We are on a diplomatic mission that leads us on a path through this region," said Rosco.

"And what is your history with the Universal Legion? I presume you saw the messenger beacons," said Norik.

"Indeed. They're hard to miss. But I need to check… are you the authors of the Declaration of Self Rule?"

The man considered this for a second. "Many people of the worlds here contributed to that declaration," he said. "If my organization had some hand in its production, that knowledge would be beyond my rank."

That seemed unlikely to be true, but it worked as an admission of what he needed to know. "Our diplomatic mission is carrying intelligence information that will be harmful to the Universal Legion."

The man at the other side of the table visibly woke up. "How harmful?"

Rosco shrugged. "Fairly harmful."

"Can you share this intelligence with us?"

"We cannot. It's information that relies on its classified nature to retain its value. Even spreading the knowledge to allies would lessen its impact."

"Couldn't we just extract the information from you?"

"Of course, I don't personally know anything genuinely valuable, for that reason," said Rosco.

The man leaned back in his chair and seemed to lose interest again. "This is all very difficult for us to verify. Intriguing, don't get me wrong. But it sounds like your project has only minimal intersection with ours. My personal advice is not to draw much attention to yourself, if you're serious about what you're saying. The Legion's spies are inept, but some of them make up for their lack of ability with enthusiasm. Even blunt force occasionally gets results. If you don't want to die, be sure you understand exactly what you're doing. Have you considered contributing to our rebellion in other ways? Financial donations are an excellent way to enable the fight."

Rosco exchanged a brief look with Fargas. It was time to bring things up a next level. "Could I show you an object I've brought with me?"

Norik seemed idly intrigued once more. "By all means."

Rosco reached into his backpack and collected a bundle. They were uniforms, or the shredded remains of them, taken from the dead bodies of the Enforcers that had attacked *Fidelity* at the Highway of Thelmia. The bloodstains were extensive. Almost as noteworthy were the laser-straight lines sliced through them, the pirates' razor-blade knives having passed through hardened polymer armor to make a grisly mess of the Enforcers. The close-combat weapons of some pirates were now kept in storage onboard *Fidelity*.

Rosco held the bundle out to the man. "As you can see…"

The man picked up one piece of the heavy jacket and held it up to the light. "Enforcers," he seemed to read it from the insignia. "I've heard of them. They're not from these parts. They're far away. As are you…" He looked up and made eye contact. "They're serious players. Not lightweights." He stretched open the gash in the armor, opening it wide and looking inside with raised eyebrows. For a moment, he and Rosco made eye contact through the hole. "And you didn't just find this thing somewhere?"

"We have more exhibits, if needed." Rosco reached for his backpack then extracted more pieces of personal equipment they'd recovered from the Enforcers. "This is a product of our work."

The man behind the table smiled warmly for the first time, somehow more genuine and relieved than Rosco had been expecting. "I'm sure some kind of arrangement can be reached between us." At that moment, the man seemed to receive a message on a personal communicator that he removed from inside his uniform. His face once again became deep and serious as he spoke quietly into the device.

He stood. "Come with me, please." He beckoned for Rosco to follow. The glass wall around the desk silently retracted into the ground, and the man led Rosco to the cavernous wall behind his desk. It looked blank and unremarkable to Rosco. The man reached out and drew a geometric pattern across the wall with his hand. Silently, a portion of the cavern wall slid back, revealing yet another hidden chamber.

Rosco was amazed. The room behind the wall seemed very similar to the room behind them, with another desk and another man sitting behind it. This man was far older and had a long gray beard and many more ornate badges on his uniform. Elements of his face appeared old, whilst other parts seemed unnaturally young. Rosco had begun to recognize this sense of chronological ambiguity as a clear marker of genetic manipulation, of an aging process that had been reversed but still left behind traces of the previous face. The man's eyes glowed with a fierce intensity. After the things Rosco had seen on his journey, he half believed that the man's eyes really were able to literally emit tiny points of light.

There were no other seats. Rosco and Norik stood before the half-elderly man, leaving Fargas waiting in the room behind them.

"You've traveled an impressive way to get here," the half-elderly man said, "in that ramshackle ship." There was a metallic quality to his voice, though there was no indication of why that was the case. Perhaps he'd augmented himself with bionics, as Leda had.

"It has been a long trip," Rosco said. He tried to look a little weary to emphasize the point.

"We've run some tests on your vessel in orbit. It's a machine that's hard to recognize, even beneath the scrap parts you've not so elegantly added to your structure."

Rosco appreciated that the engineering department's work wasn't aesthetically pleasing. The welding marks were still visible. "We've not had chance to smooth out our modifications at a repair station."

"And your hatred for the Universal Legion is what's driven you all this way?" the man croaked.

"Hatred seems a strong term," said Rosco, "but we are in a fight against them for our survival."

The elderly man's eyes glazed over for a second. "If you don't hate them, then you haven't been fighting them long enough. Here in this zone, we've been at war for nearly three hundred years."

"Even during the Makron invasion?" Rosco asked.

The old man grimaced, but it turned into a bitter chuckle. "Those were exceptional times. Humans must band together against inhuman enemies. But we finished that period still at war with each other. As for you, there are elements of your ship that we place as from the Sirkallion region. But you clearly do have some secrets to keep, and in the interests of friendly relations, perhaps we shouldn't pry further. You have come to us already knowing who we are. Are you a friend to our cause?"

"We are." Rosco felt the weight of the words as he said them. It was true. Vale Reach would happily see the Legion defeated by these rebels.

"Ours is a grand tradition," the man said. "It is not for nothing that we are called the Crusaders of Freedom. We embody noble goals. In a galaxy full of corrupted morals and selfish minds, we strive to liberate all, regardless of class or religion. We are fighting against as bleak a system of evil as humanity has ever devised, a death machine to which nations must be fed, one after the other, to satisfy its bottomless hunger. The truth is, the Legion needs to wage war to survive. If the conflict stopped, they would have no purpose. It is unthinkable. In a very literal sense, their wars can never end. Make no mistake, Major Rosco, the Universal Legion are rabid dogs that must be put down. And it will take all of us working together to do that. You would need to be a knight to join us, Major. Does that word translate for you?"

"It does," Rosco said solemnly.

"Can you uphold what that word means? Can you commit to sharing our values and being comrades through hard times?"

They were being invited deeper into the Crusader's organization. Captain Haran and Rosco had discussed this. Meeting the Makron had refocused their priorities, as had the knowledge that Makron invasion fleets could expand

and contract their empires unexpectedly. A new set of secondary objectives had been proposed to gather weapons data, study combat doctrines, and compile a dossier for Vale Reach.

In the event of an interstellar invasion from something like the Makron empire, breaking the Binding Treaty would be the least of their concerns. A secret dossier on advanced tactics and new technologies could be decisive for protecting their world. *Fidelity* could also potentially transmit such files quickly back to Vale Reach through the FTL lines, though this had some risk of interception. Rosco was tasked with assessing how any temporary alliance with the rebels could provide long-term benefits to their homeworld.

"Yes," said Rosco. "We can uphold that ideal." Somehow, the words resonated. It was inspiring to hear someone from outside of Vale Reach, someone with centuries of experience, speak of fighting the Legion. This man was living proof that what they had been told was impossible could be real¬—defiance against the Universal Legion.

"Then you may join us," the old man said, "and we will see for ourselves just how much you believe in this fight. We are a network that stretches across a thousand worlds. We have eyes everywhere, men and women willing to die for us. It's because they believe in our cause—to end the abuse of the common people of these worlds. My lieutenant here will accompany your ship. He has his own vessel, though some of your food and supplies will be required for him. If you wish to be part of our movement, as very many rebel groups have before you, then you'll find we are willing to accept any whose intentions are pure and who has the courage to stand up against tyranny."

"You'll find we have that," Rosco said.

"Brutality is the first and last tool of the Universal Legion," the old man said. "Remember, each time they strike, your resolve must harden and never waver. That alone is the path to our eventual deliverance."

"Let's not delay," Lieutenant Norik said. "My interceptor craft is nearby."

*

On the return to orbit, Rosco signaled to *Fidelity*, advising them he would not be returning alone. He studied Norik's interceptor as they traveled through space together, but he could only make limited sense of it. He swapped seats with Marraz to pilot the shuttle himself so that his more experienced spacefaring comrade could give his full attention to analyzing Norik's craft. The two of them would have the opportunity to discuss their findings before they returned to *Fidelity*.

The interceptor, as the name implied, was built for both speed and attack power. It stayed close by *Fidelity*'s shuttle as they headed back to the rest of the crew, carrying several clusters of rocket weapons, yet as Marraz indicated, it could not hold enough fuel for extended journeys. Its engines seemed built to consume its fuel as quickly as possible. The cockpit was designed to reduce all acceleration forces on the occupant, once again raising the craft's maximum velocity. These features combined to create a high-speed attack craft capable of rapidly crossing the distances between starships in a typical shipping lane. There was no storage at all aboard Norik's vessel, nor even room for him to leave his seat. It was a fighter in need of a carrier ship—and *Fidelity* could fill that role.

There was no doubt that the interceptor could be a security threat to *Fidelity*. Its weapons would easily be able to disable their whole vessel. Rosco felt a sense of trepidation as they approached *Fidelity* and it grew larger in their sights. He'd transmitted all of the information to the ship already. He also noted that Norik had transmitted a series of call signs to *Fidelity*, though Rosco didn't understand them—it was likely no one else aboard the ship did either.

Fidelity opened its shuttle bay doors and kept them open to allow the interceptor to enter too. Their ship possessed three shuttlecraft and only a single additional empty bay, so all the spaces became filled when Norik's craft touched down. A group of armed guards were already waiting as they all disembarked, and Norik was checked for weapons much as Rosco had been. Then they were escorted directly to the bridge of *Fidelity*.

Norik must have been aware that Rosco had briefed the captain already. The door to the bridge opened, and they stepped inside and walked toward Captain Haran's podium, where she waited to meet him. The bridge seemed just a little shabbier than Rosco remembered it. It really had taken a beating at the hands of the pirates. He wondered if the fresh weld marks on the ship would make them look impoverished. The repair station had patched up the many bullet holes, but there were still a few suspicious burn marks in the corners of some units.

They reached the center of the bridge and stood in front of the captain's chair.

"I present to you Lieutenant Norik, sir," said Major Rosco. "He is a member of the Crusaders of Freedom, an armed resistance movement willing to offer us support."

Haran stayed impassive, her eyes narrowing in faint judgment.

"Lieutenant, welcome aboard. My name is Captain Haran. I bid you formal greetings from our homeworld. I hope this is the beginning of a relationship built on mutual understanding and respect." She didn't move a fraction as she spoke.

Norik smiled and performed some kind of salute. "Greetings, noble Captain. Indeed, I do represent the Crusaders of Freedom. It's an honor to be a guest on this vessel."

"A guest you may be, but I note that your interceptor voidcraft has plenty of weaponry—more than our own vessel, as I'm sure you are aware. Ours is an inherently unequal relationship, in terms of firepower. Though I also note that your craft is intending to be dependent on ours for food and maintenance supplies."

Norik nodded casually. "My voidcraft is a fighting machine. Without its weapons, it is nothing. I carry a load of ninety-six rockets, able to inflict precise damage on much larger vessels. But this is standard for someone of my rank. The interceptor is my personal weapon, and with it, I have liberated many souls in this star system and the systems around."

"You may keep your weapons if they're a mark of your personal rank. We are being generous in affording you these rights," Haran said.

"It is appreciated both by myself and the people I represent. If the bonds of honor between us become strong, then it'll be my craft and its rockets that defend your whole vessel when the time of battle comes."

"Let's hope it doesn't come to that," she said.

"There's a good chance it will," Norik said. "My commander on the moon below has authorized me as such."

"We don't plan to be part of any conflicts unless absolutely necessary, given the nature of our ship," said Haran.

"Neither do I, though I have a limited ability to speak on behalf of the other chapters of my organization throughout the Liberated Zone."

"Nonetheless, my command of this ship remains inviolable, Lieutenant," Haran said. "You are of course free to operate your own voidcraft as you wish. An arrangement can be reached regarding fuel. However, you are not to use lethal force without my permission. You are not to deploy your rockets unless I am in explicit agreement."

"Understandable, Captain," Norik said with a nod.

"One of your rockets is to be provided as a sample for our scientific and engineering departments to study, under Chief Engineer Palchek," Captain Haran said.

Norik hesitated for a moment. "I advise your engineer to take great caution if they are unfamiliar with such things."

Haran gestured for Leda to reply. "My work will be very careful," Leda said. "I'll proceed slowly."

Norik looked at where she sat at her desk. "Are you seeking to produce something similar for yourselves?"

"Of course," Leda said.

"Lieutenant Norik, if you stay aboard this ship, you will also be prohibited from accessing any of our data files. As Major Rosco has informed you, maintaining the confidential state of the information we carry is our top priority in our operation against the Universal Legion. You are of course welcome to take a personal bunk in our living quarters, and you have unrestricted access to our canteen and social areas."

"That is a kind offer, Captain. My own interceptor is capable of keeping my body alive and healthy, but one thing it cannot offer me is a chance to walk. However, Captain, I must point out that I'm not here simply to observe you."

"No?" Captain Haran raised her eyebrows. "Then tell us what you're here for."

"I hope you understand that I've left my post and my mission on the moon below in order to serve a greater purpose for the Crusaders. Securing your allegiance to our larger fleet is that worthy higher purpose. If you wish to join us, it will require we travel away from here to a location deeper into Liberated Zone."

"That's acceptable to us," Haran replied in a flat, neutral tone. Rosco saw how this could provide what they needed. "But can you assure us safety and protection in such an undertaking?"

"I cannot do that with my interceptor alone." Norik offered a small apologetic shrug. "But there is a carrier ship nearby that can transport you to join to our great fleets. It is highly advisable that we rendezvous with the carrier as soon as possible. As my commander has already advised Major Rosco, we Crusaders are operating on over one thousand planets.

"You see, the reason the Legion has never defeated us is because it essentially can't. No matter how many resources the Legion commits to the fight, it can't be everywhere at once. Eventually, it always runs out of manpower.

"Exploiting that gap in manpower is exactly where we come in. We connect a thousand indigenous rebel bands together. We make all of the small wars into one big war. That means that the Legion fleets are constantly in motion, moving from one crisis to the next. And they are very large fleets in this region, large even by the standards of a Universal Legion battle force. After the long years of their losses here, the Legion dare not split up their formations into anything smaller. If you encounter one of these war fleets, you wouldn't stand a chance. They might ignore you, or they might vaporize you—it can go either way. Either you must hide, or you need to join a fleet of your own, one that can keep track of the Legion's movements and is always able to stay a few steps ahead."

"A fleet of the Crusaders of Freedom," Captain Haran said.

"Exactly," Norik replied. "I will vouch for you as worthy to be initiated into our numbers when we arrive there."

"Your offer requires a degree of trust. We've seen how poorly the Universal Legion treats its auxiliary troops, with no concern for their ultimate fate. You are telling us that the Crusaders are very different and would never do such a thing. Our experience tells us it's so easy to become expendable."

"It is unimaginable for the Crusaders of Freedom to do that," Norik said.

"Give the coordinates to our navigator, Operator Heit," she said.

Norik produced a datapad from one of the pockets of his uniform and held it up. Cal stood and walked over to Norik to collect it.

"Major Rosco," said Captain Haran, "you've spoken more with this man than any of us. You've met his commander. You get the final say. Do you verify Lieutenant Norik here as ready to become part of our crew?"

All eyes were on Rosco. He saw Cal and Leda appraising him, as well Marraz and Yendos, still weary from their journey. He thought back to Norik's commander, deep below the hard earth of that windswept place. The locals had trusted them. "I do, Captain," he said.

"Welcome aboard, Lieutenant Norik," said Haran.

They were dismissed back to their duties. Lieutenant Norik left the bridge, and Rosco followed him out. On the other side of the door, Norik stopped and put a hand on Rosco's shoulder for a second. "Thank you for supporting me there."

Rosco shrugged. "I didn't do that much. I was just being honest."

"You've taken a chance on me," said Norik. "Your career and your reputation are on the line."

Rosco nodded slowly as he realized this was true.

"Not many people in your position would do that. I've seen a lot in my service with the Crusaders, but someone actively practicing honesty is hard to find. You're willing to see the best in people, Major. It's a rare quality in a military man, but you could go far with it." He shook Rosco's hand with an approving look. "Good luck."

*

Cal and Yendos stood on the bridge, surveying a detailed set of coordinates on the main screen. It was the route Norik had laid out for them, the next two jumps through star systems. Cal frowned as he studied the glowing line on the map that streaked away to unexplored regions. He sensed that somewhere beneath that black hood, Yendos was concerned too.

"Do you recall much of either of these star systems?" Cal asked.

Yendos shook his head. "I remember seeing them on a map, but they looked dull. Of course, that was before the Legion began their war operations in the area. Conflict can completely change these places in so little time. That's why I always preferred terrain to political maps."

"So, it's entirely possible we could be heading toward some kind of a trap, then?"

"From the Legion or the rebels? It hardly makes a difference, I suppose. We've chosen one to protect us from the other. And now, we're walking into the mouth of the beast once again. At least this place isn't as unpredictable as the systems around your homeworld," he added. "A warzone like this leaves little room for criminal gangs. The immense fleets of the Universal Legion and the constant presence of the rebels are the two most dangerous things we'll encounter. But Lieutenant Norik claims he can keep us far away from one and even keep us in the good graces of the other. He seems to travel these routes regularly."

"I suppose it's Norik that leads the way for us now," said Cal. He subtly watched Yendos for frustration. He was in the same position Cal had been in, secondary to the guidance of another.

Yendos's head twitched. He was annoyed, Cal could tell.

"Norik's flying around us outside, you know, right now," said Cal.

"Is he?" Yendos sounded intrigued.

"He went straight back to his little voidcraft and checked out of the flight deck into space. He's patrolling around and around, just circling us, really. I heard he pees in that cockpit."

"That's nothing. I urinate in my suit whenever I need," said Yendos. "And none of you can tell."

Cal decided to change the subject. "Your assessment of the jump routes?"

"Relatively direct," said Yendos.

"Agreed."

They were silent again, studying the map, calculating subtle parameters that could affect their jump vectors. The gravitational pull of objects in nearby star systems would cause the need for small corrections. Cal had begun to observe that transit points had a natural wobble to them that shifted in phases.

"I think Norik annoys me for some reason," Cal said. "I suppose he claims to mean well."

"It's something about that silly uniform," Yendos replied.

"It's the velvet material."

"Completely ridiculous," said Yendos.

*

Leda felt a degree of trepidation as they neared the jump to Norik's carrier ship. They were placing significant trust in him already. For the first time, *Fidelity* was approaching a larger fleet out of choice.

The call went out across the bridge: "Prepare for transit."

The main screen changed in an instant. New planets and stars appeared. A few seconds later, the starships and settlements in the region appeared too. It all matched Norik's description. A leviathan vessel was present in the system. A name appeared, encoded into the signals it broadcast, which translated to *Cyclops*.

In most situations, no starship could hope to be seen by the naked eye across the vast distances of space, but even from far away, *Cyclops* was visible as a gleaming speck. The monitor screens displayed ships as computerized images, but Leda somehow felt the scale of *Cyclops* on a physical level despite the abstract nature of her view. Like most starships, its color was a mix of gray and brown from metal and grime, with deep black shadows in the recesses hidden from the sun's light. Some panels had been painted with strings of blue and green symbols, indecipherable as ever to Leda.

Cyclops had approximately one hundred other starships scattered around it in close proximity. They varied in size from some of the largest battle cruisers *Fidelity* had seen to small frigates barely equal in size to their own ship. Leda could see a mix of every kind of military vessel imaginable, including fuel tankers and supply ships, but they all looked insignificant compared to the main vessel.

Cyclops made no effort to hide itself. Presumably, it either knew the locations of nearby Universal Legion fleets or it was confident that it could successfully disengage from them if a fleet appeared.

It was roughly equal in size to the largest civilian shipping vessels that they'd seen on the Highway of Thelmia. Those had been bulk liquid tankers, designed for storage and transport, whilst this was a heavily armed military ship built with thick armor plating on all sides and numerous shield generators along its surface, creating overlapping energy protection. The ship had a faint glow, a cloud of light like a mist, around its perimeter. Row after row of weapons banks and docking ports covered its surface, clusters of miniature objects, the guns arranged like spines down its flank and rotated to face forward. Equally significantly, Leda saw launch bays of huge diameters along its structure. Thick metal shutters closed over each one, angled to deflect the power of any incoming attack away from *Cyclops*'s structure. It's ability to launch attack craft would be equal with any fortress they had seen.

"It's good that we got here so soon," said Norik. "They're preparing to leave."

Leda heard *Fidelity*'s bridge crew communicating with *Cyclops*, exchanging a handful of codes, as advised by

Norik. They were authorized to begin their docking maneuver and were directed to one of the smaller docking gates on *Cyclops*'s exterior.

As their vessel neared *Cyclops*, Leda saw the other ships move into similar docking positions around the massive carrier vessel. Leda had never heard of a starship capable of carrying military cruisers inside itself. She saw a handful of vessels, battleship class from their size, indicate that they would latch onto *Cyclops*'s exterior and be towed. The entire rebel fleet could combine into a single object.

Inside the starship docking bay, with its thick protective shutter raised open, she could see complex mechanical docking structures. A series of enormous robotic arms and rotating clamps were ready to hold their entire ship in place within *Cyclops*.

"We won't be aligned with the center of the carrier ship," said Leda, calling across the bridge to Norik. "What's our artificial gravity situation going to be?"

Norik chuckled. "A lot of vessels just shut off their own gravity systems, but yours isn't exactly built for that. *Cyclops* does have facilities to allow a ship like yours to maintain its own internal gravity. Your docking bay is part of a rotating drum that spins to counter our larger vessel's own artificial gravity. You should feel no change at all."

Fidelity passed inside. The main screen became a mosaic of smaller camera images showing exterior views from a dozen different positions, but beyond a close perspective of the huge mechanical hardware, little could really be seen. There was a series of loud banging sounds as the clamps engaged to hold *Fidelity* tight, matching *Fidelity*'s current rate of spin. They finally stopped.

"Very good!" said Norik. "Bravo!"

Chapter 8

The crew exited through their vessel's hatchways in a narrow but steady stream. There was a checkpoint ahead, where they would officially be cleared for entry into *Cyclops*. Diplomatic communications had already been sent. Leda made sure she was near the front of the group. Rosco was supervising things at the front, whilst Cal was somewhere behind her, perhaps feeling anxious. She'd noticed how hesitant he was to leave the surroundings that he'd grown accustomed to. Leda had cajoled him slightly into leaving the ship. It wouldn't help his mental state to stay cooped up like a caged animal.

As she stepped across the threshold and left *Fidelity*, she caught her first glimpse of *Cyclops*'s interior areas. The metal bulkhead walls had been painted a dull turquoise that was somehow soothing. A few patches had been scraped away to produce a silver gleam. It somehow reassured her that a starship as advanced and powerful as this was subject to the same imperfect standard of maintenance as their own. Her studies had shown that starships were made of alloys that were able to resist metal fatigue through centuries of heavy wear, perhaps even indefinitely, but friction would scrape away at anything. The electric lamps were bright, flooding the space with white light to create maximum visibility, perhaps so *Cyclops* could better study whoever was coming to join them. There was a large yellow sign ahead that she couldn't read and a wide metal doorway.

"Security," said Ontu, who was walking next to her. He pointed to the sign. She nodded in gratitude to the large man. "It's a scanning machine. I've seen this type before."

The first group of *Fidelity*'s crew, around forty, entered into the scanning area of the room, and a series of colored flashes occurred. Leda saw bright stars floating in her vision, and she was amazed. She had no idea what had just happened, but they were surrounded by sophisticated technology. So many things around her held her attention at once. The wide door in front opened, and small floor lamps activated to show them the way. They continued ahead, arriving through a short tube into a large open space, where a delegation of three people in uniforms identical to Norik's were waiting. They were calm, seeming almost disinterested in their jobs.

Perhaps it was just a welcoming committee. *Fidelity* hadn't done anything to warrant special attention. They weren't significant, given that over a hundred more powerful ships were already present in the fleet.

Captain Haran was at the front of the group. She stopped and gave a salute back to the *Cyclops* crew. The other members of *Fidelity* followed suit. Leda noticed that the officers from *Cyclops* were holding a stack of pamphlets. Haran took a bundle of them and distributed them to the crew herself. "Produce a decent translation of these for our people," she said to Cartographer Yendos as she passed him a stack.

Yendos passed them on to Ontu, who dutifully carried them. Leda took a copy from Ontu and studied it closely. She'd been developing some ability to read common languages, and her personal datapad was able to perform basic translations on the go through a link back to the main *Fidelity* computer. "Introduction," she read, a large word at the top. She checked with a scan of her datapad. "Orientation," it confirmed. The pamphlet contained a map, she saw, a list of areas they were allowed to visit and the borders beyond which they were prohibited to cross.

Norik greeted the others in green uniforms with big smiles and handshakes, even a hug here and there. Presumably, they were all members of the Crusaders of Freedom. Leda tried to imagine the number of crew it would take to operate something like this vessel but concluded that she didn't have enough data to even guess. Perhaps *Fidelity* had stumbled upon something magnificent. Leda was skeptical of any military that presented itself as entirely virtuous, but she couldn't argue with the efficiency of what she saw.

They arrived at a common area, where they were told that they could move freely. Apparently, Norik and Haran had filled out the necessary paperwork, granting them access to this particular area of the ship and its basic facilities.

Cal, Rosco, and Leda studied a map displayed on a large wall. The interior of *Cyclops* generally had low ceilings and regular hatchways, as other military ships had, but occasionally, there was a junction where many stairwells and passageways converged. These junctions were large and open by design, forming locations where hundreds of crew could be gathered in the same place together. Looking around, the *Fidelity* crew could see that approximately only a quarter of those aboard *Cyclops* appeared to be Crusaders of Freedom. The rest were an eclectic mix of cultures, presumably recruited from all around the Liberated Zone.

Using their datapads, they read the many labels on the map. The directory of the various decks was extensive. There was a train station, indicating that multiple train lines ran through the inside of the ship. "We aren't allowed aboard any trains," said Rosco.

That was an effective way to contain them in a particular section, Leda considered. Captain Haran had strictly instructed them to follow all the rules of *Cyclops*. Every crew member was expected to report back to her every six hours, to ensure they stayed ready to follow her commands. Leda felt there was more to see in this place than she'd get chance to investigate.

"This ship is like a city," said Cal, "And this is just one minor section. It's amazing, really. The internal volume of the ship is so densely packed, like an insect hive. There are facilities arranged like a fractal around each of the docking bays on its surface."

"We could split up from here, try and investigate the sites that would be valuable to our mission," Rosco said. "We may be docked at this ship for the long term or just the short term—that's yet to be determined. Don't cause any disturbances, but this is going to be our best opportunity yet to improve our knowledge and gather intelligence."

It still hadn't entirely sunk into Leda what she was dealing with. "We're free," she said in awe.

"Free within the confines of what we see on this map," Rosco reminded her.

"More than enough," she replied.

"You know, according to what I see here, *Cyclops* is about to complete a transit jump," Cal said, reading from his datapad. A series of glowing symbols appeared on a star map on the display. "But the approach vector they're using really doesn't make sense. I don't understand what they're doing. Unless..." The symbols vanished again from the display as the transit jump occurred. As usual, they had felt no change. "My gods," Cal said. He showed his datapad to the other two. They had jumped through four star systems in a single transit. "I need to go and do some research."

*

Cal hesitantly stepped through a doorway and into a spacious area with seating arranged around tables and people talking idly. He smiled. The calm atmosphere was pleasing to him. It would have been difficult for these people to fake being so at ease. The sitting area seemed near to full capacity, and the noise of conversational chatter was high.

Tentatively, trying not to disturb anyone, Cal pulled aside a chair, sat, and stretched his legs. The common area here was larger than the entire recreational space of *Fidelity*. Above Cal was a terrace of balconies going up five stories, allowing people to look up into the core of the ship. On each level, Cal saw fluorescent lights. There were food vendors, he realized, as well as what looked like bars.

Whether they were juice bars or regular ones, he intended to find out, but not yet. Rosco was correct—there were more important duties to attend to.

Cal took out his datapad.

Some of the upgraded features of the *Fidelity* computer systems were still accessible remotely through his portable equipment, and he intended to put them to the test. He adjusted a few settings and rebooted the datapad several times. He shook it violently to clear any dust inside then blew into the small air vent at the back to cool the internal components. Then he turned it back on and pressed his ear against it, listening for some specific piece of the internal hardware to initialize. The noises were promising.

Cal made a request for information from *Cyclops*, searching for a diagram of the transit jump they'd just made. It appeared on the datapad. Cal blinked in surprise and began to smile. The pleasant chatter of the food hall around him faded as he became totally engrossed in his reading.

It was obvious that a new form of transit jump was possible. Perhaps these were linked to the hidden transit routes that Yendos claimed only he could find. In that moment, Cal understood what his error had been. He'd presumed that all FTL drives were of a similar type and operated by similar mechanisms because he'd been able to envisage only one solution to the problem. He'd been naïve. The transit routes available were as much a product of the starships entering them as the transit points themselves. It was obvious, but everything always was, in retrospect.

By his own estimation, Cal was Vale Reach's leading expert on transit points. *Cyclops* was comfortably operating on principles that he'd once struggled even to put into words. *Fidelity*'s FTL drive functioned well enough for the basic type of jump that he'd built his career by proving existed. But there was far more to the situation than that. *Cyclops*'s transit jumps were layering multiple forms of harmonic resonance. He could see now that they mapped across space when projected holographically.

He was scrawling patterns, he realized, doodling enormous arcs with his pen on the surface of his datapad. Crossing the entire galaxy in a vessel like *Cyclops* might be a viable possibility within the span of a single modestly extended human lifetime. He chewed his pen for a second. Plus, if he figured out the nature of the extended jumps, he might finally be on even terms with Yendos. He was confident that he would figure out that man's real motivations one day soon.

*

Leda couldn't visit the engine room—that wasn't allowed. She could, however, visit a capacitor, which would satisfy her for the time being. She examined it. Despite her expertise, she wouldn't have known it was a capacitor without having read a description. She stood in a narrow chamber that seemed rarely visited, looking at the device from across some railings. It wasn't cylindrical, appearing instead as a collection of odd egg shapes made of thick metal, emanating from a central stem. She'd expected it to be big—its role was to supply peak-demand energy to the entire docking bay of the region—but it wasn't even double her height. She couldn't tell if it was also connected to any of the nearby laser weapons mounted on the exterior hull. That would have been important to know. For such a significant item, it was disappointingly small and silent—the size of a large room, yes, but she had expected more. Leda understood that there was true power in its small size. A convenient reactor was an ideal thing. She could just about reach out and touch it, but she was hesitant to poke around at a potentially charged object.

She'd experienced painful migraines since she had used her implants to slow time to study the *Tenebrous* reactor. She'd pushed the implants as far as she dared, and she didn't plan on doing so again anytime soon. She would need to upgrade the implants before she attempted a larger task. Dealing with the aftereffects wouldn't be manageable otherwise. Her vision was still blurred, and her concentration had been drained in recent days. Leda would recover, but her ability to perform her duties was still impaired. Upgrades were the only way forward, to take the strain off her biological components. Her neurons were still doing too much heavy lifting.

Leda took out her pamphlet and studied the route to her next destination. She was engaged in a self-guided tour of all the key machinery in the area. She had a checklist of things to see. She'd already visited the recycling plant and air-filtration systems. Counteracting the sweat and grime continuously produced by humans was a major challenge for *Fidelity*'s own systems, so the problem would be proportionally larger on *Cyclops*.

Her next destination was one of the large motors that operated the revolving docking bays to which *Fidelity* was connected. The route involved a long series of stairwells and ladders. She frowned—there had to be a quicker way to reach her destination. She just needed to connect to a nearby adjacent region. Leda looked around in the room she was in. There was a hatch on the wall, clearly large enough for a human to enter. The screws that held the front grill in place were missing. She carefully prised it open and peered inside. She shone a small flashlight, illuminating the space. It seemed to go in the direction that she wanted.

She double-checked the list of rules printed on her pamphlet. There was nothing she could find that prohibited her from journeying deeper into the tunnel. After all, the entrance had been left partially open, so she should treat it as she would any other unlocked door. There was no need for her to crawl—simply to hunch was enough. She ventured in to discover where it went.

*

Rosco took cover behind a concrete barricade then crawled forward as fast as he could. The sounds of battle surrounded him—strange shrieking explosions and the bark and roar of unfamiliar guns. As he moved forward on his stomach, he caught sight of his teammates crouching behind a similar block of rubble up ahead. He held his own weapon in both hands, trying to judge whether he should peer above and take a shot at their enemies.

He had pieced together facts about what equipment they were carrying, trying hard to maintain a sense of situational awareness, to stay cognizant of how many opponents were in his sector. He knew there were two shrapnel cannons out there. They would be less effective at long range. From that distance, the chain guns were the greatest danger to him. But those were very heavy weapons. Maybe he could move too quickly to be caught by them.

He popped out and fired a few shots as quickly as he could. Everything flashed red, and he was paralyzed, seeing nothing but the bright color. He could feel the floor underneath him but nothing else.

He waited. After twenty more seconds, it was all over. His vision returned. He got unsteadily back to his feet and subconsciously rubbed his training vest. He wasn't sure how it disabled him when it detected he'd been hit, but it was an effective part of the exercise. His muscles ached. He'd been working in the arena all day until his energy was spent. The other trainees in the artificial urban space were walking toward the exit doors. Rosco emerged into a simple sitting area with metal chairs and tables scattered around and many scuffed crates of equipment, both opened and unopened. He flopped down into a chair and swung his arms, exhausted.

"Hey!" someone shouted at him. Rosco looked around, slightly dazed. At a table next to him was a group of five soldiers wearing heavy armor over their whole bodies. Their helmets were off and resting on the table, revealing their greasy hair and short beards. They were waiting for a response from him.

He nodded back. "Hey."

"So where the fuck are you from?" one of them asked.

"Uh… Sirkallia."

They looked uncomprehending and gestured for him to say more.

"It's far away from here. You won't have heard of it." He shook his head.

The large, armored men seemed amused. They gestured for Rosco to come and sit with them. After a moment's hesitation, he got up and joined their table. He couldn't understand any of what they said to each other.

"And you?" he asked.

"We're the last generation of the battalion of Karatarn," he said.

"From the remnants of Malguud sector," one of the men added. They all gave a somber nod in unison.

"You've been here all day," another man said to Rosco. "That's a lot of stamina for someone with a traditional physique like yourself. It's very old-school, like you're from a barbarian tribe or something. Is that what Sirkallia is?"

Rosco laughed. "No, I don't think so."

"Does our Basic Form communication sound good to you?" one of the other large men asked.

"What exactly is that?" He'd heard it mentioned before, but he'd never gotten a clear explanation.

More rumblings of amusement came from the men around the table. "How are you not familiar with this?" the first man asked him.

"Well, as I said, I'm not from these parts. I guess there's a lot I don't know."

"Basic Form is a kind of common language. It was designed to be understandable for everyone," the second man explained.

"And that works?" asked Rosco.

"You tell me," the man said.

Rosco was amazed. "But you understand me?"

"Yes, little man, but just barely." The bearded soldier smiled again and patted Rosco on the arm. "Tell him a story!" the man shouted to one of his comrades, pointing a finger at Rosco.

"Which one?" the other man asked.

"Tell him the one about the man with two heads."

"What?" Rosco shook his head. "No, I refuse to believe that. There's no way that's true!"

"The man with two heads was fine," the other man said, letting out a sigh. "It's the man with two cocks that was a problem."

Chapter 9

Cal sat at a computer desk in a facility he'd found in the directory of *Cyclops*'s services. Sweating slightly, he tried to settle his nerves about what he was planning to do.

Cal decided to verify things one final time before he got started. "Excuse me, excuse me." He waved his hand for a moment. Someone from the *Cyclops* crew came over to where he sat, at a booth in a long line of computer terminals.

"Yes?" the crewman said, sounding disinterested.

"So"—Cal paused, a little awkward—"if I make an FTL communications call, there's absolutely no way that it can be traced back to our current location? Or compromise the ship here at all?"

"No," the crewman said. "Definitely not. All the signals are dampened and sent through numerous relays. Ensuring that the calls out of *Cyclops* are untraceable is literally the purpose of this facility."

"Okay, okay. That's good," said Cal. "And what if I accidentally let something slip out while I'm talking? I won't—I'm actually very careful with what I say, but there must be some kind of safeguard in place?"

"If you say anything that jeopardizes the safety of the ship, our auto-censorship system will instantly disconnect the call. Given the slight transmission delay, *Cyclops* can prevent the transmission from ever leaving."

"Good, good. Good work!" *So, this will be foolproof,* he mentally noted to himself.

He focused on the computer terminal in front of him. After a few hours of investigation, he believed he'd figured out how to make the machine to do what he wanted. Back at the repair station, he made careful note of the exact location that he was looking to connect to. Cal would put everything into a report for Haran once he was done.

He used the camera on his datapad to check his appearance. His hair had grown long without him realizing, and strands hung chaotically around his face. His *Fidelity* uniform had become a little dirty around his neck, but that wasn't too noticeable, he thought. He realized that he was procrastinating. He hit the call button.

"Eevey!" he said as she appeared on screen. She was wearing familiar pajamas, and for a moment, he could remember exactly how the material felt, like a memory experienced by his fingertips.

"Cal!" She smiled, clearly excited to see him. "You've managed to call! I'm amazed you found a connection."

"Yeah," he said. "I found a way." He couldn't tell her any details. For a moment, the silence felt difficult.

"Are you okay?" she asked. "I know things weren't good last time we spoke. Are you still hurt?"

"Same old injuries," he said with a shrug. "They're much better now." He still wore bandages under his uniform. "I did get blown out into space… and chased by a whole bunch of Makron, actually," he said with a chuckle.

"Oh my god!" Eevey's eyes widened, and he regretted telling her.

He laughed nervously. "It's fine, though. Really, don't worry about it."

She laughed slightly, too, breaking the tension. "Oh, good. As long as everything's fine," she said sarcastically.

"Yeah, I mean… Okay, you're right. That was a stupid thing to say. I guess I've had some close calls, overall. I can't really deny it."

"Gods, Cal," said Eevey, shaking her head. She wasn't smiling as much anymore. "I'm glad you're alive. I'm not kidding myself about how bad it is. I'm praying for you."

"Well, rest assured I'm still doing everything I can to come back in one piece."

"I'm waiting for that," she said. She didn't look any different to him despite the two years that had passed for her since he'd left. She might have to wait years more for him to return, assuming that he didn't get imprisoned or trapped somewhere.

Eevey smiled again, watching him. She didn't need to say anything—she just seemed happy he was there.

He knew he wasn't much to look at, but perhaps he was looking better than she'd expected, given everything that'd happened on the journey. Eevey looked in good health, maybe even better than she had when he'd left. Cal remembered the feeling of her cheek against his and the warmth of the bright daylight shining on her in their apartment.

"How's life on Vale Reach?" he asked. Once, he would have been afraid to ask that question, but a certain weariness about the apocalypse had set in. He just wanted to hear about her day. The mundane details of Eevey's world would feel comforting.

"We're managing to keep on going," she said. "The Legion has issued more threats that we can't understand. More of their ships have arrived in the system, but I don't know much about those. I think they've begun some construction work throughout our solar system around Vale Reach. Since the Tylder Ambassador set up her research facility here, they've even sent a few delegations down to our surface, though they only seem to want to talk to her."

"The Ambassador's opened up a facility in Arkstone City?"

"Yeah, that's where I'm working now," said Eevey. "I'm managing one of the analytical departments."

"The Ambassador's not there with you now, is she?" Cal asked. "Like the last time I called?"

"No." Eevey shook her head. "That was just one time, when she had a message that she needed to share with you. I offered for her to use our flat for the call, since it really was so urgent." Eevey paused. "Have you had any change of heart about what she said?"

"That's all above my pay grade, Eevey," said Cal with a shrug. "Our captain has her orders, same as I do."

Eevey nodded. She understood. Obviously, she knew things that she wasn't telling him, but he didn't want to push her in the search for more information. Maybe he was afraid he would lose her if they argued, that addressing the gulf that was forming between them would cause them to tumble into it. He feared their paths were diverging, just as their separate timelines had literally diverged. Or perhaps he was afraid to face a darker truth, that Eevey had aligned herself with their enemies. It was unimaginable.

"If the Ambassador has created a research facility on Vale Reach, can't she force the Legion to stand down? Surely, they can't attack our planet if she's there on it," he said.

"She can't just order the Legion around like that," Eevey said. "It's too much to ask of her."

Cal laughed in disbelief. "Eevey, what do you mean by that?" There was no way Eevey could have betrayed their world.

"It's too much for the Ambassador to ask that of the Legion. She's a diplomat, but in practice, I think her authority has its limits. In theory, she could tell them to treat our planet as an exemption to their protocols, but then why doesn't she do that for every single planet? She would lose her credibility, lose her influence. The best option for us is for her to maintain her diplomatic channels with the Legion," Eevey said.

"You admire her, don't you?" Cal said.

"She's reasonable, as far as I can tell," Eevey said. "More so than the Universal Legion or any other offworlders that Vale Reach has ever met. I can respect her even if I don't agree with everything she says."

"Pretty sure she threatened to kill me." Cal raised his voice slightly in disbelief.

Eevey looked horrified. "Cal, you know I don't want that. She was giving you an honest warning. There are forces at work that you just don't know about. I really can't tell you. Your captain is doing what she thinks is best for Vale Reach, I understand that. If the Ambassador's allies try to stop your ship before it reaches the Ruarken Senate, that's not something I have any kind of influence over. She doesn't want things to get to that point. In fact that's exactly what she wants to avoid. I hope you… I hope you turn back." She stopped, clearly shocked by what she'd said. "Or… I hope you do get past her, get to Ruarken, and then you make it back home. Either of those work for me."

"Even if she's your boss?" said Cal with a smile.

"Even then," said Eevey. "I've been working with her to discover the truth about Vale Reach's history. That's what I want. I still work to protect this planet the same as you, Cal. That's what matters."

"Turn back now or succeed at everything?" he asked. "That's not bad advice."

"Both outcomes are good," she said, "just as long as you come back. That's what I care about."

He felt all the weight that he carried easing away. His hands stopped shaking for the first time in months. He hadn't even realized he had such bad tremors until they stopped. He felt in his muscles as if he were returning to a time before he'd ever heard of the mission or stepped aboard a single starship.

"I want you back, Cal," she said. "And I want this planet not to disintegrate."

"Tell me more about… anything," he said. "Your choice. Anything. I want to hear it." He sat back in the creaking metal chair in the unfamiliar confines of the booth aboard *Cyclops*, flickers of something close to serenity appearing inside him. He was a lucky man to have her. His heart rate slowed, and a soothing sense of calm came over him. Something deep in him remembered his old life. He shut his eyes, and the sense of immersion was complete. Eevey's voice was the only thing in his mind. He truly believed in that moment that he would get back to her. He would never stop trying.

*

Rosco boarded *Fidelity* alone to attend a restricted meeting. The ship was near empty as he walked through its corridors. After the months spent seeing it packed with people, the change in atmosphere was striking. It was as though even the ship itself was resting at last, its internal hive of activity dulled to the lowest murmur. A small crew remained, mostly to ensure that the reactor remained operational. The bridge contained only three officers, who barely looked up from their consoles. As he walked through, he saw Advocate Fargas heading in the same direction.

"Conference room?" Rosco asked.

Fargas nodded. They proceeded into the room where Captain Haran waited, and both sat at the table.

She adjusted some documents. "The next phase of our mission is beginning, Major." Captain Haran looked up briefly as she spoke. "We must be clear about the procedure for what comes next."

"Yes, sir," Rosco agreed. He wasn't exactly sure which procedure she meant.

"At the present time, the Crusaders and *Fidelity* are fellow travelers. We are being taken to a rendezvous point deep in the liberated zone, which is acceptable, as it brings us significantly nearer to the Ruarken system. At some point, it's inevitable that our journey with *Cyclops* will no longer take us toward our destination. At that point, we will have to disengage from the larger ship and continue our journey alone."

"And that would be legally allowed?" Rosco asked.

"It all checks out," Fargas said.

"You are next in rank to take over the ship in case anything happens to me, Rosco. This vessel is yours if for any reason I'm no longer captain."

"Understood, Captain." The weight of that responsibility made him nervous for a moment. "I understand the requirements of my job here. If it ever reaches that point."

"As established, our prime objective is to reach the Ruarken High Senate and negotiate for the protection of Vale Reach. The issue is further complicated by the existence of the Seed of Steel. Only in a scenario where we have absolutely no other choice to prevent the destruction of our world are you to trade any knowledge or rights to the Seed with the Ruarken Senate." Something about her intense stare emphasized the desperate nature of what she was suggesting. "If it's ever a choice between saving Vale Reach or losing control of the Seed, then you must preserve our homeworld."

"Absolutely. Yes, sir," Rosco confirmed.

Fargas stared ahead, seeming already familiar with what was being said.

"In the event that *Fidelity* is destroyed, we have protocols to follow," she said. "Get all of the crew to safety. The lives of the people on this ship are your responsibility. Secondly, and this is vital, destroy all information relating to the Seed of Steel that could be salvaged from this vessel."

"What was that?" Advocate Fargas exclaimed.

"Here's a dossier I've prepared for you, detailing all the necessary steps to do this." Captain Haran passed a thick folder of papers toward Rosco. "You must ensure absolutely no details remain that could further attract any offworld powers to go in search of Vale Reach."

"That's a mistake, Captain," said Fargas, looking alarmed. "It's not justifiable."

"It's easily justified," Haran said. "If that information falls into the wrong hands, we have no idea what danger it would cause to Vale Reach. Worse, if a hostile power were to actually gain control of the Seed of Steel, Vale Reach could be annihilated. If any knowledge of its location spreads in this part of the galaxy, we can't anticipate what kind of people might go in search for it. The release of that data could prove catastrophic to our world. To be frank—" She paused. "It may have proven catastrophic to Vale Reach already, given the Legion and the Ambassador's arrival, but we're fighting against it now as much as we can. All data describing the Seed of Steel must go down with the ship."

"We are getting closer to the Ruarken High Senate." Fargas seemed genuinely concerned. "Consider that before long, we will be in FTL communication range of Ruarken. Our new computer systems have totally changed the calculus of what's possible here. We'll be able to transmit the data directly to them from a long distance."

"Not an option," Haran said firmly. "That would reveal to them our situation before we filed our case with the Senate. Theeran specifically outlined this. Our delegates need to be at the Ruarken High Senate in person to file the petition."

"You could send the data to them under the agreement that they would allow you to enter the petition later." Fargas smiled.

Haran's expression grew displeased, and she shook her head. "We'd be foolish to indulge that. I don't believe in trusting the good faith of any great power. An agreement to file a petition is not the same thing as filing the petition. We need some concrete guarantee before we give away our most important bargaining chip. If we transmit the data, we have nothing left that we can use. We don't know these Ruarken people. Neither did Councilor Theeran. We have no idea what the Ruarken High Senate will ultimately conclude is an appropriate resolution for Vale Reach. If Ruarken receives the information about the Seed without any safety guarantees established, our homeworld could potentially be in a worse position than before."

"Captain," Fargas said disapprovingly, "the Ruarken Senate will be ready to reward Vale Reach for an act of loyalty. To miss the opportunity to present them with our data and to reap the benefits that would bring would be criminal negligence."

"Get the hell off my bridge," she said. "I will not allow you to corrupt the purpose of this mission."

Fargas's eyes widened, and his jaw muscle tensed, whether in shock or rage. He was inscrutable, to a degree. Without a word, he got up and left.

Haran turned to him. "Major Rosco, do not let that man take control of the ship. He does not represent us."

*

Leda couldn't be in enough places simultaneously to measure everything that needed measuring. She had a solution that was potentially viable though by setting up devices that could compile their findings without her there. Once again, she'd checked the terms of their residency onboard *Cyclops* and found nothing that prohibited her from doing such a thing. Now she was ready to begin collecting the data that they'd recorded.

She pushed at the piece of metal hatchway in front of her, and it detached from its position with a creaking noise. She squeezed out through the narrow gap and arrived in a room on her way to the next location. She realized she had become covered in a layer of filthy grease and was glad she'd chosen to wear googles.

"Are you all right?" someone asked. It was a familiar figure.

"Ontu," she said in surprise.

"Leda!" He seemed equally shocked to realize it was her.

There was a moment of awkward silence.

"Don't let me get in your way. Please, carry on with whatever you were doing here." Ontu backed away from the hatchway and gestured for her to enter.

"I'm just here to…" Leda had hidden her recording device in a nearby air vent, but she wasn't sure she wanted to disclose that. There were tall glass cylinders full of red and white light. "What is this place?" she asked.

"It's a horticulture lab," said Ontu. "They've been collecting plant samples from all the regions they've visited."

"Plants?" said Leda, looking into a tube. She saw green shoots poking out from dark soil.

"Exceedingly rare," said Ontu.

"Well, I guess that is impressive…" Leda said, almost begrudgingly.

"There's a real art to maintaining living bio samples like this," said Ontu. His head wobbled slightly as he talked. "Different temperatures, humidity levels, wind levels, solar cycles… nature can be infinitely capricious. Truly, it's only personal familiarity with the plants that can allow you to preserve them. It's a tremendously pure form of knowledge."

"And why do the Crusaders do it?" Leda looked up from the glass case.

Ontu seemed taken aback. "Likely, this is the design of some director of research. How familiar are you with this kind of work?"

"Not very," she replied.

"Have you heard the theory of common descent?"

"That all the galaxy's species are on some level related to each other?"

"More than that," said Ontu. "They have all emerged from a single planet, likely even from a single mineral-rich ocean. A single colony of floating cells that gave birth to us all on a Homeworld Prime. Thrilling to imagine, isn't it?"

"How did they all get off the original homeworld?" Leda asked.

"A fascinating question. They were likely brought from the old world in samples by the earliest spacefaring humans. Somehow these samples ended up on all of the many different planets, where they were left to grow and adapt to the pressures of their conditions."

"And that explains everything?"

"Yes," said Ontu. "That covers everything. Except the Xenos."

Leda remembered seeing the Lizard King with her own eyes. It was not a comforting memory at all.

"From what I can tell," Ontu continued, "the Crusaders have been tracking the genetic drift of species across the whole region. It's something I'm fairly familiar with myself."

"Is that what you do?" Ontu's work had always been deeply mysterious to much of the crew. "Is that why you were taking samples of people from Vale reach?"

"N-No, I didn't," he replied.

"I caught you doing it once, Ontu. In the engineer's workshop on *Fidelity*. You were measuring me. You admitted it."

"I'm not..." He paused. "I'm not supposed to confirm those kinds of things. But I suppose it's too late to hide it now."

"Somewhat," Leda said. "So, what have you learned about us? Are the people of Vale Reach actually from Vale Reach?"

"Yes, you are. As much as anyone is actually from anywhere. Originally you weren't, but your genetic traits have been there for as long as any records go back."

"What are you looking for in our genes, then?"

"I really can't tell you." He shuffled his feet in obvious distress.

Leda stared at him. "I already know there's something about our genetic code that matters to you, Ontu. That's enough information for me to eventually figure out what you're doing. You might as well tell me, or I'll just piece it all together by myself. Do you really want me to find out that way? On my own? I might jump to a very negative conclusion. Wouldn't it be better for you to show me the information yourself, so you can guide me to what it really means?"

Ontu seemed deeply uncertain. For a brief moment, Leda became concerned that she'd upset him too much. Finally, he sighed and seemed to relent slightly. "It's not as if I know anything important."

"I'm sure you know plenty. I mean, you've been studying my homeworld."

"We didn't originally mean to study Vale Reach. We didn't realize what was on your world until quite far into the process."

"What was, Ontu? We need to know. We're sure to find out soon, anyway."

"It's the Seed of Steel," he said. "I know you've heard the name. It's buried on Vale Reach, and it's almost impossible to find. We've tried everything we could think of. We were even looking for evidence that could help us on other planets. That's what our ship was doing when you first found us. Well, we were stuck when you first found us. We'd crashed. Our current hypothesis is that exposure to the Seed over long periods of time must have left trace amounts of exotic particles in your bodies. It would be subtle, nothing harmful. Those who live closer to the site of the Seed's burial place will have higher rates of the particles. So, you see, if we measure you all and determine where you spent your lives on Vale Reach, we should be able to properly triangulate the Seed's location."

Ontu had begun to talk faster as he spoke, growing in excitement till he seemed almost joyful to share this news with Leda. He couldn't disguise his happiness at the prospect.

"So how exactly are you measuring us?" Leda continued on with her questioning.

Ontu's happiness diminished. "Well, we're not entirely sure what we're looking for. That's the difficult part. So, we're taking a holistic approach, you know? Maybe what we're looking for is lots of small things working together?"

They had no idea what they were doing, Leda realized. "You're trying to get your hands on the Seed of Steel, just like the Ambassador?"

"Everyone is, Leda. Everyone is. Before…"

"Before?" said Leda. "Finish your sentence."

"Before the Makron take your world."

"What!" Leda exclaimed. She was in shock. "What do you mean by that?"

Ontu looked surprised. "Were you not aware? Have I said the wrong thing?" He seemed to panic slightly.

"Is that true? The Makron will take over Vale Reach?" It was urgent that she take this opportunity to get all the information out of him that she could.

"I'm not qualified to say!" Ontu protested.

"But you do know something about what's going to happen."

"It's far from guaranteed. The expansions of the Makron empire in that peripheral region are essentially subject to chaos theory." Ontu shrugged as if trying to emphasize that he was not to blame. "But the odds of your planet becoming isolated and under threat are high. In theory, the Makron have no reason to go there, but they are unpredictable."

"Isolated?"

"A Makron blockade would make your world impossible to reach," Ontu said.

"That's what's bringing the offworlders from all around to search for the Seed on Vale Reach…" Leda suddenly understood. "Offworlders like you."

"Your world is like a precious treasure about to slip out of reach," said Ontu.

"Is my homeworld doomed, Ontu?" She had to know for sure.

"You've managed to last this long," he replied. "No one comes to Vale Reach, not even the Makron. Let's hope it stays that way. You've got a chance."

*

Rosco followed the sound of gunshots. The people around him on *Cyclops* seemed unconcerned by the noise, suggesting that it was nothing unusual. It stood to reason that there was an armory aboard. A military ship of such size would absolutely need a force of marines. Rosco had learned during his briefings back on Vale Reach how boarding actions could be a regular occurrence during certain types of starship combat. They'd all been caught in a boarding action not so long ago, during the fight for *Fidelity* between the Lizard King's pirates and the Enforcers.

His body was still healing wounds from that, not least the significant stab wound in his leg. That knife had been shiny silver, like a mirror. The engineers of *Fidelity* had been unable to determine how it'd been made or what gave it such alarming cutting abilities.

It was still in an engineer's workshop on *Fidelity*. Rosco didn't see himself planning on using it, partly because it lacked a sheath and partly through his personal preference, but those blades were perhaps the only weapons they had with any significant armor-piercing capability. Perhaps he could find something more suitable for the defense of their own ship, whether just for his own use or for all the security staff aboard *Fidelity*.

Rosco arrived at a door that had many bright warning signs outside. The small illustrations, cartoons demonstrating various different ways to mishandle a gun, were obvious in their meaning. One depicted a person walking in front of a shooting range, a bright-red line through it. It all seemed straightforward. He stepped inside and entered a small booth-like space. Just as when they'd had disembarked from *Fidelity*, a series of colored flashes seemed to scan him rapidly. Then the door in front opened, and he was allowed into the next room. Weapons racks filled the walls, holding all kinds of rifles and pistols and other guns. Half a dozen other people were already in the room, examining the weapons, some intently and some aimlessly. A heavy, closed gate at the far end seemed to lead to the actual shooting range. It all felt familiar to Rosco, somehow. He knew the place on a professional level.

The people in the room were a mix of the green-uniformed Crusaders and the more eclectic crew, who seemed to wear a battered mix of flight suits of very many different kinds, likely representing the huge range of ships docked aboard *Cyclops*. Perhaps the uniforms worn by the crew of *Fidelity* were not so very different, and they actually blended in amongst the inhabitants of *Cyclops*. It seemed these ships and crews had been collected from far around. He began to see how *Cyclops* had built its own patchwork fleet as it traveled.

Rosco walked up to a wall-mounted rack of rifles. These weapons also seemed to represent a range of cultures, with some as bare shiny steel and others covered in elegant carved wood. He walked up and down the whole length of the wall, trying to determine whatever he could about them. Magazine loaded. Ammo-drum loaded. Single shot. Breech loaded. A handful were muzzle loaded. Some had ejection ports for spent cartridges, but others didn't.

The ammunition types puzzled him more. A few of the magazines had transparent sections, where he could see bullets directly, but most were opaque, leaving him with no clue about what was inside.

He passed a set of items that he recognized as plasma grenades. A plasma grenade had killed his comrades Major Lee and Major Oryx not so far out from Vale Reach. The bodies had been reduced to ashes just feet away from him. The memory hardened his resolve. Rosco pressed on with his investigations.

He came to a collection of weapons that had hosepipes attached instead of ammunition, connected to a small tank of chemicals. He decided not to touch them, although there was a worrying amount of such chemical weapons, especially given the implication that they were for use in the corridors of a starship. He selected a weapon he was reasonably confident he knew how to operate then used his datapad to scan its labels. Low-voltage auto railgun.

Self-explanatory. He gently took it down from the shelf and looked around. No one had shouted at him for taking it.

It was only a little longer than the typical battle rifle he used, though with more of a thick cylindrical design than what he was used to. He carried it to the door of the firing range, selecting a pair of large ear protectors and a face shield from a plastic basket nearby. There was at least some risk that he would blow out his eardrums if he was totally wrong about what he was doing, but he'd done that a few times in his life already and regarded it as an occupational hazard. He pushed a button, and the door to the shooting range opened. The sound of gunfire was punishingly loud even through his hearing protection. He took a second pair of ear protectors and managed to fit them over the first, which improved the situation to some degree.

People in a mix of uniforms were firing their weapons in a line, all facing the same direction. The mix of noises was strange, some loud and familiar, others long and shrieking. The way the noises combined further added to the deeply disconcerting effect. At the far side of the room were targets and presumably an exceptionally solid piece of wall. Rosco took his place in the line of shooters. After spending several minutes studying what he believed to be the safety setting and shot selection, he put the thick gun to his shoulder and aimed down the top.

He pulled the trigger. Nothing happened. He again flipped the switch that he thought was for safety. An audible electric hum emerged from the weapon. Rosco aimed and fired a second time. There was a crack and a white flash like lighting that left a glowing afterimage in his eyes even through the protective goggles he wore. The recoil, while still plenty, was less than he'd expected. The internal magnetic systems of the rifle were doing something to absorb the force. At the far end of the target range, he saw a glowing dot on the wall, white and orange. Maybe those were where the metal slug ammunition was liquefied by the pressure of impact. He would have to ask Cal or Leda. He fired several more shots then went back to try another weapon, carefully returning the rail rifle to its original place. He felt a tingle of anticipation as he picked up the next gun. He realized that he was having fun.

Hours seemed to pass very quickly. A message appeared on Rosco's datapad, buzzing with urgency. He removed the magazine from his current weapon, made sure it was empty, then set the weapon down on a nearby bench and looked at the message. It was on a channel they kept for receiving official orders, yet he'd never seen anything quite like it before. It was from *Cyclops*. He engaged an auto translation on the datapad.

"All new arrivals," it began. That would include everyone from *Fidelity*. "Attend the mandatory orientation event this evening cycle at your local auditorium. Your participation will be recorded. Failure to give the presentation its due attention will offend your hosts, the Crusaders of Freedom."

The datapad buzzed again immediately with a message from Captain Haran to the whole *Fidelity* crew. "All crew, report back to the muster points on our vessel for an immediate in-person briefing from the captain." There was an urgent tone to the message. He put his weapons back on their equipment rack and headed directly to his own ship.

*

The crew stood aboard *Fidelity* at their respective stations under the supervision of their commanding officers and waiting to hear Captain Haran speak. Her message would be transmitted through each deck. It had the effect of reminding everyone of their roles aboard the ship and their original purpose. Captain Haran stood at the ship's center, radiating a sense of authority. She seemed like an extension of the ship in that moment, Rosco thought, and *Fidelity* was the embodiment of her will, as though they were one and the same.

"Crew of *Fidelity*," Haran said, audible through the earpieces they wore, "we've all left families behind. We pledged to defend them, even at the cost of our own lives. What stronger bond can there be than that between family, planet, and culture? Today, I know you will be asked by agents of the captain of another ship to make another pledge. If you refuse this pledge, it is likely that you will be confined aboard *Fidelity* for the immediate future, unable to move through *Cyclops*. I will not ask you to lie for me. Whether you pledge or not is a matter for your own conscience.

"What I seek to instill in you now is a single word to guide your judgment. That word is 'primacy.' This vessel and this mission must have primacy above all else. When this vessel reaches the entry point to the Ruarken system, we will claim political asylum within its territory. Our petition will be accepted. It is Vale Reach that loves us, that has given us their absolute trust. It is to Vale Reach we must be loyal with all our energy.

"If our delegation does not make its case at the Ruarken High Senate at the earliest possible opportunity, our planet will be colonized by the Universal Legion. The people who crew *Cyclops* share some of our goals, and for that, we are blessed. I have been in communication with the leadership of their vessel. We are currently traveling through the center of the Liberated Zone. We are drawing nearer to our final destination with each passing hour. Keep your faith in our mission, crew. This is a critical moment for our homeworld and for our loved ones. Report back to your positions here at the same time tomorrow."

*

Rosco, Cal, Leda, and the rest of the crew of *Fidelity* walked into a huge auditorium. The space was dark, almost pitch black. They could see several other groups entering—unknown starship crews arriving through a series of doorways. Officers from *Cyclops* seemed to act as ushers, directing them quickly and arranging them all around a gigantic central platform. Still, there were no lights—the platform was obscured from view.

The room was already deeply quiet, as though filled with a soundproof lining, but the low-level ambient noise dropped to zero through some artificial means. Time passed slowly in absolute darkness and silence—around five minutes, from Leda's guess, though it felt far longer.

Blue lights exploded across the stage with thick white sparks flaring away from crackling balls of plasma. It was beautiful, the way the liquid energy fell away in chunks or burst into a spray as a jolt of lighting extended like some reaching tentacle. Eight spheres of blue light multiplied into more, then hovered, multiplying again above the surface of the stage and arranging themselves into a circle. The circle rotated, spinning rapidly, emitting a painfully loud electric crackling sound. Links of energy reached from one sphere to the next, wavering and shimmering, dividing until a flat surface was formed. Suddenly, the thin film of plasma burst outward, gaining a complex three-dimensional shape. A face formed—an entire head, in fact—many meters tall, male, and with long hair and a beard. Huge sparks tumbled down as it talked.

"My name is Paous Ultrarch. Welcome aboard my vessel. Welcome to *Cyclops*! Welcome to our work together. I am a deacon of the Crusaders of Freedom. For centuries, I have traveled aboard my ship, recruiting willing souls for the battle of good against evil."

The giant head of blue plasma shattered in a wave of flashing particles, revealing a man floating at its core, flesh and bone and not blue but wearing robes of red and black. "Before that, I lost someone I loved to the Universal Legion. Perhaps you have too?" His voice was normal, human. Then the blue electric head reformed, hiding him from view.

"They told me there was nothing I could do. Does that sound familiar? What can one man and one world do against a fleet of the Universal Legion? It gives me no joy to tell you that everyone who spread that message to me has since faced justice in the years that have followed, felled by the consequences of their own actions. No single planet has the power to defeat the entire Universal Legion, not even the Technocracies themselves. But our starship has consolidated enough power to defeat a full Legion battle group in direct combat. Isn't that exactly what you want to see? Our vessel liberates worlds one by one, fearing no one. As long as the Legion remains spread across the expanse of the Liberated Zone, we may puncture their defenses as we choose.

"Can you imagine how many worlds I've seen where a military terrorizes the population? Since the dawn of history, weapons have separated mankind into those with power and those without. A warrior caste is born. They concentrate their weapons and build fortresses, be they physical or mental. They deem themselves invulnerable. Like parasites, they suck the power and capital out of us all, contributing nothing. Ultimately, the Legion answers only to itself and serves itself. It operates as it chooses and for its own benefit. Violence is inevitable, many would say." The vast blue face became sad, its brow frowning in regret. "They aren't wrong. And yet, it is also contagious. It is a toxicity, being pumped into our environment, polluting our societies. I've seen the terror of the military. But we've also seen the alternative. We've seen worlds with peaceful hierarchies. Planets where each citizen knows their role and works hard. Societies where the military is strictly a tool of the civic body—that is, each one of us.

"We are the civic body that must stand above them. They must answer to us. That is what our movement is all about. Otherwise, we will be answering to them. And, friends, I do not like where that road leads. It is only when a civilian takes up arms to fight that true justice can be achieved. Those who are called to fight in spite of their own good nature. Some call what we do vengeance. Let it be vengeance if you wish. Many of you have had family, comrades, whole cities, and worlds destroyed by them. But it can be more."

Rousing music began to play. "A noble society. A genteel society. Civilized and sophisticated. It could be everything that's been stolen from you. It may sound like a utopia, friends, but we've seen it before. We know that we have. Within the borders of our Liberated Zone, citizens triumph over the Legion. Their continued existence will be down to our mercy. Armies exist to serve the common people. The Legion just have yet to realize that."

The blue face disintegrated slowly in somber fashion, revealing the man within. Eventually, the blue light vanished entirely, and Paous Ultrarch was lit by a single white spotlight from above.

"Alone, we are atoms drifting in the endless void. Banded together, we become infinitely stronger. That is what *Cyclops* represents. That is what the Crusaders provide to you. Raise your hand and swear your commitment to your brothers and sisters on this ship."

Rosco, Cal, and Leda each raised a hand, as did everyone else in the auditorium.

Then the deacon spoke in a language they didn't recognize. It was hypnotic and undulating, seeming to come from deep within his throat. The rhythms seemed like something that couldn't have been produced by one man alone. The white light faded, and Paous Ultrarch was gone. The room was illuminated as normal, its painted metal walls visible for the first time. The abrupt return to reality was a huge shock. Several other groups in the auditorium seemed in a state of such high emotion that they were close to tears. In a daze, they walked out of the entrance.

*

Cal saw Leda as they emerged and came over to join her. He needed to speak to someone, to try and express what they'd just experienced.

"That was crazy," he said.

Leda nodded. "It was. I guess he did make a few valid points in there…"

"I mean, literally, that guy was crazy. Ultrarch whatever-his-name. I'm telling you not to trust anyone who puts that much effort into a presentation. They're always up to something."

"No one forced you to make that pledge," said Leda. "Though I suppose it was required of us to maintain our access to *Cyclops*."

"I only did it because everyone around me did, and I didn't want to seem different," said Cal. "I didn't mean it, so it's not really a proper pledge for me, you see? I just said it because I needed to. Do you think that pledge is going to be binding for us later?"

"I mean, that is the point of a pledge."

"Well, once we cross into Ruarken, we can put all this behind us," he replied. "I doubt somewhere as prestigious as the Ruarken High Senate will care about agreements made with completely lawless rebels, as these Crusaders claim to be."

"But do we still believe that the Ruarken Senate will seriously listen to us?" Leda said with a hint of bitterness.

"We're official envoys from the sovereign nation of Vale Reach. That should matter. Besides, my oath to the Vale Reach military predates my oath here, and I can't be expected to fulfill both of them at once."

"Right…" said Leda. She wasn't sure if she was annoyed or impressed by Cal's attitude. It didn't seem difficult for him. "So, when you give your word to someone, it doesn't actually mean anything?"

DEFIANT SYSTEMS

"It means the same as anyone else's word, I can assure you of that. I'm honest that my first loyalty is to myself... and Vale Reach," he added quickly. *Because of Eevey*, he thought to himself.

Leda seemed to know exactly what he was thinking. "You're lucky to have that woman back home, Cal. She makes you into a better person."

"That, she does."

*

Lieutenant Norik appeared from the crowd and joined Rosco. "Wonderful, isn't it?"

Rosco nodded, unsure how to respond. "That was incredible." He was still slightly stunned from the experience. "Not what I expected."

"I always get a thrill every time I see Commander Ultrarch perform, even though I've seen it many times now. It reminds me of the early days."

"How often does he do it?" It felt inappropriate to describe a military ceremony as a performance, but based on what he'd seen, it did seem accurate.

"Every time he collects new ships for his fleet," Norik said. "You're lucky to have seen it from this deck. The visuals are especially dramatic here."

"It happens on multiple decks?" said Rosco. His confusion must have been evident, because Norik smiled as if amused.

"I will tell you something I perhaps shouldn't," said Norik. "He does that routine on every deck at the same time."

"So that's not really him?"

"Commander Ultrarch is in a lot of different places. Who's to say what's really him?"

A loud alarm sounded from every direction, and red lights began to pulsate in the corridor.

"Gods, that doesn't sound good at all." Rosco felt a weight in his stomach, an intuitive sense that something was going terribly wrong.

"I have to go," said Norik. Without another word, he sprinted down a corridor.

Rosco needed to get to an information point and find out what was happening. He turned a corner and arrived at some kind of control room. Inside, a dozen crew from *Cyclops* urgently surveyed several walls that were covered in dozens of monitor screens. Cal and Leda were also in the room, looking extremely concerned. None of the *Cyclops* crew paid any attention as Rosco joined them. He quickly studied the screens under the pulsating red light. A cluster of starships had transited into the system, and more were incoming. The ships were large and heavy—that much, he could tell.

Cal turned to Rosco, wide eyed. "They said it's a full-scale engagement."

Rosco's heartrate accelerated as though he were fighting for his life. "That's never a good thing to hear," he said. He searched for information on the control room screens.

"*Cyclops* is turning around so its front armor is facing the incoming fleet. First laser strikes are likely to hit the shield at any time," Leda said.

DEFIANT SYSTEMS

"The entire ship's already gone to battle stations," said Rosco. "All the crew are reporting to their assigned combat positions. *Fidelity* hasn't been assigned any battle duties within *Cyclops* yet, but—"

"Most of the other vessels held within *Cyclops* are scrambling to launch," said Leda. "Maybe all of them are. The rebel ships are deploying into a fleet to engage the Legion. It is the Legion we're engaging here, right?"

"Must be," Rosco replied.

Cal walked up to a particular monitor and scrutinized it. "I see many Legion cruisers registered among the incoming ships. Whole squadrons of them. I'm seeing a larger class too, Legion battleships. I don't think we've seen those before, now there's three of them, and maybe more still incoming."

Rosco ground his teeth to suppress his nerves. He couldn't show fear yet. "Does *Cyclops* stand a chance against all this?"

"Maybe. I don't know," Leda said with a frustrated shrug. "With all the Crusaders' ships fighting together, it's possible they might. The whole fleet that *Cyclops* carries inside has a lot of combined firepower."

"Could *Cyclops* launch *Fidelity* into this fight?" Cal asked him.

"We never received an official role in the Crusaders' fleet," said Rosco. "We're still being processed as new arrivals."

"Gods…" Cal muttered. "Imagine if we'd docked here any earlier. We could be sent out into this battle. It's going to be a close one. A real firestorm. Devastating. The

Legion has brought a lot of ships, but… I can't tell if it's going to be enough." His face grew pale.

Rosco saw what Cal meant as he looked at the screens. It appeared the battle could go either way. "That doesn't make sense," he said with a frown. Once again, he sensed something deeper was wrong. "Why would the Legion attack when they don't have a clear advantage? Nobody would intentionally choose such a risky assault."

"I doubt *Cyclops* was expecting it either." Cal gestured at the other people in the room. He was right. They seemed afraid and confused by what was happening. It was abnormal, even for an ambush.

At that moment, they all received a voice communication from *Fidelity*. "This is Captain Haran, aboard the bridge of *Fidelity*. All crew, return to your stations aboard our own ship immediately."

"We should get out of here," Rosco said.

Cal and Leda headed toward the door, not hesitating to get where they were told.

"Captain Haran," said Rosco. "I'm at an observation post on *Cyclops*. I can see their tactical analysis of the situation from here. Requesting your permission to stay in place on *Cyclops* and report back to you on the Crusaders' view of the battle."

"Agreed," said Haran. "Don't end up left behind. We probably have only twenty minutes until all of our crew return. After that point, an emergency launch of *Fidelity* could be a necessity if we need to escape our situation here."

"Understood," Rosco said.

Cal and Leda turned and came back to him. "What are you doing? Hurry back to *Fidelity*," Rosco said to them.

"You need us here, Major, to make sense of what you're seeing," Leda said.

"You can't really do the calculations fast enough," Cal added, "so I'll guess we need to stick with you for now." He gave an unhappy sigh. "This section of the ship is pretty sturdy, right?"

One of the screens began to flash more brightly than the others, attracting their attention. The Universal Legion cruisers had formed approximately into a delta shape and were converging directly on *Cyclops*'s location. "They're coming right at us, no doubt about that." Rosco felt a dizzying sense of powerlessness at the sight of the deadly vessels coming their way.

"With so many ships, they're going to get into very close range," Leda said, an edge of fear to her voice.

Around fifty separate laser beam weapons began burning the energy shield of *Cyclops*. "The shield's taking hits!" said Cal. The shield's strange gaseous nature caused the heat of the concentrated white-hot points of light to disperse, but as the shield itself gained temperature, it would increase the strain on the generators that powered it. So far, there was no signs of a rupture or failure of the shield units, but the level of absorbed energy was steadily creeping higher.

Enormous clouds of missiles had been launched. It was intimidating, even as a set of symbols on the screen. It was hard to ascertain what kind of warheads they were. Worst-case scenario, they were massive fission bombs, capable of annihilating *Cyclops* entirely. The weapons had a long way to travel, however, and *Cyclops* would have the chance to target them extensively. Rosco saw a bank of anti-missile defense systems on *Cyclops* activate and wipe out a wave of projectiles before they'd covered even a quarter of the distance to the ship.

So far, *Cyclops* was holding off the Legion fleet, but the Legion's main formation was still encroaching toward them. The motley vessels of the Crusader fleet opened fire with their own laser weapons. In response, some portion of the Legion cruisers and battleships directed their firepower back at the smaller vessels.

The effect was deadly and immediate. Rosco saw half a dozen vessels break apart in a torrent of flames and vapor. It was horrifying. One large rebel cruiser absorbed multiple lasers with its shields for a moment. The cloud around the ship glowed fiercely, becoming effervescent, and Rosco could see the bright-green points of the attacking lasers dancing across its surface. Then something deep inside the vessel exploded, rupturing and spraying out debris. The shields collapsed, and in seconds, the laser beams had carved the ship to pieces.

"Gods… so many killed," Cal whispered.

But they had taken pressure away from *Cyclops*'s systems. The level of harmful energies in the shield generators began to return to normal. The Crusaders could yet win the battle. Rosco saw a new order appear on one of the screens, a string of text he was able to recognize. The allied ships of the Crusader fleet were being commanded to increase their attack power, to draw more attention away from *Cyclops*. It was cold-blooded, Rosco thought. The auxiliary ships' losses would be severe. He felt immense relief that *Fidelity* was not among their number. Cal was right. Making their pledge of allegiance any earlier could have been fatal for their own ship. It was a matter of bureaucracy that had saved them.

The Legion cruisers were still drawing closer. There was no need for them to approach to such a short distance. Fresh alarms went off, adding new shades of color to the pulsating red. The terror of the *Cyclops* crew became overtly apparent.

"What is that?" Leda hissed in frustration. New symbols they couldn't recognize were pouring out from the Legion cruisers, icons with intricate features, in the numbers of hundreds or even thousands. "What does it mean? What are they doing?"

Cal laughed slightly in demented disbelief. "I honestly have no idea."

One of the *Cyclops* crewmen turned to Cal. "Void-kin," he said in an anxious tone.

Rosco understood. "Boarding parties." He suddenly lost confidence that *Cyclops* was going to survive the attack. "Let's get back to *Fidelity*. Hurry! Now!"

The three of them ran out of the control room and dashed through the corridors. At each junction, they passed by the crew of *Cyclops*, in position behind barricades and readying heavy weapons with well-trained efficiency. They seemed grim, ready for death. Rosco, Leda, and Cal increased their speed, desperate to get out of the direct line of fire. They passed stairwells, hatchways, and more *Cyclops* defense troops preparing to repel the boarders.

There was an audible crash nearby, a shrieking tear of metal. It reverberated through the structure of the starship's decks around them. Rosco felt his heart pounding even harder inside his chest. Heavy-looking doors began to descend across some of the corridors, limiting movement throughout the ship's interior. Next to each door were screens showing a view of the other side. Through one camera, Rosco saw a section of corridor violently exploding into a cloud of dust. The dust and debris were sucked out rapidly and thrown into space. People were sucked out after it, their bodies bouncing against the walls of the corridor as they went.

"That's a hull breach! It's right by us!" Cal said in horror.

"Don't slow down," Rosco replied.

They rushed past another door with another camera showing something walking around in the depressurized area, but he wasn't sure what.

"Is that even human?" Cal asked.

It had to be, Rosco thought. Someone was walking in the corridor section that had been ripped open to the vacuum. They were humanoid, but the proportions seemed all wrong.

They were getting nearer to *Fidelity*, still passing barricades of *Cyclops* crew whose weapons were aimed in the direction of the hull breach.

"She has mechanical limbs," said Leda.

"It's a woman?" Rosco asked.

"I think so."

Ahead of them was a damaged screen, its image frozen from the broken camera on the far side. For a fraction of a second, Rosco saw the void-kin clearly. He took a mental note. The humanoid woman had what seemed to be steel claws for hands and feet, carried some kind of gun in each hand, and wore a large unit on her back that looked like it enabled flight. An angular metal helmet, pointed almost like the beak of a bird, sat on her head. She seemed entirely armored.

"Is that really a void-kin?" Cal asked in clear disbelief.

"She's elite," Rosco replied. "None of the others looked like that."

They heard a grinding and crashing noise terrifyingly nearby. Rosco expected to hear the wailing hiss of air escaping to space, but their stretch of corridor remained unbreached.

None of them said anything, each listening for any sign that the void-kin was coming closer.

They passed another junction, and a series of doors closed behind them to mitigate any effects of decompression. They'd reached a labyrinthine section of hallways, nearing the entrance to the docking ports of the ships.

An enormous explosion of metal shook the corridors around them. Rosco looked to his right and saw the void-kin break into an adjacent section of corridor through a doorway.

There was a bright spurt of blue fire from the back of the woman's flight pack, and she launched down the corridor like a human rocket. Ahead, Rosco heard screams and a violent crash as the void-kin slammed into the *Cyclops* crew at a section of the barricades. Rosco was surprised that she could withstand such a hard impact, but as she flew past another open doorway, he saw that she was unharmed. More *Cyclops* crewmen opened fire, the noises audible from all directions.

Doors began to seal around them as the crew tried to enclose the void-kin in that location. Nearly all of *Cyclops*'s crew had switched to fully protective helmets in case she ripped open the hull. There was no indication that she was slowing her attack. Cal and Leda had come to a halt, looking in all directions, trying to figure out where the void-kin was, afraid she was already ahead of them. She moved so quickly that it was impossible to tell. They heard her flying down the corridors at a relentless speed, a shrieking engine noise coming from her flight pack.

"Take cover here," said Rosco. He pushed Leda and Cal out of sight behind a large stack of crates and peered out to try and confirm the void-kin's location. Farther down the corridor, he saw her pounce into a team of *Cyclops* crewmen, pulling off their heads and dismembering them with ease. She hadn't even needed to use her guns yet.

He turned and saw that Leda and Cal had both gone deathly pale, probably from the screams echoing through the corridor.

At least the void-kin was no longer between them and the entrance to *Fidelity*'s docking berth. Rosco peered out from around the crate again to be sure she was distracted.

The void-kin held down one of the *Cyclops* crew members and paused, leaning toward him and shouting, her voice distantly audible over the gunfire. After a few seconds, she killed him with a strong punch then rocketed away once again. The crewmen fighting back with their guns seemed to be unable to hit her. Rosco saw her corner another of the crew and hold them down.

It was an interrogation, Rosco realized. She was speaking in the universal language that he'd begun to recognize.

"Where... is... *Fidelity*..." she croaked.

Rosco felt a sudden terror that they were already doomed. Cal and Leda hadn't figured out what the void-kin was saying—he could tell from their lack of reaction. He hit the button to call Haran.

"Captain, there's at least one hostile void-kin aboard *Cyclops* near our position. She's searching specifically for *Fidelity*," he whispered.

"All crew, commence the emergency launch procedure from our *Cyclops* docking berth," Haran replied to the whole crew. "Rosco, get back on board now. There's no time left."

"Yes, sir," he replied. He nudged Cal and Leda, putting a hand on their shoulders to reassure them. "Let's get back to *Fidelity*. We need to move now, or we're going to die here." Even with the sealed doors, they had a route back. It was about a thirty-second dash to reach the gates of the security checkpoint. They had to evade the void-kin for that long.

He gave Cal and Leda a small shove in the right direction. "Go."

They ran through the corridors of *Cyclops* as quickly as they were able, hurrying through the twisted confines of the hallway. The clamor of battle, the screech of the void-kin's engines, and the frantic firing of guns surrounded them.

They reached the main entrance to the dock that *Fidelity* occupied, but the security system of the checkpoint was still active and would not let them through till it had verified them.

"Don't pace," said Leda. "Resist the urge to move. Just remain still for the scans."

Once again, a series of colored lights flashed. Rosco wondered if *Fidelity* had launched already, and they'd been left behind. Finally, the door at the far side opened, and they saw the boarding pipe that led to *Fidelity* still open. They desperately sprinted through, adrenaline suppressing all signs of fatigue.

"All crew registered aboard. Commencing launch," said Captain Haran the moment they were aboard. The hatchway behind them closed automatically with a loud clang. A few seconds later, *Fidelity* shook violently as it accelerated away from its position inside *Cyclops*. Their ship would have to use the chaos of battle to try to escape the whole star system. Rosco had forgotten already how much the interior of *Fidelity* would shake and rattle during its maneuvering. The ship's motions could be intuitively sensed by the human body.

"Captain," Rosco said, "I'm heading to the bridge now with Operator Heit and Chief Engineer Palchek."

"Excellent," the captain replied.

"Our ship is clear of *Cyclops* and out in open space," Leda read from her datapad.

Their vessel was exposed to the space battle raging around them, but at least they'd separated themselves from the rampaging void-kin. They needed to remain unnoticed in the melee around them. *Fidelity* had no weapons, which could work in their favor. Likely, they'd be identified as a supply ship of low priority and minimal value by the attacking Legion fleet. They were gambling everything on that, Rosco thought, but perhaps it was a safer gamble than staying docked and facing that thing that was tearing its way through *Cyclops*'s interior. Still, without any real defensive systems, they faced potential destruction at any moment.

"Ahhh…" Leda tried to say something to Rosco, but it turned into a scream as she spoke. He'd rarely heard such a noise.

Cal grabbed her datapad and took a look for himself "Oh, fuck! Fuck!" he shouted. "The void-kin has broken loose. She's out in space again!"

"She's coming right at us," said Leda, "through space. She's crossing the distance like it's nothing at all." She sounded awestruck.

"Captain Haran, the void-kin is inbound toward our ship," Rosco reported urgently.

"Acknowledged," said Haran. "I see it here on the screens."

There was a reverberating impact that Rosco could only interpret as the pursuing void-kin striking their hull. External cameras showed her standing on the surface of the ship.

Rosco made a split-second decision. He doubted himself for a moment, but then went ahead with it. "Captain, we can't fight her. I've seen this void-kin at work. She can destroy our entire ship. We have to attempt a surrender."

"She's heavily armed?" Haran asked after a pause.

"Yes," said Rosco.

"Then we activate the personal-evasion protocol," she said.

Rosco nodded as regret filled him. The personal-evasion protocol was one of the final contingencies that he'd been briefed on. It would abandon the ship. Most of the crew would stand down at their posts, on the assumption they could safely remain in place. Meanwhile, the diplomatic staff necessary for contact with the Ruarken Senate would evacuate in secret, along with other significant senior officers, to attempt to continue the mission without the starship *Fidelity*.

That list included him, given that he'd been promoted since the mission had begun. It included Leda, too, he realized, as the ship's chief engineer, though she would not have known that. She hadn't been briefed on the contingency plans yet.

"Chief Engineer Palchek, we need to report to the shuttle bays of *Fidelity* immediately. There is an evacuation order for key bridge staff," he said.

"What?" She looked shocked. "I see. Right…"

Rosco looked back at Cal. He wasn't included in the order. Though he didn't have any idea what was happening, he looked forlorn and isolated in that moment.

Rosco owed Cal his life after the events on *Tenebrous*. Plus, Cal had some connection to the Ambassador. It was potentially more dangerous for him to be left behind on *Fidelity* and captured by the Legion. "Come with us," Rosco said to him.

The three of them quickly made their way to the docking bay. There was a shrill metallic squealing as the void-kin broke into the ship, but mercifully, they heard no gunfire. Her metal footsteps clattered on the decking, but she was heading to the bridge, away from them. They arrived at the shuttle bay and saw that *Fidelity*'s two shuttles were already prepared for launch, their engines glowing hot and the entrance ramps open.

The door at the far end of the hangar bay opened, and Rosco saw Captain Haran marching into the area, followed by around a dozen other crew. Most were the diplomatic staff who'd been continuing the work of the mission's original leader, Councilor Theeran, after his death. *Fidelity*'s purpose above all else was to transport these people to Ruarken. Captain Haran nodded to Rosco and kept moving. "Let's get out of here."

"Where's Marraz?" Rosco asked as he started up the ramp of the nearest shuttle. Cal and Leda rushed inside.

"Marraz opted to stay," Haran said. She switched to headset communication as she boarded onto the other shuttle. "He thinks he can reason with her, as one void-kin to another. He wants to negotiate some truce for the safety of our crew."

"Does he stand any chance?" Rosco entered the shuttle and hurried to the pilot's seat.

"Unknown," Haran said.

Rosco turned and looked back toward the crew compartment. "Is everyone aboard and ready to launch?" he called over his shoulder to the passenger seating area of the shuttle.

"Fargas is here. He's just come on board with us," said Leda.

"I'm sealing the ramps. We're launching immediately," said Rosco. A few seconds later, the lights on his dashboard confirmed that the shuttle was ready for takeoff, and the wide outer doors of *Fidelity*'s launch bay began to open. There was a rush of air as the atmosphere was blown out during the urgent launch maneuver. First, Captain Haran's shuttle lifted from its landing pad and streaked out into the black vacuum. Rosco held the flight controls firmly and directed his own shuttle to follow hers.

He switched to a private voice channel. "What's stopping the void-kin from just following us out here?" he quietly asked Haran.

"We have a secret asset. Both of our shuttles are equipped with small scrambling devices that can hide our positions. These were privately obtained by Theeran from offworld. I've activated them in response to the personal-evasion plan being engaged," Captain Haran replied.

For a moment, Rosco was surprised by the depth of Theeran's resources. "Offworld technology? Do we know for sure if it'll work?" he asked.

"It's our best chance. We can't hope for anything more," Haran replied.

He looked around at space using the shuttle's external cameras. He could see the laser strikes and huge explosive flares of the Legion fleet battling the Crusaders. The destruction was as bright as ever.

"We can still be located visually," he said.

"Agreed. We need to find shelter," Haran replied. "Head to this location, and we'll rendezvous on the planet's surface. We can power down the shuttles and hide. That'll make us very difficult to detect."

"Acknowledged," said Rosco. Captain Haran had sent him the coordinates of a specific location on a nearby planet, somewhere that seemed filled with rocks and jungle.

Rosco entered the commands into the shuttle's autopilot system. He looked back at *Fidelity* through one of the shuttle screens. Cal and Leda had joined him at the doorway to the pilot's compartment, having changed into space suits as a precautionary measure. *Fidelity* seemed quiet as they watched. No fires or sparks erupted from within it. It seemed almost as if nothing at all was happening.

Then the electric lights along its surface went off one by one till *Fidelity* was entirely dark. The orange fires of nearby burning starships cast long and eerie shadows across its hull. The shapes seemed to dance slowly over *Fidelity*'s surface, their vessel illuminated by the destruction of all those around it. It seemed so small, shrinking till it looked almost like a children's toy, tiny and fragile.

Cal stared pensively through the shuttle window, watching their ship as it disappeared. Rosco shared the despondence. Leda pushed the helmet of a space suit toward Rosco. "You might need this, Major," she said. "We have to stay ready."

*

Advocate Fargas sat in the back of the shuttle, holding a small pen made of mirrored chrome. It slowly slid between his fingers. He stared at it, seeing his own face in its reflection.

Fidelity was lost. The ship was in the Tylder Ambassador's hands, but Fargas knew she'd gained nothing valuable. Captain Haran had transferred all of Theeran's notes regarding the Seed of Steel away from *Fidelity* and onto both the shuttles, likely encoded somewhere inside the secret stealth devices. If the mission continued, as was the plan under Vale Reach's personal-evasion protocol, the remaining crew on the shuttles would intend to carry on to Ruarken and submit the petition as originally proposed.

It would probably take quite some time to recover from the setback, and the mission would travel painfully slowly without their own vessel, but they could get within transmission range of the Senate and be able to send the information they carried. These people would have no chance of making it to the Senate themselves. Transmitting Vale Reach's most valuable data forward was the only way. Captain Haran would never agree to it. She'd made that clear. But he could make Rosco do it.

Fargas rotated his thumb along a few points of his silver pen, checking that the data that mattered was stored in the shuttle's stealth device. It emitted small signals to his nervous system through tiny electrical discharges that created visual images in his brain. Both shuttlecrafts contained a complete copy of all the information that Theeran had compiled, material that had now been completely deleted from the main ship, just as Fargas expected.

He rolled the pen in his hand, weighing the options. Would the negotiators from Vale Reach be needed? Unlikely. He could take care of everything himself.

The pen continued to roll before he let it settle in the palm of his hand.

There was nothing else that could be done. Besides, a smaller party would travel faster and hide easier.

He pressed a particular sequence of code with his thumb. The stealth unit in Captain Haran's shuttle ceased operating.

A few seconds later, her shuttle exploded apart in streaks of hot metal, pierced by a stream of plasma larger than the shuttle itself.

"No!" he heard everyone in the cockpit scream. They exclaimed in disbelief and confusion.

There would be nothing left, he knew. Fargas jumped to his feet and slid the metal stylus into his pocket.

☐

Chapter 10

The shuttle set down with a crunch in a flat section of scrubland. Everyone sat in shock. The sudden silence of the shuttle engine finally shutting down felt deafening. There was only the creaking of the turbines and the rustling of the wind, a sound unlike anything they'd heard in months. Cal thought he heard what sounded like a bird in the distance.

They had spent the entire remaining journey down to the planet in a state of certainty that they, too, would be annihilated by one of the plasma weapons that had destroyed Captain Haran and her vessel. According to Leda, the captain had been accurately targeted by a weapons turret on a Legion warship. Why they had escaped a similar fate was unknown. The fear and trauma were still too great for them even to probe what'd happened and find answers.

"Get away from the shuttle," Rosco said after a moment. He sounded close to exhaustion. His skin seemed grayer and wrinkled, as though he'd aged years.

It hadn't been until the shuttle had entered the lower reaches of the atmosphere that Cal had allowed himself to consider that they might not die. For that entire duration, Rosco had kept a perpetually vigilant watch for any sign of danger whilst flying the craft through atmospheric entry. He seemed so weary even beneath his military composure. "We should get clear of it, just in case," he said.

The shuttle's sensors showed a difficult but breathable atmosphere outside. The ramp lowered, the outside and inside air merging with an audible pop. There was a strong smell to the planet, not entirely pleasant. Cal saw plants and trees through the open doorway. He wanted to go toward them, suddenly overcome by an overwhelming desire to be among the greenery. He felt tears rising inside and squeezed his hands angrily. Things had gone wrong more than ever. He didn't have time to count the cost. Cal exited the shuttle.

*

The four of them sat a circle in a small jungle clearing, resting and recovering.

"You are the mission now," Fargas told them.

Rosco nodded slowly. "We are," he agreed then turned to Cal and Leda. "We have to get to Ruarken High Senate. Somehow. We have to keep going." He exhaled and seemed to grow more resolute. "It's our mission. We're all part of it, each one of us. Haran is gone, but our journey to save Vale Reach remains."

"What can we do when we get there?" Leda asked.

"I'll handle that," said Fargas. "You are the captain now," he added to Rosco after a pause.

"My god," Rosco whispered under his breath. He was quiet for a while.

Nobody felt like talking.

*

There were tents and rations stored in the shuttle. The group collected everything of value from the craft, and Rosco carefully repositioned it to be deeper under tree cover. The planet around them was a mixture of forest and bushland. Farther away on the horizon, the landscape became a steep rolling ridge with deep ravines and canyons cut by fast and powerful rivers.

Leda waved for the others to join her. "Look at this." She'd retrieved her datapad. "I've deactivated any of its connections, so we can't be tracked, don't worry. Make sure you do the same to yours. But look. It received messages as we were coming down through the atmosphere. These were sent out on a wide bandwidth to a whole area but with a signature that our machines can pick up. Here's the first."

The screen on her datapad played a video image of *Fidelity*'s bridge, mostly as they remembered it. At the front of the image was the void-kin as she'd appeared on the cameras aboard *Cyclops* but with a handful of fresh burn marks and scratches across her armored body. She'd removed her angular helmet, and they saw her face. She had what Leda could only assume was artificial skin, its texture synthetic and colored different shades of gray. In her eyes, though, she looked the same age as Leda herself, if not younger. In the background, Leda could see a handful of the bridge crew of *Fidelity*, still at their stations but seeming dejected and in a state of surrender. There was no sign of Marraz, she noted.

The woman spoke, her voice metallic and electronic, a poor imitation of a natural speaker. "All remaining crew of starship *Fidelity*, stand down and submit immediately. You have one chance to surrender peacefully. I am Special Agent Belara, and I am in command of your ship. Lethal force will be used against any elements of your mission that do not immediately comply."

The transmission ended abruptly.

"At least we know they're still alive," said Cal.

"Since when did you become our voice of positivity?" Rosco laughed grimly.

"*Fidelity* is one piece. Our comrades are okay, mostly, we can hope," said Cal.

"You're right," Rosco said. "The ship itself lives. But it's not under the command of Vale Reach anymore."

"You're a captain without a ship," said Fargas.

The other three turned and looked at him. He was the odd member of their group, wearing his offworlder civilian's outfit and noticeably very different from them in his age.

"I'm quite serious," he said. "Let us hope it is only a temporary inconvenience to your mission."

"There's another message," said Leda. She pressed a button to play it. "This one's audio only."

"Survivors of *Fidelity*, this is Lieutenant Norik," said a familiar voice. "I've registered that your ship has been captured intact by the Legion. I'm so glad to see that you avoided destruction. I thought you would have been killed while following our carrier's battle orders. That would have been... regretful. You didn't deserve that. Gods bless you for living, however you did it." They heard Norik sigh.

"I'm sorry I can't help you more. *Cyclops* has disengaged and exited the system, and much of the Legion fleet is leaving in pursuit of them, but there are still Legion cruisers on patrol here. What remains of our rebellion is... quite minimal, but there are some surviving rebel vessels hiding or dormant in the area and refugees on many of the planets. I'm going in search of them now. My interceptor is still operational. I hope we find each other again one day soon. Don't give up. I've seen people come back from worse. Lieutenant Norik, signing off."

A musical tone played on Leda's datapad, and another voice automatically began to play.

"Paous Ultrarch's farewell address," said a female voice.

"Fantastic," Cal said sarcastically.

"Brave crusaders!" Ultrarch's distinctive voice said. "Glory to you for a courageous operation today. Your sacrifices here will be celebrated for generations to come. Our precious mothership, *Cyclops*, has been saved by your heroism. Before long, it will return to lead our fight for justice. The struggle against the Universal Legion never ends. Have no fear, for the Crusaders will be back to avenge the lives of our fallen warriors in this place. I expect all our remnants to be ready to greet us when that day comes. Until then, good hunting, you righteous souls."

No one spoke for a moment after the messages ended.

"Kind of feels like dying to help *Cyclops* was the whole purpose of the rebel fleet," said Cal.

"The life of a mercenary…" Rosco shook his head. "Easily disposed of."

"Or of a peasant crusader," said Fargas. "What is a crusade without martyrs?"

"Perhaps the Crusaders inadvertently gave us what we needed," said Leda. "They brought us this far, and we aren't dead like any of their other auxiliaries… but we have lost our ship." She looked sad.

"Inadvertently…" Cal let loose a bitter laugh. "Only because the whole place blew up before they could arrange to send us out to die."

"Sometimes a good escape is exactly what life is about," said Fargas. "In fact, that's what my profession is built on."

"We're fortunate compared to most of the others on that ship," said Leda. "We didn't get in too deep."

"We are completely trapped down here on this damn planet, though," Cal replied. "I don't think this mission has ever felt so hopeless."

"That's not true at all," Fargas replied sympathetically.

The others looked at him in confusion.

"You're nearer to the Ruarken High Senate than ever before!" he explained. "You are close now. Just a handful of decent FTL jumps are all that remain between you and saving your world. All we need is to find some way to get you back up into space and away from the Legion. Unfortunately for once, I cannot help you in that department…"

"The Crusaders are still out there…" said Rosco. "We'll likely meet them again." He looked around at the landscape. "If we ever leave this rock."

"So, what do we do?" Cal asked. "What do we do, Captain?" he said, correcting himself.

"Norik's right. We aren't alone here. We don't surrender. We have Fargas and others who can assist us. The void-kin woman, Belara, may have taken *Fidelity* and our comrades… but the mission was never about the starship. It's about protecting our world. There's no way we can stop. Even if we have nothing but our tents." He glanced around at the empty jungle clearing.

"You all can be the delegates. I will advise you," said Fargas "The four of us are enough to achieve what we originally set out to do."

"We still have the operational shuttle, at least for now," said Leda. "Which means we're not trapped here."

"It's too much of a risk to use the shuttle," Rosco said. "The Universal Legion fleet will stay in orbit above us for some time, especially if they're hunting survivors. If we used the shuttle to leave the planet, we'd very likely be destroyed as soon as we tried to exit the atmosphere."

"We've got to get away from here somehow, though," said Leda.

Cal kicked a few small rocks as they all thought about their predicament.

"For now, we sleep," said Rosco. "We can formulate ideas in the morning."

*

Cal was back in his apartment, seated at the familiar wooden kitchen table once more. As ever, someone sat opposite him, surveying him with alert eyes. The walls of his house were shadowy and formless, as if made of some thin gray gas. The woman became shadowy, too, the more that he looked at her. At certain moments, she almost seemed to fit the proportions of Eevey, but that was brief and fleeting. Generally, she seemed large and unnaturally still, like a cat. Behind her, a white light flickered like strikes of lightning without thunder.

"Ambassador," Cal said.

"Caladon." Her voice sounded warm and welcoming.

"You're meeting with me in my dreams."

"We are meeting each other in this place."

Cal became angry at her. If he was in a dream, she couldn't hurt him. He was free to demand she listen to him. "You sent that void-kin woman to attack our ship."

"Belara is my agent, perhaps one of my best. She has been successful, as ever." For a second, the Ambassador became fully visible, her purple dress and uncanny orange eyes appearing before the dream once again dissolved her details back into something invisible.

"She's part of the Universal Legion fleet," he said, "but that's not where her allegiances really lie. She works for you." Cal put his hands flat on the table, feeling the soft, smooth wood. "Do you control the whole fleet that jumped into this system? Is that why they jumped here? To find *Fidelity*?"

"What do you think?" she asked.

Cal laughed to himself softly. "That confirms it." He nodded to himself. "I've figured out what you are."

"Have you?"

He nodded to himself. "I have." He pointed at her. "I'm not talking to a real person. The Ambassador hasn't implanted anything in me, nothing physical, anyway." Cal tapped his head. "You can't get to me like that onboard *Fidelity*—not by my calculations, anyway. So, what you've done to me is psychological." He felt as though the person across the table was smiling at him, though he couldn't see her face.

He continued, sensing that he was correct. "That flickering white light... I see it every time we meet. But I didn't see it the first time we spoke, the real time, on the call with Eevey. You haven't told me a single thing that I didn't already know. You only ever present old facts, or tell me what I'm most afraid of. Nothing new. You're a program, aren't you? An imitation that's been imprinted on my subconscious and creeps out at night when my mental defenses are down. The flickering light appears when you activate yourself. I'm right, aren't I?"

"And what would that mean?" she asked.

"It means you're not the Ambassador," said Cal. "You're just something that she's put in my head to haunt me."

The Ambassador clapped one single time, seemingly to signal her satisfaction. "You have some wisdom, Caladon."

"So you can't be physically tracking me. There's no way for you to communicate back to her, the real her," he said, growing in confidence. "You didn't follow me to find *Cyclops*. I didn't cause this." He stood.

"That is true," she said. "And yet, I did find you successfully. And I sent a whole fleet of the Universal Legion to stop you, many of whom are now burning at the hands of your rebel friends, who are also mostly dead. That, Cal, was all caused by the stubborn intransigence of your ship not to turn back."

"Why did you bring Eevey into it?"

"We met on Vale Reach before I even knew who you were," the figure across the table said. "She chose to become part of my work. I thought using her presence would set you at ease."

"Look at you, pretending to be her," said Cal. "You can't pick what form you want to take."

"When the brain sees something it doesn't understand, Cal, it invents something to fill the space." The voice was Eevey's.

"When I get back to Vale Reach, I don't want to see you in our lives. You're a nightmarish thing."

"When you return, you'll find that Eevey and I can't be separated." It sounded as if Eevey and the Ambassador spoke simultaneously. "*If* you return."

After a moment, Cal felt afraid. "Something's coming toward us, isn't it?"

"Another of my agents," the Ambassador said. "A giant, a titan. It's coming down to the planet. You are progressing through the branches of a tree of possibility. I have prepared for all eventualities. You can never escape my parameters. Every action you ever take is within the scope of my plans. Surrender, Cal. Surrender."

Cal awoke inside his tent.

"Something's coming!" he heard Rosco shout from outside.

*

Leda rushed out of the tent, not bothering to put on her boots, standing barefoot in the dirt. Cal and Rosco were looking up into the sky, witnessing a brightly burning orange streak. Leda joined them. Beyond the fiery intensity of the falling object, it was hard to make out much detail.

"That's a heavy kind of planetfall," said Cal. "It's coming down fast, and it's big."

Fargas joined them. Over several minutes, they watched the flaming mass grow larger and larger. It seemed like it wouldn't ever stop growing, looming larger than any starship or satellite, but the true scale was impossible to tell. Amidst the blazing-hot atmospheric entry, they could even make out the shapes of a few dark, sharp angles. It was going to hit nearby.

As the three of them looked across the flat scrubland plains, the falling object struck the planet with a tremendous eruption of dust. A vast cloud of brown ash, like the mushroom cloud of a nuclear weapon, rose from the dirt. A fraction of a second later, the deafening sound of the blast wave hit them, a thunderous roaring that caused them to clutch their ears in pain and fall to their knees as the ground shook beneath them.

When the dust settled, something was standing in the crater, something that was unfolding itself to stand even taller, almost as tall as the erupted cloud itself. It strode toward them through the smoke.

It walked on two legs. Leda was paralyzed with fear as the machine came their way. She decided the moment had come to employ her implants and speed up her mental actions to study the huge mechanical construct. Brief usage shouldn't affect her badly.

The bipedal machine was at least three hundred meters tall, maybe more. Its legs connected at a pelvis, but that was where its humanoid qualities ended. Its torso was a rounded dome like the inverted hull of a ship, smooth as polished steel. On sockets along its surface, mechanical arms of many kinds were mounted, each probably dozens of meters in length. Leda couldn't tell which objects were sensors and which were weapons, but at least ten gun-like appendages waved through the air above its armored core. Most ominously, it flickered with an energy shield, as the starships had, a gaseous cloud that crackled with flickers of electrical discharge.

She could barely speak. "Wh-What do we do?"

"Hide!" said Rosco. "Get behind some rocks now!"

They all dived into action and hid behind a large bolder. It was scarcely big enough to conceal the four of them, and they pressed close together against it.

"Now what?" Leda asked.

They could still hear the deafening noise of the giant's footsteps as it approached. The tremors from the force of each stomp were terrifying.

"Stay quiet!" Rosco waved for them not to talk.

The thunderous stomping abruptly ceased. Despite her overwhelming terror, Leda dared to peek out from around the bolder, using her implants once more to see it clearly for a fraction of a second.

Various radar dishes and scanners on the machine's surface were rotating. It was searching, she realized. It hadn't found them yet, though it was trying. If they were to have a chance of evading it, they needed to determine how it searched. Visually was obvious. Audibly was a strong possibility too. Carefully, Leda took out her datapad and typed a message to show the others: *Is it searching for sound? If we get to the river, the water covers our noise.*

The others nodded. Cal took out his own datapad. *How else does it search?* he wrote. *Thermal? X-ray?*

To avoid visual detection, they'd need to crawl on their stomachs, away from the boulder and down into a ditch that led to the ravine. There was a chance they could stay out of sight if they were extremely careful. *The big rocks should be enough to hide us,* she wrote back.

Cal nodded. Rosco and Fargas watched their exchange. Leda looked at a high rock ridge that rose along one side of the landscape. If they could reach the other side of it without detection, they might have some chance to lose the mechanical giant, but the ridge was still so far away.

Leda heard a loud metallic whining that sent a fresh jolt of fear through her nerves. It sounded both immense and distant. Again, she dared to peer out. The walking machine was rotating at the hips, aiming its appendages in various directions. *It's still looking around. Some of the devices must be directional.*

Wait till they're not pointing at us, then we move, Cal wrote.

Some point in all directions, she replied.

We take our chances, Rosco wrote to them. *Pick the best moment.*

Fargas poked at them to get their attention. He made a gesture as if to say he could hear something else, but Leda couldn't tell what. She decided to risk one more brief glance at the machine. Some kind of flying aerial unit had detached from the top of the walker—several of them, in fact. A search from above might find them soon. They had to quickly get under the cover of the trees in the ravine.

"Flying drones. Get out of here," she mouthed silently and urgently to the others.

"Stay low," Rosco whispered, signaling to them. "Don't create any noise." He pressed himself flat on the ground and crawled as quietly as he could away from the mechanical roars of the juggernaut behind them.

*

The metal giant followed them as they anxiously crept through the thick jungle and pulled themselves over sharp rocks. They quickly became muddy and soaked in water from the boggy soil. The machine seemed to have a vague understanding of where they were, but it was circling the area in an attempt to pinpoint their position. Through the dense green trees, they could glimpse its feet when it got close to them, crashing through the foliage, threatening to smash them beneath its tread and grind them into the dirt.

To stay hidden, they continued to crawl as they headed deeper into the ravine, moving gradually from behind one boulder to the next. Rosco led them from the front, searching for a way to carefully approach the tall rock ridge and cross it without being seen and caught.

Without warning, the machine fired one of its huge cannons, launching a screeching torrent of green plasma. The liquid projectile hissed and crackled as it moved in a high arc through the air, streaking past them and out of sight. They heard it crash into the jungle not far away.

The group made slow, gradual progress for hours, growing exhausted. Suddenly, the sound of rockets came out of nowhere, and they looked up to see the skies filled with what appeared to be small black fragments.

"Cluster bombs," Rosco whispered. "Get deep down into the rocks."

They pressed themselves as far down into the cracks as they could. Dozens of bombs landed around them, a rippling series of explosions, painfully loud, so violent that it rattled their teeth. Pillars of black smoke rose in many directions, and the air developed a fiery red tinge. Leda felt as though they were insects being exterminated.

They had no other option but to keep going. Climbing the ridge was their best plan. Rosco kept them disciplined, preventing them from growing impatient from fear or making any noise, ensuring they took no risks even as they were filled with fatigue. Crawling on their hands and knees was immensely more tiring than any trek. Leda felt as though she'd run a marathon. Her muscles were aching from holding her weight so carefully to prevent rocks and gravel from scraping loudly beneath them.

The sun began to set, and the sky rapidly grew darker. They had no idea how long a daily cycle was on this planet. Leda's whole sense of time was distorted by constant fear and adrenaline that renewed itself each time the titanic walking machine came near them. Leda realized she didn't know how long they'd been crawling. The period of heightened awareness seemed to stretch into forever.

At some point, the hard ground beneath her started to become steeply inclined. They were rising toward the top of the ridge. Rosco had found a path that kept them hidden from the machine's sight, winding up through the remnants of a dried stream. Leda risked a look back at the gigantic walker, which trampled the forest as loudly as ever, and saw a multicolored glow of energy emanating from its direction.

The rocky terrain grew steeper till she was climbing a cliff face. Leda welcomed the sense of reaching higher ground. Crossing the edge of the ridge would change their situation.

The skies above grew slightly brighter. A sun was rising on the ridge's far side. The light shone with an orange glow amongst the bluish gray. The machine was still near, its loud motors never ceasing. Leda sensed they were nearing a critical moment in their journey. The terrain flattened suddenly. The rock around them was bright pink in the morning light, and she saw they were at the top of a narrow plateau, the far horizon visible. She had no time to look around.

"Go. Hurry," Rosco whispered. He stood slightly then ran at a low crouch. Leda did the same, her legs struggling to carry her. She saw Rosco dive down a steep bank a few meters ahead, tumbling down the far side of the ridge. Leda tumbled after him, vaguely aware of Cal and Fargas behind her. Their falling, rolling bodies came to a stop, and they lay dazed, recovering their breath, no longer crawling.

The walking machine that hunted them was on the other side of the ridge behind them. Its aerial vehicles hadn't been seen in some time. They were beyond its view.

Leda's eyes adjusted to the new light of the sunrise, and she took in a series of hills and sweeping cliffs stretching into the distance. But something else caught her attention, an artificial structure only a few kilometers away. It looked like a castle or a temple, with towers and buttresses and tall gray stone sides carved in vertical and orthogonal patterns.

She pointed to it, too tired to say anything.

"I see it too," said Rosco. Leda looked around at the others. They seemed pleased by the sight, just as she was.

"Maybe we could get there," said Rosco. He turned to Fargas. "Is there anyone in that place? Would they let us in? A sanctuary? Do you know anything about it?"

Fargas looked weary. He was likely the least physically fit of them all, but he was three hundred years old. His physiology was a mystery. The blue robes he wore were stained black from water and mud. "I don't know…" he said.

They lay still for another few minutes, resting from their weariness.

"Okay," Rosco whispered, "let's move. Stay quiet. It can't see us, so walk fast and low. We should be able to reach that structure in under two hours."

Leda's fatigue was still intense. It felt impossible for her to stand and walk again, but somehow, she managed it. They set off at a careful, tired pace.

Before much had passed, they heard the sound of whirring mechanical motors in the distance behind them. They all instinctively dived into a nearby ditch, throwing themselves against the earth once again and crawling to be flat on the soil.

Leda looked back. The machine was towering above the edge of the ridge. It had seen the stone fortress. There was a new noise, electrical crackling, rapid like a torrent of rain. Then one of its largest cannons discharged with a blinding white flash. Leda could see nothing but the whiteness as she felt the ground tremble underneath her like an earthquake. It sounded as though the hills themselves were breaking apart.

Slowly, her vision returned. Where the stone castle had been, an expanding mushroom cloud rose to the sky. Huge fragments of rock tumbled back down and landed with a distant crash as pieces of stone wall cascaded across the plains. It had been disintegrated, a hole in the ground where it had once stood. Leda felt her heart sink into despair. There was no escape. Waves of exhaustion overcame her. Her vision faded, and she slipped out of consciousness.

☐

Chapter 11

They woke up in a hot, darkened room. Rosco opened his eyes and looked around as best he could. A pale-blue light was visible, and he saw wide black columns in the darkness that reached some kind of high ceiling above them. He felt as though they were underground. Cal, Leda, and Fargas were with him, also slowly waking. They were held in some kind of metal frame that restrained them from moving, keeping their arms by their sides and forcing them to stand upright. He couldn't see anything else in the darkness. Someone must have brought them here. Liquid dripped loudly in the distance.

"Hello?" said Rosco.

"You are in the inner sanctum of the Graven Monks," a deep voice said. The reverberating bass rumbled off the walls.

"Why are we here?" he asked the empty room.

"It is not your place to ask questions of the assembled council. You are to answer them, as best as you are able. Why have you come here?"

"We didn't intend to," said Rosco. He saw the others stirring. It was likely they could also hear what was being said.

"You were found on our planet, interloper. You are from the fleets above. Explain why you have trespassed on our world and attacked our brothers," came the slow, powerful voice.

Rosco began to understand. "I am Captain Nurten Rosco, commander of the starship *Fidelity*," he said. His voice was firm, but he spoke without shouting. "I am the enemy of the machine that has invaded your world."

There was silence for several seconds. Then, in front of the four of them, a disk descended, wide enough for three figures in red robes to comfortably stand on top. Complex gold embroidery covered their heavy, hooded outfits. Rosco assumed that they must be the monks.

"We abstain from the affairs of the wider galaxy," the voice said. One of the monks raised a single hand, presumably indicating that he was the one speaking.

"These are ancient hermits," Fargas whispered, "but they're not in any records I've ever seen."

"Have you heard of the Universal Legion?" Rosco asked them.

"Captain, you were told that we do not answer your questions here," said the monk. "It is regrettable that the name of the Universal Legion has penetrated our consciousness. They offend the sacred vaults of our mental space."

"The Legion are trying to kill us," Rosco replied.

Another monk raised his hand, and the first lowered his. "They have already killed far more than you."

"That was your monastery they destroyed," said Rosco. "The machine must be stopped somehow."

The third monk raised his hand. "You speak the truth," he replied.

"Where are we?" Cal mumbled next to Rosco.

"Cal, we're being held in a dungeon by some monks," said Rosco.

"That's arguably better than where we were before," Leda added.

"Do you have any weapons that can be used against the Legion's war machine?" Rosco asked before he remembered the monks' rule against questions. "We need weapons to stop it," he said simply.

"Weapons are strictly against the Graven Monks' code," they said.

"Damn!" Cal replied.

"That's not helping," Fargas said.

The first monk spoke again. "One of you bears the signs of contact with an ancient superhuman."

The group hesitated in confusion, looking to each other for answers.

"It has been many centuries since we had such a fascinating specimen in our presence."

The lead monk drifted from the floating disk and came toward them, flying using some method hidden beneath the robes. He was tall, Rosco saw, and seemingly without feet or a face. He drifted directly toward Cal, who responded with clear horror and confusion but remained quiet. The monk hovered, surveying Cal closely. Still, none of them could move.

"We need to find a way to stop the Legion's war machine," Rosco said. "It's urgent." He hoped to distract it from interrogating Cal, who seemed in danger of panicking.

"We shall slumber and hibernate," the monk said. "The machine will never find us. Our monasteries can be rebuilt." It leaned closer to Cal by a few inches. "Your neural pathways are unnatural."

"Is that g-good or b-b-bad?" Cal asked after a long pause.

"They bear the fingerprint of someone so very far beyond you," said the monk.

Cal nodded, seeming to understand, somehow, what the monk was telling him. "The Tylder Ambassador?"

"Tylder," the monk said, his voice inscrutable. "So that is who you have met."

"Not physically," said Cal. "Just a phone call."

The monk finally seemed to look Cal in the eyes. "She has inserted herself into your brain."

"We"—Rosco hesitated—"we're not part of the Ambassador's agenda," he said. "We're from a simple planet, just looking to travel. But the Legion is hunting us."

"The machine that wanders our land bears a similar imprint. It contains some form of living tissue inside, something that the Tylder Ambassador has spoken to just as she has spoken to you. Her technology is remarkable, but it is not untraceable to our sight. What draws her to mortals such as you is harder for us to understand. The worlds outside this monastery must have changed in ways we do not comprehend."

"We can help you, if you help us," said Rosco. "We're willing to be of assistance."

The monk finally turned away from Cal, moving to face Rosco. "Perhaps something can be done to stop the machine, but it will require his brain."

"You can't cut him open," said Rosco. "That's not acceptable. Don't harm him."

"A device could be produced that would allow the brain to remain in its original skull," said the monk.

Cal nodded enthusiastically. "That's much better."

"His life matters to us," Rosco said. "You need to treat him carefully."

"We will seek to establish a link between his mind and the machine," said the monk. "If a connection is made, we can enter the machine's thought space and disable its systems."

"Keep him safe," Rosco said.

"That cannot be not guaranteed," the monk said.

Rosco turned as much as he could. "You don't have to do this, Cal."

"First, let us move around," said Cal. The metal restraints suddenly disappeared, and they were standing on the floor. Cal turned to Rosco. "I don't think there's any other way out of this for us. We can't go back out there with that thing hunting for us. And we can't stay down in this dungeon forever."

"I don't want you to sacrifice yourself. We'd be putting our trust in the monks," said Rosco.

"It might be the only way," said Cal. "We all need our mission to succeed, Rosco. Maybe this is what it takes. We have to get out of here, somehow. We need to keep going to save Vale Reach. Protecting our homeworld is what matters the most."

"It has to be your choice, Cal," Leda said. "We can't ask you to do something that's so… unknown." She looked down, clearly distressed. Rosco realized that she couldn't think of any better ideas either.

"We need time to discuss this with each other," Rosco told the monks.

"I think we should hear what they have to say," Cal said. "Tell us your plan to stop the war machine," he asked the red-robed monk that hovered above him.

"We will transport you onto the surface of the machine. There, we will use a neural-link cable to connect you to its internal systems, likely through your spine and through the machine's data-upload port. There are biological elements inside the war machine that have been harvested from living humans. Both Cal and the war machine contain a virtual image of the Ambassador, a simple echo that can communicate on her behalf. This creates a common point of reference between them both.

They will share a synthetic protocol for producing simulated mental interactions. This will allow us to connect one mind to the other. The necessary ports in their consciousness are already established. From there, Cal will have a chance to disable the machine."

"How are you possibly going to get him to the top of that thing?" Leda asked.

"They don't like answering direct questions, remember," said Fargas.

Leda sighed. "Tell us how," she told the monks. "Please."

"For transcontinental journeys, we possess a glider aircraft. We assure you that it can remain fully invisible to the walker that is currently attacking our land. Our brothers will direct the aircraft and ensure this Cal is connected appropriately to the machine."

"You need him for this, don't you?" said Rosco. "Your brothers can fly and operate the glider. But with no weapons, you really have no method to stop the machine. Cal here is your only way to take it out of action, or you'd have done so already."

There was silence. The monks didn't make any comment on his assertion.

"Help us reclaim our starship," said Rosco. "I assume that you have some means to go up to space, since you possess such an advanced aircraft. Our ship, *Fidelity*, has been stolen from us by a void-kin from the Universal Legion. She is in control of it right now. She is standing on my bridge, controlling my crew. Pledge that you will help us retake our ship, and you can"—he hesitated, feeling dread for what he was about to say—"use Cal for your operation, if he's not harmed by the process." Disbelief and regret hit him in the chest. Rosco's plan for the future didn't extend beyond that, but it was a start. He could adapt things from there.

Cal nodded but looked pale and afraid.

"A single starship?" the monk asked. "Stolen by a single void-kin?"

"It's not even a large starship," said Leda.

"Your proposal is accepted," the monk intoned.

Fargas patted Rosco firmly on the back, his face beaming with a smile. "Excellent work, Captain."

*

The dungeon roof above them opened like two halves of an enormous trapdoor, and they were elevated as the platform under their feet began to move. Distantly above them, they could see unrecognizable machinery, a complex symmetrical pattern of curved steel that none of them could interpret. The pale-blue light illuminated the rounded surfaces.

As the rising platform lifted them out of darkness, they became surrounded by the strange machinery. The council of monks had disappeared beneath them, and they were alone. The platform suddenly came to an abrupt halt, and out of exhaustion the group fell to the floor. A round metal portal opened like an iris next to them. There was nowhere else for them to go. Through the round gate, daylight beckoned. Wearily, they forced themselves back up to their feet and trudged into the next chamber.

They arrived somewhere recognizable as a hangar bay, where a silver aircraft awaited them. It was dozens of meters long and possessed a featureless exterior other than its wide wings and engine vents at the back.

A red-robed monk drifted down from the ceiling and hovered above the glider.

"Prepare yourself," the monk said. His voice was slightly different from that of the monks below. It didn't seem to shake the walls as much. "Engage in the final rites of your culture. Be at peace so that your soul may adequately pass beyond the veil of mortality."

"You said he wouldn't be harmed," Leda said angrily.

"I will endeavor to return him back to you safely," the monk said.

"Cal…" said Rosco. "This is your last chance to say no to this."

For a long time, Cal stared out at the crack of daylight that emerged from the distant opening of the hangar. No one disturbed him.

"Don't blame yourself, Captain, if anything happens," Cal said. "You're a good man. Send me out there. Get the starship back for us. And tell Eevey I love her."

Leda wrapped her arms tightly around Cal. He looked surprised then accepted it. After a few seconds, they separated.

"You're a brave man, Cal," Rosco told him. "An honorable man."

"A hero," Cal replied with a mischievous smile. He turned and walked away from them, accompanied by the floating monk.

*

The interior of the monks' aircraft was smaller than he'd imagined. Perhaps it had very thick walls. Cal guessed that he was being held in some specific compartment for passengers. The monk was with him, seeming not to need to pilot the plane. The aircraft was silent as it moved, but occasionally, Cal felt the floor underneath him rock slightly as it changed direction.

"Are we close to it yet?" he asked.

The monk didn't reply.

Cal checked the time on his datapad. Twenty-five minutes had elapsed since they'd set off. The monk stirred from his resting state and opened a door in the side the aircraft. Cold wind blasted at them as a powerful torrent. The monk gripped Cal with both hands, and suddenly, the two of them fell out from the aircraft.

Cal instinctively closed his eyes and kept them closed as they rushed through the air. Somehow, he vaguely trusted the strange creature who held him tightly, at least in terms of getting him to the machine.

They landed on something hard. Cal's feet felt the solid, smooth, curved surface beneath them, and the monk released him. He opened his eyes. As promised, they were on the upper hull of the war machine. Open skies stretched above him. Cal could look far into the distance, seeing ranges of white-capped mountains that had never been visible from the ground. Around him, rising at towering heights from the armored black surface upon which he stood, were the huge weapon arms of the walking machine, each with many joints and several meters across in diameter. The biggest of them raised their cannons almost into the clouds.

Suddenly, the machine took a step. It was a terrifying shock to Cal as the smooth metal floor beneath him lurched upward almost instantaneously. The monk quickly gripped him again, and for a moment, Cal clutched at the monk's robes as they were violently shaken by the machine striding forward. Somehow, the floating monk was able to hold a steady position. Cal realized that the machine was walking normally. It still had no idea where they were. No weapons had been trained on them.

"Come," the monk said, half leading and half dragging Cal to a mechanical port a few inches wide, located a short distance away on top of the moving machine. The monk produced a length of cable from his robes, barely longer than a meter, then carefully inserted it deep into the port on the machine. Cal noticed that the other end of the cable had what appeared to be a gleaming silver needle.

He inhaled sharply and tried to stay calm. Without hesitating, the monk grabbed Cal's head then stabbed the needle into the back of his skull.

*

Cal awoke somewhere completely different. The atmosphere, the air pressure, everything around him had changed. It was hot and dark, as if he was in a small room. He was lying face down on a hard floor, he realized. He looked up and surveyed the area around him.

A handful of electric lights were mounted on a low ceiling. They each glowed in different colors—green, blue, and yellow. By their light, Cal saw what looked like control panels and terminals covered in buttons and screens. He was confused and resisted the urge to call out. Instead, he quietly got to his feet and peered around.

The place almost looked like the bridge of a starship, but it was much too confined and too flat compared to every starship bridge he'd personally seen. It didn't seem to be part of the walking machine, either, given how totally silent and stationary the room was compared to the severe shaking he'd endured on the top. The heat was high, almost making him sweat. As his eyes adjusted to the darkness, he saw walls around him. The control room was not large at all—he could see its farthest extent in all directions, even in the dark. Each wall was full of switches and dials, illuminated in different shades by the ceiling spotlights directed at them.

Cal became aware that he wasn't alone. Someone else was moving in the space, someone human and around his height. He crouched anxiously then crept forward a little, pressing himself into the shadows at the side of a console desk. The other man was muttering to himself as he seemed to work on something, either unaware of Cal's presence or not caring.

He had no idea where he was, unsure whether the monk had sent him there or whether he was even still on the planet with Leda and Rosco. He cautiously waited for a few minutes to see if anything would happen. The other person in the control room moved occasionally from one terminal to the next, hurrying slightly as he went about his task. Cal looked out to watch him properly.

The man was wearing a military uniform, including a battered cap. His hair was greasy, and the man's eyes seemed hollow. The skin of his face was sagging. There was something drained and alarmingly lifeless looking about him, but he was intensely busy in his work. His exhausted face stared urgently into the depths of the screens and dials all around him. The man's uniform was badly tattered, but Cal saw a nameplate that read "Garrett." The room smelled, he realized suddenly, as though his brain had just registered the odor of human sweat and waste that had built up over many years. The man somehow never left this place, Cal suspected. His uniform was full of badges and medals, many of which Cal recognized as symbols of the Universal Legion. There was no doubt that the man was some kind of highly ranked officer. But why was he alone in here? And where the hell even was Cal?

Cal stood up a little more, no longer hiding himself. The man still paid him no attention, though he had to have been aware of Cal by then. Cal began to walk around. As the uniformed man moved from one console desk to another, Cal was clearly in his line of sight, but the man looked straight through him as though he wasn't there. Up close, the man almost seemed like a living corpse, a revenant possessed by some unending purpose.

He clearly didn't register Cal as a threat, somehow. It was abnormal. Cal decided to address him. Perhaps he had information. Perhaps he could be reasoned with.

"Hello?" Cal called quietly.

No acknowledgment.

"Hello?" Cal said a little louder, stepping closer. As the man hurriedly moved to examine another console, Cal decided to block his path slightly. As the man walked around Cal, he looked directly at him suddenly, just for a moment.

"Who are you?" the man asked. "I'm very busy." He kept walking by.

"I'm Cal."

The man seemed already to have forgotten him.

Cal had a strange thought, an idea of where he could be. He walked toward a wall and found a door out of the control room. It wouldn't open at all, no matter how he pulled it, but it did contain a small glass panel. He put his face close to the glass and looked through.

Beyond was darkness, but more than that, Cal sensed he was looking into nothing. There was a void. Nothing existed beyond the control room.

None of this place was real. He was in an artificial environment, like a simulation. He thought back to what he'd heard the monks say. He was inside the walking robot—not physically but mentally. This man was what remained of the biological components.

Cal looked around urgently, suddenly afraid for what could happen. He had to be successful. What he was doing in this place was crucial to protecting Rosco and Leda. The screens around him all showed the hills and ravines amongst which the three of them had been hiding. The instrument dials and computer consoles each described a weapon or some other critical function of the machine. But it all had to be a visual metaphor, an idea produced by his brain to help him interpret what he saw. The eerie heat and unnatural silence of the room made that clear.

Cal looked at the man who frantically worked the controls, the haggard-looking Garrett. He began to understand what he had to do, though he was not sure he could do it, either morally or physically. He approached the man again.

"Are you Garrett?" he asked.

"Captain Garrett," the man replied, his attention still entirely held by what he was doing.

"Are you part of the Universal Legion?" Cal asked.

"All my life."

Cal nodded. "Is this place real?"

Garrett looked up suddenly. He looked around as though seeing the environment for the first time. Then he returned to his work. "As real as anything is."

"How long have you been here?"

"My whole life. A long time."

"Have you ever been outside this room?" Cal asked.

"I... don't remember," Garrett said after a pause. "I have to do my job. I have to concentrate. The Legion are counting on me. I have to protect people and preserve lives."

He marched away to flip switches on some other panel on the wall. Cal followed.

"Are you a real person?"

The corpse-like Garrett stopped suddenly. The abrupt motion was somehow deeply alarming to Cal. "I don't know," Garrett said. "I really don't know. I know I think I am. I think I was, once. Parts were taken away from me." Garrett tapped his skull. "Like a brain in a jar, except you don't need the whole brain. Just enough to focus on tasks, the part that works, works, works."

The screens and dials all began to flash a violent red. Garrett looked horrified, as though awakening from a trance, and began to push buttons again at twice his previous speed.

"What are you doing?" Some level of understanding was coming to Cal. The place was a dreamworld, but it all represented very real events taking place inside the machine.

"I'm venting reactor heat, redirecting plasma flows, cooling limb motors, clearing memory blockages and logic errors…"

"What if you didn't?" Cal had to try and persuade the man to stand down, to cease operating the machine that scoured the planet's surface searching for them. He could disable it if he could just persuade Garrett to cooperate. "What if you stopped your work? Even just for a while?"

Garrett shook his head. "Impossible."

Cal needed to appeal to some kind of common humanity they shared, to persuade him to make the choice to spare their lives. "You can stop," said Cal. "You really could. You have the choice." He realized he was seeking mercy, but mercy would require Garrett to abandon his duty. "You have the power to do that."

Garrett shook his head again. "Impossible."

"My friends are outside," said Cal. "You can spare their lives. They've harmed no one. They're not a theat."

"I don't have the power to do that," said Garrett, pulling on a heavy set of levers. "I'm not authorized to stop the hunt."

"Do you think they deserve to die?" Cal needed to know if the man had a soul, buried deep inside the machine.

"Nobody deserves for anything that happens to them." Garrett exhaled. "All we can do is hold things together for the sake of future generations."

This image of a man was just a manifestation of some part of the giant war machine's psyche, yet he held no enmity toward Cal. He seemed consumed by his own anxieties, so worn down and disheveled. Face-to-face with that empty man, Cal suddenly saw how on a deep level, they were not so different. Garrett was exhausted, the same as Cal was, and trying desperately every second to fulfil his impossible orders.

Cal's understanding became something terrible. Garrett was equally as incapable of abandoning his mission as Cal was. They both had no other purpose. They were the only two sentient beings who existed in that virtual space, yet there could be no peace between them. Each was bound to different paths that transcended any commonality between them.

He saw the nature of what the monks had intended for him all along. Cal was inside the machine. He was opposed to Garrett. He was his friends' best hope. Cal had to give Garrett one last chance to back down, to be sure he'd tried everything to reach for a better way.

"Please stop," Cal told him.

"No."

"Please. It'll be so much easier for everyone. So much better."

"No."

Cal hesitated, growing desperate. "I absolutely need you to stop now."

Garrett looked up at him. "What would it even look like if I stopped? What would I be? Would I even exist? I... I can't imagine myself stopping," Garrett said. "I don't think I'm built to be able to. It's just..." Garrett looked deep into Cal's eyes, and for a moment, his facial expression flickered as if imploring Cal, as though he wanted Cal to do what was on his mind. "Not an option." He looked down at his manically typing hands as he entered commands into a terminal.

Cal would have to kill him. Cal had fought for his life before, struggling in a battle that'd left many dead. He knew what it was to willfully attack someone, to wish for their death, just in that moment. He tried to summon those feelings. This was war. It was survival. For *Fidelity* and Vale Reach.

Cal walked to stand close behind Garrett, who remained entirely focused on his work. He was so frail. Cal wondered if Garrett was allowing him to act. Perhaps Garrett was the part of the machine that secretly willed for something fatal to happen, that wished for an intervention, for things to be ended. Garrett would never be able to stop his work. He had been built that way.

Cal felt sudden resolve. He had to act. He had made his choice.

He wrapped both arms around Garrett and tackled him to the ground. They both fell and rolled on the floor.

"No!" Garrett cried fearfully.

Cal got on top of him and held him down with all his strength.

"No, let me go! I need to operate the machine!" Garrett shouted, begging and angry.

Cal tightened his grip with every ounce of his strength, pressing the man's arms flat against his chest.

The entire room began to flash red, filling Cal's vision, till all he could see was a pulsating blood red. The entire control room faded away to nothing but the searing, rage-filled color.

"Stop!" Garrett screamed. "I have to… I have to…"

The ground shook, the sound coming from far below. Cal heard Garrett exhale, and he felt Garrett's body become limp, and his face motionless, finally at peace. The shaking room became a deafening roar until Cal felt something rupture with an ear-splitting crack.

*

Leda and Rosco were watching the huge war machine from a screen in the monk's caverns, provided by the monks at Rosco's request. They saw the titanic machine falter, walking with uncertainty, as though losing control of its movements. They dared to imagine success, watching in wordless hope as the whole entity shuddered. The vast robot fell to one knee, convulsing with a clear affliction, as though in the grip of distress. One of its weapons arms exploded.

"My god, Cal!" Leda shouted.

"No…" Rosco whispered.

Another weapon exploded, then another. Fire and fragments rained down across the rest of the machine.

There was no sign of the red-robed monk.

The machine began to sway, moments from collapse. They saw a human body, a tiny form, a body that could only be Cal, sliding from the top of its surface and falling motionlessly, far down to the earth, plummeting as the machine ripped apart in a final cataclysmic explosion.

☐

Epilogue

Rosco stared into the mirror of his modest living quarters. He would soon attend a meeting with the monks. He adjusted the cap that came with his uniform. He rarely wore it, but it'd been recovered from the *Fidelity* shuttle that he'd hidden in the forest. He would wear it to show his authority. He polished the metal badges on his chest and shoulders and adjusted the angle of the cap again. He looked like a captain.

"Leadership," he said to himself without entirely knowing why. "I showed leadership. That's what I did. It was needed."

He'd always known that leaders had to make hard choices. He understood how it was true. He'd always believed it.

There was a knock at the door. The heavy wooden door to the stone room creaked as it opened. From the sound of the footsteps, he knew it was Leda. The monks noiselessly floated everywhere.

"They're bringing Cal back in the next hour," she said, her voice quiet and sorrowful.

Rosco didn't turn to face her but instead kept looking into the mirror. He could see Leda's reflection over his shoulder. "Any updates on their"—Rosco paused—"processes?"

"I asked," said Leda. "Apparently, the recovery is going according to their plan."

Rosco nodded. He almost couldn't speak. It felt as though his throat was closing. "That's good to hear," he managed.

"Do you believe what they're saying?" said Leda. "That there was no way for them to have known the machine would blow up so violently?"

Rosco hesitated before he answered. "Their own monk was injured. I'm sure they wouldn't have allowed that if they'd known it was coming."

Leda nodded. "I suppose so. These monks are few in number, and somehow, they seem so old. They also seem to be the only people on this planet. I'm sure they wouldn't risk themselves if they could avoid it. But still…"

Rosco knew what she meant. "Their promises to take care of Cal didn't amount to much," he said.

"No," said Leda. "They did not."

"But Cal is alive?" said Rosco. He wanted Leda to confirm it for him. He turned to look at her.

"That's beyond my ability to say, Rosco," she replied. "The monks tell me that they're not finished with him yet. They have all kinds of incredible machines hidden in this place, but I can't tell you much yet about what it is they do. It's possible that the monks have something that can help him, but... I think they're preparing us to expect the worst."

"The worst outcome has happened already," Rosco replied despondently. Truthfully, he felt as if he'd failed as captain on his first day. Yet there were far more days to come.

"Not yet, Captain," Leda said with a small shake of her head. "Maybe not yet." Her sadness returned. "How's the rest of your plan going?"

It was time to capitalize on the relative success they'd recently experienced. He and the monks would discuss terms for the next phase of the plan, the agreed-upon recapture of *Fidelity*.

"I'm about to determine our strategy with Fargas and the monks," he said. "We know some of the Legion fleet could linger for a while. We might be facing reinforcements when we attack Belara. But there are other Crusaders out there too. Our ship is still in the area. We can retake *Fidelity*. It's achievable. I can make it happen."

"There'll be a cost," Leda said.

He nodded. "Yes. There always is." What had happened to Cal had only happened because Rosco had allowed it. He was the mission leader. The crew were his responsibility, always. His hard choice would be the first among many. It was reckless to believe otherwise. He was prepared for it. He would do it for Vale Reach. And for Cal.

"I'm sorry for what I did to Cal," he said suddenly. He wanted Leda to know. He wouldn't say it again.

"Don't be," said Leda. "He chose to go. We should honor him." She walked away.

Rosco sat alone for a moment. He couldn't change what was already done. He had to find some way to move on, to keep moving forward. He exited the room and met Advocate Fargas waiting on the other side, a stack of documents under his arm, ready for negotiations.

"Let's get this done," said Rosco.

*

Leda was waiting at the entrance to the monks' underground fortress when they returned with Cal. She still had seen no more than a handful of monks at any given time, and she had no way to tell them apart.

Cal wasn't dead, they told her, but his brain was dying. What was left of him was being held in an in-between state by their technology. She already knew that most of his body was gone. It sounded revolting, yet in a frightening way, she was thankful for it. She'd used the monks' computers to research what she could about his condition whilst she'd waited for the recovery party's arrival.

The chrome aircraft touched down on a flat piece of land in front of her. A featureless hatch opened, and two monks drifted out.

"Where is he?" she demanded. She couldn't see any sign of Cal.

The monk in front of her held up a black metal cylinder, one foot in length and a few inches in diameter. "In here," the monk said.

Leda's heart crashed. "I don't understand."

"His body was damaged by the secondary explosions of the machine," the monk said. "This will store him indefinitely."

She stared at the cylinder in horror and fascination. She instinctively reached out to touch it, her fingertips hesitating to contact its metal surface. Not even his skull remained. She wondered what could actually survive of Cal. "You put his brain in there," she said.

"His remaining neural tissue," the monk confirmed.

"Can he be made into a"—she hesitated—"a whole person again?"

The monk laid it carefully in her arms. "We cannot provide a miracle. Yet there is always work to be done," he said.

Leda nodded, answering the question for herself. Far more work was needed—the monks were right about that, even if their arrogance had cost the life of her friend. The situation wasn't over, not with her involved. If the monks couldn't fix it, she would find a way herself.

She looked at the black cylinder and imagined the human life contained with it. It was an alien form of technology, with its inner workings invisible to her, but its existence proved what was possible.

Perhaps Leda would have time to understand the device, to make sense of it all. She didn't believe it would be quick, but she'd seen now how long a human life could be extended to last. She could work forever till she had reversed this terrible event and Cal was with them again.

*

Eevey awoke on a morning like any other in her bed in Vale Reach. The light outside seemed dim, struggling to enter through the blinds of the flat she'd once shared with Cal. It had been nearly three years since he'd left, but every day, she tried to imagine where he was. He would have seen incredible things and reached places she couldn't imagine. One day, he would find his way back, one way or the other, and they could reunite and share their stories.

And if not—if *Fidelity* had vanished into the void, never to be seen again—in her mind, Cal would be off on an adventure forever.

The Infinite Void series

Infinite Void is a science fiction space-opera series, focused on a far future galaxy of dysfunctional cyberpunk empires and frontier societies.

Danger and suspense fill each exhilarating encounter. Many brave souls will fail. Only a tenacious few will reach their goals and achieve unimaginable power.

All will bear witness to the wonders and terrors brought by mankind's inevitable transformation.

The next stage of human evolution faces chaos.

Defiant Space – Novel One

One starship against the galaxy.

When an armada of predatory warships come to annex their world, the inhabitants of planet Vale Reach must face the fearsome threats that stalk their galaxy. Terrors lurk in the uncharted depths of space, ready to crush their world and enslave its people. A lone starship is sent on an impossible journey. But is it already too late?

Caladon Heit wants to prevent the destruction of everything he knows. Together, the ship's crew must overcome the ferocious marauders and brutal empires that seek to eradicate them all.

In space, they will find a harsh and remorseless environment. Unimaginable enemies await behind every moon and asteroid. Their mission will demand sacrifices from every crew member to reach its destination. Will they emerge with their resolve and their starship intact? Or will

Fidelity and their homeworld be annihilated?

Defiant Space is the first novel in the Infinite Void series.

Defiant Systems – Novel Two

One starship against endless empires.

The starship *Fidelity* arrives on the far side of the galaxy, without power or allies. A fiery interstellar conflict threatens to pull them in. *Fidelity* must find a way through the complex web of loyalties needed to survive on the frontlines of a warzone.

Cal is haunted by dreams of a ruthless ancient being that hunts them. His comrades, Rosco and Leda, must master the advanced technology around them, and begin a perilous journey down the path of cybernetic augmentation.

Only through their ingenuity and wit can the travelers from Vale Reach hope to defy the odds and achieve their impossible mission. War machines and horrors of titanic scale will rise against them in an epic confrontation as they draw nearer to the prize of securing protection for their homeworld.

Can the crew of *Fidelity* face the full onslaught of a hostile galaxy? Or will they become just another casualty in an endless struggle between empires?

Defiant Systems is the second novel in the Infinite Void series.

Inhuman Pressure - Anthology One

An anthology of nine short stories of interplanetary conspiracy and catastrophe.

Cybernetic elder beings control the stars. Haunted wilderness planets offer no safety. The limits of the human condition are tested as ordinary people face conquest and revenge.

An impending apocalypse. A lone soldier at the end of a galaxy. Witness the fate of the universe in a startling collection of science fiction tales. A trail of forgotten lives will have vast consequences for all civilization.

Inhuman Pressure is the first anthology in the Infinite Void series.

Recurrent Immortality - Anthology Two

An anthology of nine short stories of cosmic discovery and survival in space.

The void between planets is filled with pirates and hunters seeking their fortune in the lawless chaos of the galaxy's frontiers. Unhinged ship captains, haunted machines and inhuman hybrids stalk the path of unwary travelers to the stars.

A handful of desperate souls will experience incredible transformations to escape death and become greater than human.

Recurrent Immortality is the second anthology in the Infinite Void series.

Join our newsletter for exclusive access to 'The Survivors' – a prologue short story to the Infinite Void series.

Plus early reading access, discounts on new releases, and more exclusive bonus content:

Join here:

https://cutt.ly/rimington

About the Author: Richard Rimington

Richard Rimington is a British author living in Hong Kong. He is a writer of science fiction, working for over fifteen years.

His favorite authors include Phillip K. Dick, Alastair Reynolds, Dan Simmons and Ann Leckie.

Get regular updates at
https://rimmblog.wordpress.com/

RICHARD RIMINGTON

Acknowledgements

Thank you to Indrani Banerjee and Paul Rodgers for proof-reading manuscripts

Thank you to editors Lynn, Sara and Kate at Red Adept Editing

Thank you to cover artists Kim and Jovana at www.derangeddoctordesign.com

Thank you to the readers in the ARC group for your support

Printed in Great Britain
by Amazon